The Inventors at No. 8

A. M. MORGEN

LITTLE, BROWN AND COMPANY
New York Boston

Copyright © 2018 by Glasstown Entertainment
Excerpt from *The Inventors and the Lost Island* copyright © 2019 by Glasstown Entertainment
Map illustrations by Diana Sousa
Map image copyright © Oleg Golovnev/Shutterstock.com

Cover art copyright © 2018 by Iacopo Bruno. Cover design by Karina Granda.
Cover copyright © 2018 by Hachette Book Group, Inc.

Little, Brown and Company
Hachette Book Group
1290 Avenue of the Americas, New York, NY 10104
Visit us at LBYR.com

Originally published in hardcover and ebook by Little, Brown and Company in May 2018
First Trade Paperback Edition: March 2019

Little, Brown and Company is a division of Hachette Book Group, Inc. The Little, Brown name and logo are trademarks of Hachette Book Group, Inc.

The publisher is not responsible for websites (or their content) that are not owned by the publisher.

The Library of Congress has cataloged the hardcover edition as follows:
Names: Morgen, A. M., author.
Title: The inventors at no. 8 / A.M. Morgen.
Other titles: Inventors at number eight
Description: First edition. | New York : Little, Brown and Company, 2018. |
Summary: Twelve-year-olds George, the very unlucky third Lord of
Devonshire, and his neighbor, scientist Ada Byron, join forces against a
nefarious group of criminals who steal the map to a priceless family heirloom.
Identifiers: LCCN 2017037192 | ISBN 9780316471497 (hardback) | ISBN
9780316471503 (open ebook) | ISBN 9780316471480 (library ebook)
Subjects: | CYAC: Robbers and outlaws—Fiction. | Voyages and travels—
Fiction. | Lovelace, Ada King, Countess of, 1815-1852—Fiction. | Inventors—
Fiction. | Scientists—Fiction. | Orphans—Fiction. | Europe—History—19th
century—Fiction. | BISAC: JUVENILE FICTION / Fantasy & Magic. | JUVENILE
FICTION / Action & Adventure / Pirates. | JUVENILE FICTION / Action &
Adventure / General. | JUVENILE FICTION / Family / Orphans & Foster Homes. | JUVENILE
FICTION / Social Issues / Friendship. | JUVENILE FICTION /
Social Issues / Self-Esteem & Self-Reliance. | JUVENILE FICTION / Social
Issues / New Experience. | JUVENILE FICTION / Family / Alternative Family. |
JUVENILE FICTION / Animals / Apes, Monkeys, etc.
Classification: LCC PZ7.1.M66983 Inv 2018 | DDC [Fic]—dc23
LC record available at https://lccn.loc.gov/2017037192

ISBNs: 978-0-316-47151-0 (pbk.), 978-0-316-47150-3 (ebook)

Printed in the United States of America

LSC-C

10 9 8 7 6 5 4 3 2 1

The Inventors at No. 8

To I. R.
Sorry you're not in this book.
I hope one day you read it anyway.

xx

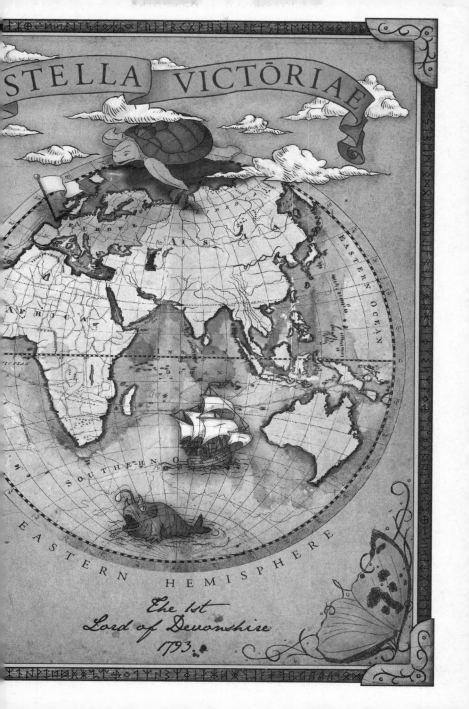

STELLA VICTŌRIAE

EASTERN OCEAN

AFRICA

ASIA

INDIAN OCEAN

SOUTHERN O

EASTERN HEMISPHERE

The 1st
Lord of Devonshire
1793.

Prologue

Most would agree that some people have rotten luck, but George, the 3rd Lord of Devonshire, was the unluckiest boy in all of London—and he could prove it.

Exhibit #1: Lady Devonshire, his mother, had died giving birth to him.

Exhibit #2: When George was four years old, he stood on his head. This so surprised his beloved governess that she promptly choked to death on a caramel candy. From that day forward, George was afraid to exhibit prowess at any physical activity, lest it kill someone.

Exhibit #3: On George's tenth birthday, his father bought him a pair of newfangled roller skates. Before

George could try them, his father insisted on giving them a spin. He skated straight out of an open second-story window and landed headfirst on the brick walkway in the back garden at the feet of his own father, the 1st Lord of Devonshire.

Exhibit #4: The 1st Lord of Devonshire, George's grandfather, was secretly relieved that his son was dead. Now he could stop stashing his valuables underneath the floorboards to keep his son from pawning them for gambling money. For reasons known only to himself, the 1st Lord immediately buried his son, the 2nd Lord, in the garden. However, the 1st Lord was no longer used to such vigorous exercise, and he suffered a heart attack and died without another word.

Exhibit #5: After arranging the 1st Lord's funeral, the butler and the cook ran away to the seashore to get married. By then, it was quite clear that the house, and possibly George as well, was under a terrible curse of bad luck. Therefore, George was not surprised when word arrived that the butler and the cook had drowned during their honeymoon swim.

And:

Exhibit #6: The housemaid left to buy flowers for the

1st Lord's funeral and was struck dead by a carriage just after leaving the florist.

Thus, by sundown of the 3rd Lord's tenth birthday, No. 8 Dorset Square had only two inhabitants: George and the new elderly manservant, Frobisher.

Frobisher had recently arrived to replace the previous elderly manservant, who had died several weeks earlier (Exhibit #7). But upon entering the house, Frobisher was immediately struck with laryngitis and a severe cold (Exhibit #8) and went to bed. Amazingly, neither his cold nor his swollen vocal cords killed him, though his runny nose and inability to speak remained with him.

In the course of one tragic birthday, George, the 3rd Lord of Devonshire, became both an orphan and the owner of No. 8 Dorset Square.

Was it sad? It was.

Was the 3rd Lord of Devonshire the unluckiest boy in all of London, possibly in all of the British Empire? Seemed likely.

Was it also possible that the unluckiest boy in the entire world could become the luckiest? Perhaps.

But only if he was brave enough to try.

Chapter One

George, the 3rd Lord of Devonshire, began his twelfth birthday in a foul mood.

First of all, it was raining. This was not so unusual, as in England it was often raining. However, it was one thing when it rained *outside*.

It was another thing altogether when it rained *inside*.

George woke to rain plopping onto the tip of his nose from several large leaks in the roof.

"Happy birthday," George said to himself.

Plop, the rain replied.

George dressed carefully in his best outfit, which also happened to be his only outfit, as he'd sold the last of his spare trousers the previous Wednesday. Then he went to the kitchen for his usual breakfast of hot water and bread crust.

Frobisher was nowhere to be found. George concluded that he must have gone to the antiques dealer already. Last night, George had asked Frobisher to sell his grandfather's old, moth-eaten seafarer's uniform. George might have run the errand himself, but he hadn't left his dilapidated home since his tenth birthday, exactly two years ago. He didn't trust the world Out There beyond the doors of No. 8. His bad luck was bound to catch up with him even more quickly Out There.

Still, he was quite lonely without Frobisher at home. Besides Frobisher—and of course Mrs. Daly, Frobisher's beloved pet rat—George's only company were the debt collectors who came by every now and again seeking payment of the many unpaid bills his father had left after his death.

Without anything better to do on his birthday, George went about his usual business. First, as he did every morning, he carefully collected the snails that had crawled in through the rotten baseboards and placed them in a rusty bucket for Frobisher to take out to the garden. Then, as he did every other day, he turned his attention to scouring the old house for more things to sell.

Over the last two years, he had slowly dismantled his family's home, piece by piece, like a jigsaw puzzle in reverse. He and Frobisher had sold the tapestries and the rich leather chairs; the cutlery and the mirrors; the chandeliers and the standing lamps and the oil portraits of various glowering relatives. They had sold the birdcage that had once held Frobisher's poor parrot, Frobisher Jr., before he had been swallowed by a much larger owl after a window was left open (Exhibit #9). If George could not continue to pay off his father's bills, the debt collectors would take No. 8 Dorset Square. And if his home was taken away, he and Frobisher would be parted. George would be sent to an orphanage, where he would eat gruel and share a bed with lice.

He would much, much rather share his own house with snails. And Frobisher.

After hours of looking into every nook, cranny, and baseboard, George turned up nothing new to sell other than a litter of baby mice. He retrieved his accounts ledger to tally revenues and expenses.

It looked like this:

Expenses	*Revenues*
1. More cheddar for Mrs. Daly, 50 pence	1. Grandfather's seafarer's uniform
2. Pastilles, 63 pence (cherry-flavored—Frobisher's favorite)	2. Seven baby mice
3. Trouser mending, 32 pence (last pair—must invest in appearances, after all)	3. Ten buckets of rainwater
	4. Frobisher's periscope

With a firm scratch, he struck Frobisher's periscope from the list. It was the manservant's sole possession, and George chided himself for even considering selling it.

George smoothed the golden-blond cowlick just above his left temple, as he often did when he was nervous. His grandfather's uniform was, truly, their last source of income, other than the clothes on their backs.

And, of course, the map.

But he hadn't even put the map on his list, because the map was something he had sworn never to part with.

A soft tap at the windowpane made him jump, which sent a series of thumps and bangs echoing through the empty house. His heart thudded as he turned his head to look out the window. What if someone had finally come to take him away? But all he saw was the magnolia tree waving in the wind.

Frobisher, he realized, had been gone for hours.

George could not remember the last time he had been this alone.

What if Frobisher didn't return at all?

What if Frobisher became the latest victim of the bad-luck curse (Exhibit #10)?

A loud creak at the bottom of the stairs broke the silence.

Then there was a soft *rap rap rap* on the glass, as if someone had tapped a long, thin finger against it.

"Frobisher?" he called out hopefully. Of course there was no answer. Frobisher was nearly deaf, so even if he had come home, he wouldn't have been able to hear George from all the way upstairs.

Another shiver ran up George's back when a faint but distinct scraping sound reverberated through the house. Careful to make no noise, George lowered himself to the floor. Last month he had told Frobisher to sell his grand-father's military saber. It was just his luck that as soon as he sold his only weapon, he needed it.

George crawled to the top of the grand curved stair-case leading down to the front door. "Hello?" he called. His voice echoed back. *Hello, hello, hello.*

He edged down the stairs and toward the drawing room, avoiding all the creaky floorboards (which was most of them). He drew a deep breath...

And with a formidable cry, leapt into the drawing room.

It was empty.

But wait.

He caught a sudden movement at the window. Some-one had left the sash up. Outside, a dark bird was perched on the sill. It cocked its head and stared at him with wink-ing eyes. *Rap*, it said, tapping its beak against the window.

"Come here," George commanded. (He was not fond of animals but thought perhaps Frobisher would like a bird to replace Frobisher Jr. Then Frobisher would have another reason to stay with George at No. 8 despite all the many reasons why he ought to want to leave. George did not want Frobisher to leave. If Frobisher left, he would be very alone indeed.)

But the bird took off, flashing through the trees across Dorset Square, only to disappear through an open upstairs window of the narrow gray house across the street, No. 5.

A bird flying indoors wasn't odd at No. 8. But a bird flying into No. 5 was *very* odd. As far as George knew, that house was occasionally used as the winter residence of the Milbanke family. Most of the time, though, the house was shut up tighter than a can of tinned oysters. The home had been visited at various points by a famous relative, the poet Lord Byron, but it had been years since the lord himself had come around. One evening last summer, through his kitchen window, George had overheard the gossipy maids at neighboring No. 7 say the man had left his unwanted baggage at the house and never returned for it.

"Stupid animal," George said. To think he'd been spooked by a little bird! Clearly there was no one else in the house. The noises must have been his imagination.

George let go of the window sash, which slammed shut with a bang. He jammed its rusty latch back into place as best he could.

That was when a heavy hand came down on his shoulder, and George screamed.

Chapter Two

When George realized it was only Frobisher, finally back from his trip to the antiques dealer, he tried to pretend that he hadn't screamed out of fear at all, but had only been practicing his vocal exercises.

But when he saw the sad look on Frobisher's droopy face, he stopped all the humming and squawking at once. His embarrassment melted into worry. "What's wrong, Frobisher?"

Slowly, Frobisher unwound the scarf from his neck, unbuttoned his coat, and took off the many hats he wore at George's insistence. Then, even more slowly, he unfolded his hand to reveal four small coins.

George counted rapidly once, twice, three times. A pit

opened up in his stomach. He counted them again. "Only four shillings for Grandfather's uniform?"

Frobisher bowed his gray head.

"Did you go to Twombly first?" George asked. Frobisher nodded. Suddenly, George's throat felt thick, as though he'd swallowed tar. "What about Wadsworth? Harris? Cotswold?"

Frobisher's face only got droopier and droopier, like a bit of browned lettuce in the heat.

George swallowed a rising sense of panic. "But it should have been worth much more. Maybe a hundred shillings. At *least* a hundred shillings! It was the antique uniform from the collection of my grandfather, the renowned maritime hero, the 1st Lord of Devonshire. Did you explain that?"

Frobisher nodded again. George's head began to ache with calculations. The money would cover expenses for a week. But soon it would run out. As would Frobisher's cherry pastilles, which were costly. They couldn't sell Frobisher's coat, scarf, or hats. Surely he'd get even sicker without them.

But at this rate, they were going to lose the house within the month, and George could already imagine the sneering faces of the orphanage masters coming to collect him—

"That's the last time I sell anything to Wadsworth! Or Cotswold! Or Harris!" He banged his fist against the doorframe to emphasize his point, biting back a yelp of pain. His eyes burned with tears. There was nothing left of any worth to sell.

Except one thing.

An item he had promised never to part with.

"Tomorrow, you will sell the map to the Star of Victory," George heard himself say. Just speaking those words drained him. The colors in the room seemed to dull around him.

Frobisher's watery eyes went wide, and he began shaking his head and waving his arms back and forth frantically (this was Frobisher's voiceless version of yelling), because Frobisher knew that the map to the Star of Victory, a priceless stone that assured its owner of success in battle, was the most important heirloom George's grandfather had left behind. Unlike the eerie portraits and rotting furniture, the map was George's real legacy.

I've seen corners of the world you wouldn't believe, his grandfather would say. *All of it here, in this map. One day, you will discover the map's secrets, with a little luck.*

The 1st Lord was once a hero, and he had wanted George to be a hero, too, to take the map and recover the Star of Victory himself.

George had no interest in being a hero Out There. The only thing he wanted to save was this house, and the little life he had. In Here.

"That's an order, Frobisher. It's the only way to pay off enough of my father's debts to save the house. I should have sold the map first, not last. I'll go get it now," George said, hoping that if he sounded firm enough, he would convince himself. "Why don't you finish chopping up the magnolia tree outside? A fire would be nice."

And so, with no other choice, George gathered himself and headed toward the library, which had once contained numerous books on history, geography, mathematics, and grammar. The only books left now were those no one wanted to buy, such as *Useful Needlework* and *The History of the Rhône*.

As he pulled the map to the Star of Victory out of its cabinet drawer, an old, not unpleasant musty scent filled his nose.

This map is your destiny, the 1st Lord of Devonshire used to say. George would listen raptly while his grandfather described the Star: as blue as the sky, as bright as the sun, and as radiant as the stars.

He had studied the map practically every day since his grandfather's death and could describe it with his eyes closed. It was split into two azimuthal projections of the Eastern and Western Hemispheres, their unexplored poles dotted with angular topographical markings. The blues, greens, and grays of the seven seas were so realistic, George heard them churn in his sleep. Knowing it might be his last chance, he admired his grandfather's more fanciful additions: colorful sea serpents that writhed in the oceans and flying turtles that soared up to the clouds. He studied the peculiar symbols that laced the map's edges, which looked like toppled statues of a long-lost civilization. These were the strange, foreign lands that had filled his dreams at night—lands where anything was possible.

But even still, he could not figure out where the Star of Victory was hidden. There was no X marking the buried treasure, no latitude and longitude to steer toward.

A loud, particularly violent *whack* inside the house jarred George, causing the map to slip from his hands and float gently down to the floor. It sounded far too close to be Frobisher, chopping away at the magnolia tree outside. Another *thunk* froze him in place. But only for a moment. On instinct, he threw himself into the cold, dark chimney.

Not that George was *hiding*, of course. He was planning an ambush, like any brave lord would.

Masked in the shadows, he listened as the stairs creaked and groaned. Someone was in the house, and from the sound of the footsteps, George sensed that the person was hunting for something (or someone). The footsteps were unhurried but deliberate . . . and they were getting closer.

Soon they paused just outside the library.

Squeezing his knees to his chest, George held his breath as the door creaked slowly open, and bit his tongue to keep from crying out. As long as he kept quiet, he would be safe. If the intruder was a thief looking to steal silver forks or jewelry, he had picked the wrong house on Dorset Square, George thought unkindly.

The footsteps started, then stopped again, this time inside the library.

The map, George realized. His most prized possession. His last hope. A hole opened in his stomach. He had left it lying in plain sight, right in the middle of the empty room.

Without a second thought, George burst from the fireplace with the force of lava spewing from a volcano. His flailing arms and legs dislodged a cloud of soot, and black ash bloomed around him. He grabbed for a weapon, any weapon, until his fingers closed around the fireplace poker. Brandishing the object like a sword, he stabbed wildly in every direction.

His throat burned. His eyes watered. "Begone!" he commanded between coughs.

When he could see again, George found himself alone in the library, holding not the poker, which had been sold, but the fireplace brush. The map was gone.

Still holding the brush like a sword, George raced out of the room—but in his rush, he forgot to skip over the rotted floorboard outside the dining room. His foot plunged through oak, and he crashed forward onto his knees. The brush spun out of his grip. By the time he retrieved it, the intruder was towering over him, blocking out all the light.

Chapter Three

The thief was well dressed, in a top hat, dark red coat, white pants, and riding boots. An abundance of thick, shiny red curls peeked from beneath his hat. Up close, he did not look like a thief, or a criminal, or a murderer. He looked quite...respectable.

Relief washed over George; his grip on the brush relaxed a fraction. Respectable people didn't break into houses and steal things. Then he spotted a rolled-up paper in the man's hand.

The blood pulsing through his veins turned to ice. It was his grandfather's map.

George propped himself up on one elbow and pointed his brush at the man's chest. He hoped the thief wouldn't see the brush trembling. "Drop that paper as you leave, thief!"

The thief cocked his head, looking down at George as if he were a puppy that he could not decide whether to pet or kick. The corners of his lips lifted into a smile as he lifted his boot to smash George's head. George flung up his arm to protect his face, but the blow didn't fall.

Instead, the garden doors flew open with a bang.

George uncovered his face just in time to see Frobisher, his teeth bared in a silent roar, swing a whiplike magnolia branch at the back of the man's head—but the thief nimbly dodged Frobisher's attack. As Frobisher stumbled forward, the man sidestepped behind him and raised his fists high in the air, then slammed them down like a battering ram on Frobisher's back.

Frobisher dropped to the floor, his limbs sprawled out awkwardly.

"Frobisher, no!" With shaking arms and legs, George crawled to his motionless manservant and shielded Frobisher's body with his own.

The thief, map in hand, opened the front door to leave. When he glanced behind him at the scattered destruction in No. 8's foyer, he flashed his crooked yellow teeth in a triumphant sneer.

Then a dark creature zoomed toward the open door, heading straight for the intruder. It was the same bird that had been perched earlier on the windowsill. George recognized its oil-dark feathers and the curious sharpness of its beak.

The thief turned his head just as the bird reached him. In one motion, the animal tore the top hat off the thief's head and drew a ragged red line down his face with its talon. Screaming and slapping furiously at the dark wings beating his face, the man staggered blindly *back* into the house.

Brush in hand, George rushed forward and grabbed for the map while the man grappled with the bird. When the thief tried to thwack George out of the way, George defended himself, parrying the blows with his brush. Finally, the bird dove for the thief's face again, walloping him with the vicious thumping of its wings. In the scuffle, George yanked the map from the intruder's hand.

Then the thief was driven by the bird, still flapping and clawing, out onto the stoop. He closed his fist around the creature's neck and flung it back through the doorway, where it hit the floor like a stone, landing with a terrible thump near the magnolia branch. Still gasping for breath, George threw himself against the front door to close it before the thief could reenter. He locked it with a satisfying click.

Stuck Out There, the thief cursed—maybe the man wasn't very proper after all. George dared a glance out the window. Luckily, the ruckus had drawn the attention of the neighbors. The sour-faced butler from No. 5 and the gossipy maids from No. 7 were on their porches, casting alarmed glances at No. 8. The thief wouldn't dare force his way inside again with so many eyes on him.

"You haven't seen the last of me," the thief said, his voice rough as gravel.

Then he darted down the front path and was gone.

George sank down to the floor next to Frobisher, utterly exhausted. He gently shook Frobisher by his shoulder. When the manservant coughed, fluttering his eyes open to give George a weak but reassuring wink, George breathed a sigh of relief.

The intruder's hat lay next to Frobisher. It reeked of

perfumed macassar oil: the same oil George's father once used to make his hair shine. George kicked the hat away.

Frobisher sat up slowly, rubbing his shoulders where the intruder had struck him. He waved away George's help. With tender care, he reached for the bird, which lay unmoving on the stone floor.

George felt a surge of pity for the creature as Frobisher took the heap of black feathers in his hands, stroking it lightly. It had helped him retrieve the map. Was it dead? (Exhibit #11?) He leaned in for a closer look. A shudder whipped through him at the sight of its lifeless black eyes and its neck, which was twisted at an odd angle. But then, miraculously, the bird chirped.

Or rather—it *clicked*.

With a jerk of its wings, the creature came to life. It lifted its head despite the injury to its neck, then hopped to its feet in Frobisher's palm.

"Would you like to keep it, Frobisher?" George said when he saw the manservant's face light up.

"*Ssss*," the bird hissed. It spread its ragged wings, and George noticed its silver talons.

His face still glowing in delight, Frobisher nodded

toward the bird, as if he wanted George to pet it. George laid the map carefully in his lap and reached out, hand shaking slightly, to place a finger against the creature's side. It was cool under his fingertips.

He pulled his hand back. The bird was not made of feathers, flesh, or bone.

It was mechanical.

George had never seen anything like it. The bird's jet-black eyes were not dead but unblinking, made of some metallic stone that rolled in its sockets.

As George stared, stunned, the bird recovered itself. Before George could react, the creature hopped onto his knee, pinched the map in its silver beak, and catapulted several feet into the air as if launched by a spring. With one sweep of its dark wings, the bird sailed out of the broken window—taking George's most precious possession with it.

Chapter Four

Soaring once again over the green lawn of Dorset Square, the mechanical bird alighted on the second-story windowsill of No. 5.

Having recovered himself, George watched helplessly as the white lace curtains fluttered inside the house and a girl about George's age appeared to greet the mechanical bird. The bird seemed to look back at No. 8 with a smug shuddering of its wings, map still in its beak, before it disappeared inside. The girl banged the window shut after it.

A girl? He had never seen a girl inside No. 5.

"I'll take care of this, Frobisher. Go to bed. You've had a nasty blow, and you need to rest."

Frobisher, who was now wobbling upon his feet,

looked knowingly at George with watery eyes. He patted George on the back and lumbered up the steps to his room.

Only when he opened the door did George remember how exposed, how vulnerable, how alone he would be Out There, where he hadn't been for two years. His heart began to hammer in his chest. The sun had dipped below the rooftops, and the sky above Dorset Square had dimmed to the color of a dirty sock. A squirrel raced by, causing him to leap back.

His father's voice taunted him in his head: *spine of a snail, brains of a bowl of porridge.*

"Buck up," George whispered to himself. It wasn't that he was *scared* to leave the house. His isolation was for everyone else's safety, not his own. So far, Frobisher was the only person who was even moderately immune to his bad luck. If George began to meet more people, who knew how many of them might die? He didn't want to be responsible for the next plague or Great Fire.

George combed his fingers through his hair, straightened his jacket, and inched onto the stoop, shutting the door behind him. In front of him, gas lanterns smoldered in the streetlamps. The evening breeze felt too harsh against his cheeks, and the smell of grass burned in his nose. But no carriages came tumbling apart, nor did any houses burst into flames, so he took a step toward narrow No. 5 across the square, and another, and another, until he was down the rotting garden path and out onto the street.

Breathing heavily, he covered the distance between No. 8 and No. 5 in thirty-five tense paces, his annoyance increasing with each step.

What nerve, George thought, glaring up at the second-story window where the abominable bird had taken refuge. As he got closer, he noticed uneasily that several of the windows were nailed shut. Others had extra locks and were crisscrossed with thin metal chains. He had always assumed that the house was shut up tightly to keep intruders out. But what if it was to keep someone *in*? Surely no one but a lunatic would keep a mechanical bird for a pet. And surely no one but George, the unluckiest boy in London, would have a dangerous lunatic for a neighbor. Still, he forced himself to keep going, because *someone* inside No. 5 had his map.

Lifting the heavy brass knocker, George rapped one, two, three times.

A bolt unbolted with a clunk. Then a lock unlocked

with a click. A chain unfastened, then another bolt and another lock. At last, the door swung open a few inches, still secured by a chain.

The sour-faced butler looked George up and down, taking in George's soot-covered, sweaty, disheveled figure. "We didn't call for a chimney sweep."

"I'm not a chimney sweep," George huffed. He nearly gave his name before thinking better of it. If the butler knew of his family, admitting he was the 3rd Lord of Devonshire might inspire questions about where the 1st and 2nd Lords of Devonshire had gone. "I have very important business here."

The butler began to close the door, but George thrust his foot into the door's path. "What I mean is that, for me, chimney sweeping is not only my business, it's my, er, personal mission. Proper chimney maintenance is my life's calling." George swallowed, inventing wildly. "Just last week, I discovered a chimney clogged by an umbrella. Umbrellas," he added when the butler raised his eyebrows, "are extremely dangerous to chimneys, you know."

"Come in," the butler said at last. "But don't move from this spot. If my mistress, Lady Milbanke, says to send you away, you will go at once."

"Thank you," George said with a fake smile. (It was a charming smile, nevertheless.) He waited until the butler was out of sight before stepping quickly into the narrow corridor that led to the staircase. Lining the sides of the first few steps were precarious stacks of newspapers and books, which made the stairs even narrower. George picked his way around them, careful not to make any noise as he climbed.

On the thirteenth stair, the floorboard dropped suddenly under his weight. He had to grab the banister so he didn't tumble backward. Looking down, he saw that beneath his shoe, the step had lowered at an angle like a switch on a machine.

The banister vibrated as some kind of metal mechanism began to grind loudly inside the wall next to him.

He quickly stepped backward. Not a second later, an enormous bag of flour hurtled from the ceiling and, with a heavy *whoomf*, landed directly where George had just been standing. The mechanical whirring stopped as suddenly as it had started.

George squeezed the banister so tightly his knuckles turned whiter than the cloud of snowy flour drifting onto his boots. A fit of dizziness seized him. If he had hesitated a second longer, he would have been knocked to the bottom of the staircase like Humpty Dumpty. He fought back an overwhelming urge to flee all the way to the safety of No. 8 Dorset Square. Instead, wiping flour from his brow, he tiptoed cautiously over the deadly bag of flour and continued up the stairs.

At the top, George heard a very faint clicking and the fluttering sound of the mechanical bird's wings. The noise seemed to be coming from a small red door across the hallway. As he walked toward the sound, he smelled sawdust and a hint of smoke.

The door was slightly ajar. A brilliant sliver of light shone through the slim opening. Though part of him feared that another rogue bag of flour would fall from the ceiling, he pressed his eye against the crack to see inside.

As his eyes strained for a glimpse of the bird, or the girl, or his map, George hoped that his adventure would end soon. When he saw what was behind the door, however, he got a dreadful inkling that it was only just beginning.

Chapter Five

The room was almost identical to George's bedroom in size and shape—a rectangle the length of two carriages put back to front—but dissimilar in every other way.

Unlike his bedroom, which was bare except for the massive four-poster bed whose four posts had been sawed off for firewood, this room was bursting with colors. Hundreds of drawings of birds and other animals papered the walls. On the many shelves, a thousand clay models of trains and ships, owls and seashells, miniature houses and mysterious faces jostled for space. Scraps of wood and metal were piled on the floor, some alive with movement and the same mechanical clicking he had heard earlier.

In one corner, a figurehead of a winged woman held a strange orb of light in her wooden hand. To George, it looked as if she were beckoning him to enter.

Behind a workbench, the slender girl with dark hair whom George had seen briefly through his window now stood bent over the mechanical bird, seemingly too fixated on it to even notice his entrance. An array of mirrors surrounded a single gas lamp, bouncing the light and focusing it into a bright beam. A hatch in the bird's neck was open, exposing its metallic inner workings. George watched the girl adjust something inside the bird with a pair of long tweezers.

Apparently, this was the maker of the thievish bird.

A girl. About his age, from the looks of it. It was not what he'd expected at all.

George nudged the door open a little more. A bell attached to a string tied to the inside doorknob jingled, and the dark-haired girl whirled around. Her eyes were five times the normal size, or so it appeared until George realized she was wearing a pair of enormous goggles, strapped to her head by what looked to be a man's silk bow tie.

He was caught. Taking a deep breath and squaring his shoulders, he flung open the door. "Now, look here..." he began, in the stern voice of the lawyers and creditors who regularly appeared on his stoop.

But before he'd taken two steps into the room, his ankle snagged on something invisible, and he yelped in surprise. Tumbling forward, he landed on his hands and knees. His chin bumped the floorboards, and his hair fell over his face.

Before he could stagger upright, the girl had crossed the room.

"Who are you?" she demanded. She brandished her pair of sharp tweezers menacingly in front of his face. "Did the Organization send you? Answer my questions or I'll pluck out your eyes."

George tried to speak but succeeded only in sneezing. The room was very dusty. He pushed his soot-powdered hair out of his eyes and scrambled to his feet. When he finally stood upright and met her eyes, which were still begoggled, the girl sighed and lowered the tweezers.

"Oh, it's just you. Beg pardon. I couldn't see you very well with my goggles on. I thought for a moment you must have been a spy sent by the Organization. As Mother always says, one can really never be too careful. Do you like eggs?" She said these things all in a row, very quickly, as though it were normal to move from talk of spies to talk of eggs in one conversation.

George shook his head in bewilderment.

She pulled a hard-boiled egg from the pocket of her purple dress and began to peel it.

The longer he stared at her, the more ridiculous she looked. Her hair was dark and massed in unruly curls on top of her head, like something sprouting. Her eyes kept changing size as the lenses in her goggles shifted, seemingly of their own accord. Where were her manners, her civility? *Had* she recently escaped from an asylum? That would explain why George had never seen her before. But it didn't explain why she seemed to know him.

"I know why you've come," the girl said, with her mouth full of egg. "First, I'd like to apologize."

George felt a rush of relief. But before he could say a word, she barreled on. "I'm sorry about the mollusks."

He stared at her. "The . . . mollusks?"

She nodded somberly and pushed her goggles onto her forehead. "Last year I was studying adhesives and viscosity," she said matter-of-factly, as if this would make him less and not more confused. "I collected one thousand shelled and unshelled mollusks of different sizes, from the common garden slug to the rarer South American blue-shelled snail. That's over two hundred more than Charles."

George's mind turned with questions as if some-one had set his whole head spinning on top of his neck. "Charles? Who's Charles?"

"But wouldn't you know, I must have forgotten to close the tank one day! It was surprising how fast they escaped, I'll tell you, for animals that move so slowly. I'm so glad that Frobisher thought to relocate them to the garden, but really, you might think of asking him to take them farther afield."

George smoothed down his cowlick. "How did you—?" His cheeks heated up. "Have you been *spying* on me?"

"Of course," the girl reassured him, widening her eyes, as if otherwise he might be offended. "Every day for close to a year now. And it finally paid off! For you, of course." She grinned and dipped into a low curtsey, lifting her skirt and sweeping her right hand to her chest. "Ada Byron." Her introduction might have been elegant if her mouth hadn't still been full of egg.

George bowed, as one is supposed to do when greeting a lady. "*Lovely* to meet you, Miss Byron," he lied. "My name is George, the 3rd Lord of Devonshire. I come not about the slugs and snails, but about that creature." George straightened up and pointed at the bird. It looked rather pitiful lying exposed on the workbench with its mechanical guts showing. "I have a complaint to lodge against it."

Ada frowned. "A complaint? This bird saved your skin."

"I had it all under control," George said quickly. "I was chasing the man out of my house before he could steal anything valuable." He blushed, hoping that if she had been spying, she hadn't noticed that he had no valuables to steal. "He was on his knees begging for mercy when your bird attacked."

Ada tilted her head, as if inspecting him. "That's a lie. Sometimes lying is acceptable, but it serves no purpose in this case except to protect your ego."

"My what?"

"From what I saw, if my bird hadn't come to your rescue, that man would have left your house with this very valuable map," Ada said. She pointed to her workbench, where the scroll lay unopened.

"I was doing fine on my own," George said, stepping toward the map with his hand outstretched.

But Ada snatched it up first. "I think you owe *me* an apology. I helped you."

George opened his mouth to argue but stopped. "How do you know the map is valuable?"

"Because someone wanted to steal it. Because it's practically the only earthly possession you haven't sold, by the looks of it. So what is it?" she said, almost as if she were talking to herself. She smoothed the map out on the workbench and produced a magnifying glass from her pocket to examine it more closely. "It's beautiful. Unique, surely."

George flushed with pride. The girl was odd, but she didn't *seem* like a thief, even though she'd snatched his map. "It's the map to a precious gem of great historical significance. It is completely singular. I know because my grandfather made it."

Ada's magnifying glass paused briefly over the Latin phrase *Stella Victōriae*. "The Victory Star," she said.

"The Star of Victory," George replied warily. Did she want to steal it, too? But if that were the case, her bird could have simply flown away with it . . .

"This map is a work of art," she continued, making

George's regard for his grandfather swell in his chest. "Except for these blemishes and the typographical errors like this one over Switzerland."

"Blemishes? Errors?" he snapped. The suggestion was preposterous. He followed her finger, which was pointing to two triangular shapes over Lake Geneva. "That's not an error, Miss Byron. That is the Greek letter *lambda*—in other words, the lake's initials. They're a bit crooked because my grandfather had a unique style of script. I know the map better than anyone."

"Interesting," Ada said, staring at him, or through him, rather, as if she were thinking very hard about something. "Don't you think it's odd that someone stole this map on the very same day Frobisher went to the antiques dealer?"

George glared at her. She knew about that, too? "Just bad luck," he said. "Which reminds me, I really must be tending to him. He's quite frail and your bird gave him a fright. Now, if you'll give me the map, I'll be on my way."

"Wrong again." Ada straightened. "I'll tell you what I know."

"I'm not interested."

Ada didn't seem to hear him—or care, he couldn't tell which. "It must be the work of the Organization. They are no common criminals," she said, raising a hand when he started to protest. "They hide in the shadows, never revealing what their true purpose is. My father used to tell stories about them."

Used to. Ada's words stoppered his throat. He didn't know what to make of this girl. But George knew what it was like to lose someone.

"Miss Byron," he started softly. "I'm sorry to hear that your father is . . . gone." He paused, waiting for her to clarify, but she only nodded. He must have been right. Ada's father had passed away, like his own. "But this wasn't the work of an, erm, organization."

Ada blinked at him, which was the longest she had paused before speaking. "Lord Devonshire, I didn't believe in them at first, either. I didn't even believe my own mother when she told me they were responsible for driving my father away. That he left for *our* own safety. Then my letters to him went unanswered. Then I noticed men lurking around Dorset Square. Then a thief broke into your home—a home that, no offense, clearly offers nothing of value besides this map," she said, fluttering her fingers in the direction of George's dilapidated mansion. "I have a scientific mind. I can't just ignore evidence. They must want the Star of Victory."

"But it was just a man," George insisted. "A redhead with a stupid red coat who smelled like macassar hair oil."

Ada crossed her arms. "Criminals can use hair oil, too, you know. And these criminals are like termites. They're everywhere, hidden in plain sight, all the while eating at the foundations of society until the whole kingdom crumbles to dust."

George scoffed. "I've never seen or heard of a criminal like that."

"That's because you stay inside your house and have never had anyone like me to warn you."

George blushed again fiercely, but Ada didn't seem to notice. "You're absurd. Surely one small organization couldn't topple an entire government."

"It's not *one* organization, it's *the* Organization." Ada clucked her tongue. "You are naïve. So was I. The Organization could have members working for the army. Or for the *King*. I haven't yet determined the source of their current funds, but...imagine what they could do with a fortune," she said. Her eyes began to gleam with a ferocity that made George uneasy. "Yes, they must want the Star. It's valuable."

George wasn't sure what to make of the strange girl

with the strange theories, but she spoke the truth about one thing—the map had value.

"We'll have to leave right away," she said.

"Leave?" George asked.

"To get the Star of Victory *first*. They must want to do something terrible with it." She looked at him. On a shelf, a clock ticked away loudly. Its brass pendulum swung back and forth, slicing the silence between them. "You've nothing better to do."

For a moment, as he had countless times before his grandfather died, George imagined how it would feel to discover the Star for himself in a distant, frosty place. He would leap off the boat and ride an iceberg to the beach, where he would take a deep breath of icy air and yell, "I declare myself to be King George, Ruler of the Unknown Continent, Rightful Owner of the Star of Victory!" and would plant a flag with the Devonshire crest in the frozen ground.

Then he imagined the earth cracking open to swallow him—and anyone unlucky enough to have accompanied him—whole.

Ada's voice burst into his thoughts. "I'd be doing you a favor. You must be bored. And lonely."

41

He snatched the map away from her. He'd stayed too long already. "I'll thank you to keep out of my affairs from now on, Miss Byron. Good day."

As she watched George slip the map into his interior pocket, Ada's eyes grew huge. She looked as if she was about to plead with him, or maybe swipe the map from his grip. But then, at the same lightning speed with which she spoke, Ada's entire demeanor relaxed and she simply shrugged. "Suit yourself."

George marched out the door, down the stairs, and across Dorset Square to his house, still fuming. Who did Miss Ada Byron think she was, with her goggles and her machines and her airs and her pocket stuffed with hard-boiled eggs?

Who did she think she was, calling *him* lonely? He wasn't the one tinkering with toy animals all day long. He had Revenues and Expenses and the study of *The History of the Rhône* to occupy him. Soon he might even have enough money to provide a proper home for himself and Frobisher, buying the manservant a lifetime supply of pastilles and a doctor's visit and even paying his back wages.

If anything, Ada had made him more certain. The map would only bring more daydreams, which a young man of his age should not be indulging. George's father's fate should have been warning enough. The whole preposterous idea was bad luck waiting to happen.

Tomorrow he would sell the map, no matter what, for the highest price he could get.

Or he would have, if the red-haired thief hadn't rounded a corner and snatched it out of his hand first.

Chapter Six

The thief was up onto his horse in one practiced, graceful leap. His face and neck were covered in angry pink streaks from where the bird's talons had scratched him earlier. George caught a brief glimpse of a red saddle blanket edged in gold, the elaborate royal crest, and the initials *KPS* gleaming in gold threads before the man galloped away with his curls streaming behind him and the map held high over his head like a trophy.

For a moment George stood there, gasping for breath, his hands clenched in rigid fists, his heart a drum in his chest.

"Told you the Organization was after you."

The flutelike voice came down from the window

of No. 5. Ada Byron was watching him pityingly. "You should have let me help."

"I don't need your help!" George shouted back.

"Fine," she said primly, and slammed the window shut.

Almost immediately, he regretted it. She had been right about the theft. Might she have been right, too, about the Organization? He was no match for an international criminal ring. Even the snails weren't afraid of him.

But he would have swallowed a bottle of macassar oil before he'd admit he needed her help.

The initials *KPS* tumbled through his mind. KPS. A royal crest, the thief's red coat and riding boots, the expensive hair oil, and now the initials all pointed to one place: Kensington Palace Stables.

When George was younger (and the curse had not yet claimed its second victim), his governess used to take him on long walks down to Hyde Park to watch the ducks swim in the Serpentine. He remembered that if he headed south, he would find Kensington Palace—the home of the royal family—next to Hyde Park.

After what seemed like hours, he reached the iron railings and gates that surrounded Hyde Park all the way to the Kensington Gardens, which were even grander than he recalled. He skirted the park until he saw the redbrick chimneys of the palace rising above the treetops. The tall iron gates, which were decorated with the same gold crest he had seen stitched onto the thief's saddle blanket, were guarded by six men wearing bright red jackets and tall hats.

Careful not to be seen by the guards, he continued along, searching for another way in. Rounding the corner, he saw a side gate swing open to let a line of several carriages pass through. Quickening his pace, he joined the procession of carriages. He jogged beside one of the tall, rolling wheels until he entered through the gate, unseen.

Dodging several horses and a flurry of men with rough accents, he slipped into the stables. The smell of wet hay and manure was thick. Horses neighed and stamped in their wooden stalls. Beside every stall, identical red-and-gold saddle blankets hung from iron hooks. There was no sign of the redheaded man.

George's stomach tensed. It had taken him over an hour to get to the palace. What if he was too late, and the thief had already made his escape with the map? What if he hadn't come back to the palace at all? George peeked into a stall, hoping to find the thief crouched inside, but found nothing but a sodden clump of straw.

"George." The whispered voice made him start. "George. *Psst*. Over here."

He backed quickly out of the stall and caught a glimpse of a grubby, unfamiliar boy at the stable doors, gesturing for him to follow. The boy had streaks of dirt on his cheeks and wild dark hair under a flat-topped cap. Before George could ask what he wanted or how the boy knew his name, the urchin had darted away.

George sprinted after him through the stable yards and, trying to keep up with the boy's racing shadow, plunged past a cluster of shrubs that had been trimmed into pointed triangles. On the other side of the shrubs were steps leading to a sunken garden and a pool filled with white ducks swimming among green lily pads. By the time George made it down to the edge of the water, the boy had disappeared completely.

George stopped for a moment to catch his breath. Ada's words echoed in his head: the criminals were hiding in plain sight. A grimy little boy would be the last person he would suspect of being in a secret organization. Perhaps he shouldn't have been so quick to follow a stranger.

It was too late to turn back now. After a few twists and turns through a lush, quiet grove, he came face-to-face with the boy, who was wearing a threadbare brown suit and *staring* at him with fierce dark eyes. He was a stranger. And yet...

George blinked. He recognized the pale face smudged with dirt.

It couldn't be.

"Good afternoon, George. I thought you'd never get here." Ada Byron pulled a hard-boiled egg from her pocket and began to peel it. "My disguise fooled you, didn't it? I borrowed a trick from the Organization and dressed the part."

George could only stare.

"You should close your mouth," she said. "You'll swallow a fly."

George closed his mouth. With his bad luck, he could die precisely that way. Then he opened it again, because he had to know: "Are you *following* me?"

"Following you?" Ada laughed, wisps of her dark curls slipping out from beneath her cap. "Lord Devonshire, I'm *helping* you." She swallowed her egg in several large bites. "I came to get your map back."

For the first time, he noticed the roll of yellowed paper neatly tied with a red ribbon and tucked into her jacket pocket. His map. A strange, light feeling ran all the way down to his toes.

"How . . . ?" he began. "What . . . ?"

"How did I know the map was stolen by a stable hand from Kensington Palace?"

George nodded. He had seen the royal crest stitched onto the thief's saddle blanket. But there was no way Ada could have seen it from a distance.

Ada smiled. "His demeanor. His clothes. But especially his smell."

"His *smell*?"

"Delcroix's macassar oil. You mentioned it when you burst into my rooms without announcing yourself," Ada said. "Yes, it's much too expensive for any ordinary footman to own. But if the Organization is employing him as well, then he will have extra money to spend on making his hair glossy and thick." She shrugged. "I caught a glimpse of him. The King's footmen are generally quite tall and wear red coats and riding boots when they exercise the horses."

"That's . . ." *Amazing. Incredible. Brilliant.* ". . . absolutely preposterous," George finished instead.

"Do you want to know how I got the map back?" Ada

brushed her fingertips against its yellowed edges, then handed it to George, who snatched it before she could use it as a napkin.

"No thank you," George said. "I must get back to Fro—"

"I had already come up with several plans to get the map back if you were unable to protect it, but I didn't think I would have to put them into action so soon."

"I had everything under control!" George interjected.

Ada shot him a stern look and continued. "At any rate, I arrived in the palace gardens only a few minutes after the thief."

"A few minutes?" George repeated. "Impossible. How did you get here so fast?"

"I'm here, aren't I?" she said. Ignoring his questions seemed to be a habit of hers. "In my disguise, I asked around for a redheaded man—his name is Roy, by the way—and found him in no time."

George crossed his arms. "And I suppose you merely asked for the map, and he gave it to you?"

"Of course not." Ada snorted. "I told him I had a letter for him." She motioned for George to follow her through a row of hedges while she continued to talk. "And I did. Nobody questions the messenger. They only care about the message. I had written a letter that told him his instructions had changed and that he was to put the map inside the large white flowerpot outside the orangery."

"And he left it there? In a pot of dirt next to a greenhouse?" George inspected the edges of the map for cleanliness.

Ada beamed, holding a tree branch for him to pass under, which revealed a narrow dirt path. "Of course. It was all quite simple."

George's cheeks burned hot. "I could have managed it—"

"Alone. I know." Ada rolled her eyes. "And you're welcome."

"I was going to say I could have managed it with less dirt, but thank you," he mumbled.

"Best to keep the map hidden. We're not safe yet."

George nodded and slipped the map under his shirt. They had walked deeper into the grounds, down more gravel paths, these narrower and more twisting. As George followed Ada, who navigated the palace gardens with the confidence of someone who had come this way often, he noted (again) how easily she could have stolen the map from him. But she hadn't.

So why was she helping him?

It suddenly occurred to him to ask where they were going. "Miss Byron, where are we—"

"Shortcut!" she chirped happily, forging ahead with hardly a backward glance to see if he was behind her.

After so many years between the same crumbling walls of No. 8, he had forgotten how green everything was. Everywhere he looked was a different shade: the hazy green of the drooping willow trees, the glossy green of the thick boxwood hedges, and the radiant green of the grass. Overhead, a thrush trilled, and the song filled his chest with a strange feeling, as if someone were opening a music box that had been closed for a very, very long time.

George felt the map, tucked safely into his shirt. In the past few hours, it had brought nothing but trouble, he reminded himself. He would be *lucky* to be rid of it—lucky, perhaps, for the first time in his life. If only Ada would hurry up and lead them home. The sun was sinking lower in the sky, the trees casting long shadows across the grass.

Two rust-colored shapes shot from the bushes and zoomed across the gravel path. George yelped and jumped backward, but it was only a pair of squirrels chasing each other.

"It's good to stay on your guard and be aware of your surroundings," Ada said. "When dealing with the Organization, you can never be too careful."

"It was your father who told you so much about this Organization?" George asked, recovering quickly from his embarrassment. He still wasn't sure whether he believed her or not. Why would the organization Ada described want his map? He didn't have an answer, but he knew hardly anything, really, except for his rooms at No. 8 and its leaky roof and *The History of the Rhône*.

Ada's dark eyes sparkled. "*The* Organization. Yes. My father knew all about it. He left hints of it in his poetry, even—encoded, of course. He told my mother all about it and she in turn told me. He wanted to protect us, you see. That's why she's always taught me to keep my inventions a secret. They're after them. I just know it."

She explained all this as though it were perfectly natural to be wanted by criminals, and to live in a house fortified with locks and chains.

George wondered at the coincidence of it all: that after

Ada's years of watchful avoidance of the Organization, it had been he who had finally attracted their interest. But just as quickly, he realized that it wasn't a coincidence at all.

It was, quite simply, the curse of his bad luck.

Ada took the left fork where the path diverged in front of them. They passed through a grove of trees, and then, suddenly, they were at the entrance to a small cluster of glass pavilions surrounded by a high iron fence. Emblazoned upon the arch over the iron gate were the words *The Royal Menagerie.*

George stopped beneath the sign. "A menagerie on the palace grounds?" he asked suspiciously.

"Princess Victoria loves exotic animals. The more extraordinary, the better."

George was about to object, but Ada had already passed through the gate. When it clanged shut behind her, an unearthly roar erupted inside the central glass pavilion. The roar was joined by screams and howls that surely no human ear was meant to hear and live to tell about.

Chapter Seven

George wished more than ever that he would be magically transported back to No. 8 Dorset Square. He wasn't fond of domestic animals like chipmunks, mice, and rabbits. Exotic animals were far, far worse. But he stepped through the iron gate after Ada and wedged open the pavilion door just enough to stick his head inside. He was greeted by a curtain of vines with huge leaves.

"Ada, this does not look like a shortcut."

Ada's voice rang out clearly from beyond a screen of foliage. "I've decided that you should meet Oscar. Just trust me."

Trust her? Her strange demeanor still made him uneasy. And yet, she seemed to be on his—well, the map's—side, and lingering outside where he might be caught at any moment seemed ill-advised. So George tugged the door wide open and stepped through it.

Before he could get very far, someone sprinted past him.

"Excuse me," the boy said quickly to George. He was wearing ragged clothes streaked with stains of a thousand different colors and carrying what appeared to be a toddler swaddled in an orange fur coat. The toddler turned to look at George and grinned, its mouth protruding as if it had swallowed an apple. With a start, George realized it was not a human child wearing a fur coat at all. It was an ape. Other than its wrinkled, eerily human face, the rest of its small body was covered in wispy orange hair.

"Indeed." George followed the boy and the creature into the pavilion at a safe distance. It was warm and humid inside the glass building, even though tall tropical plants draped with thick vines blocked out most of the remaining sunlight.

"Ada, I need your help," the boy said. "Ruthie's eaten my pestle. I'm scared she's going to die."

Die? George's mouth went dry with fear. Was he somehow responsible? Was this Ruthie the latest victim (#12) of his curse?

56

"Over here, Oscar," Ada replied. Her calm voice slowed George's pulse. She took the ape into her arms and began to press her fingers into its stomach. The ape made a soft, pitiful whimper but otherwise did not seem to be in mortal danger. "George, this is Oscar, and his companion, Ruthie. Oscar is studying to be a painter and I'm assisting with his training. Ruthie is an orangutan."

"How interesting," George said awkwardly, his rules of decorum failing him utterly in this situation. Did one introduce oneself to an ape? Did this Oscar character have a last name or a title? While George stalled by patting down his cowlick several times, still lingering a few paces away from them, a flock of pink flamingos with long necks and even longer legs strutted through the glade. A rainbow-colored bird swooped down from a tree and began preening itself on top of Oscar's head. This did not help George with decorum in the least.

The little reddish ape was now dangling from Ada's neck by its spidery limbs, making a terrible retching sound. Oscar looked on in concern.

"Open your mouth, Ruthie," Ada told the ape.

Ruthie glanced at Oscar, who straightened his arms, then wheeled them around to various positions as if his limbs were the hands of a clock. Ruthie responded by raising her own arms and parting her wrinkled brown lips to stick out her pink tongue, which looked exactly like a human tongue.

Was Oscar...talking to an ape? Impossible. George inched closer.

Oscar was a few years younger than George, with a round, open face that showed every change in his emotions like a mirror of his thoughts. His hair, skin, and eyes were brown, except for his fingers, which were stained a vivid green color as though they had been dipped in pea soup. He orbited Ada in meandering circles with one eye trained on Ruthie.

When he noticed George watching him, his worried expression brightened with a gap-toothed smile. His grin resembled a cheerful jack-o'-lantern's; there were several spaces where his adult teeth hadn't yet grown in all the way.

"Hello," said the boy sunnily. He waved, and with the other hand gave the orangutan's head a gentle, loving pat. "Did you fly here with Ada? Are you one of her scientist friends?"

"We're neighbors," George said.

"Oh. Did you come to see the birds? Ada studies them

to see how their wings work. She shows me how they move and then I draw them. Every great artist should understand anatomy and how things work, Ada says."

"Oscar is a great artist." Ada's fingers were still pressed against Ruthie's belly.

"And Ada is a genius. She knows the most fascinating people. Any friend of Ada's is a friend of mine," Oscar said, beaming now.

"Miss Byron and I are acquaintances, *not* friends," George replied.

Oscar's smile vanished as quickly as it had come. He squinted his big brown eyes as if he were trying to see through George's skin to somewhere deep inside. "Pity for you. Ada's mother doesn't let her have many friends. If her mother doesn't think you're suitable, then maybe you could be her protégé like me and she could teach you things."

"I'm the 3rd Lord of Devonshire," George clarified stiffly. Ada's mother should be the one vying for George's favor, not the other way around. "My grandfather was a maritime war hero."

"A mariner!" Oscar brought his arms across his chest in the shape of an X, though George had no idea why. "I have salt in my blood as well. My father is a sailor. A pirate, actually. A very good one." He said this as if it were something to be proud of. "One day I'll join him and we'll go sailing the wide waters together. In the meantime, I have Ruthie to keep me company. And Ada. And my paints. I make my own pigments out of bits of plants and rocks. Would you like to see my mineral collection?"

"I would not," George said more harshly than he had intended. "I have very important business. Some other time, perhaps." He looked down at the map tucked inside his shirt to avoid seeing Oscar's hurt expression. Any delay in getting back to No. 8 could put him in danger of losing the map again, or worse—his bad luck could claim another victim. "Ada and I were about to take a shortcut home. Weren't we, Miss Byron?"

Oscar's eyes brightened further than George would have thought possible. "Oh, I love flying. It's much faster than walking, isn't it? Ada promised to take me on another trip soon to look for rocks."

"Flying?"

"I was hoping you could convince him, Oscar. Go on. Show him. I promise Ruthie is perfectly fine. I'll bring her along in a minute," Ada said.

Relieved, Oscar turned and beckoned George to fol-low. He trailed after Oscar through the heavy plant growth one cautious step at a time.

"What are you going to show—"

Pushing aside a wet fan of leaves, George stopped short, dumb with wonder. Of all the strange things he had seen today, what was waiting there in a small clearing of growth was by far the strangest.

Because in addition to the towering, smelly plants and exotic creatures, the menagerie housed a gigantic mechan-ical bird. It looked identical to the smaller bird that had invaded his home, except that it was the size of a large horse and had cushioned seats in a hollowed-out portion of its back. Two large wheels took the place of talons. Behind them were two flattened trails of grass that led to a large set of double doors at the opposite end of the menagerie.

Instinctively, George staggered back. So *this* was the shortcut. He remembered the drawings of wings in Ada's room, and the black bird soaring over Dorset Square, and now he understood how Ada had gotten here—and how she intended to transport them both home.

The taste of a coming disaster was bitter on George's tongue and he swallowed hard, realizing he'd made a grave mistake in leaving his home. Perhaps an even graver mistake in following Ada this far. What downfall had he invited into his life by getting wrapped up with this genius who flew through the skies in a mechanical bird?

Ada joined them next to the contraption. She unhooked the orangutan's arms from around her neck and handed the creature back to Oscar.

"There's nothing to be done but wait," she said. "I can tell she ate something very hard because she cracked her baby teeth. But she'll be just fine."

Oscar flashed his gap-toothed smile, all worry gone from his face. "Why would she eat my pestle? I use it to grind all my pigments. It's my hardest stone and the loveliest shade of Prussian blue."

"She may have a touch of geophagia caused by a lack of minerals."

George cleared his throat. "If you'll excuse me, I'm leav—"

"Geophagia?" Oscar interrupted. "What does that mean?"

"Some animals and even people have a tendency to eat dirt or clay or pebbles to aid their digestion. It's not surprising, I think, given how sick she was when we rescued her from that wretched cage at the traveling circus."

Perhaps Oscar and Ada wouldn't notice if he just slipped out the door. Taking small, silent steps, he began to slink away.

"She eats minerals all the time! Just yesterday she ate some of the glauconite I use to make my Verona green," Oscar said, wiggling his pea-green fingers as Ruthie nuzzled her head against his shoulder.

Ada sighed. "Well, that confirms it. She definitely has geophagia. She's been through worse than this, Oscar. What goes in must come out, never fear." Ada turned back to George, who had one foot into the curtain of leaves that hid the bird from view. "Are you ready to go?"

George froze and turned to face her. "Go?" he replied, his voice as wilted as the garden lettuces behind No. 8 Dorset Square.

"Yes, go. Leave, depart, quit this place, et cetera. My mother is taking a health cure at the seaside for the rest of the month. If we're going to go, we need to go now." She hopped up into the mechanical bird with a graceful leap. "Pull out the map. You'll have to navigate while I fly."

The word *fly* seemed to drive a spear of lightning through him, jolting him alive.

"You're crazy if you think I'm going in that thing!" George jutted his chin at the giant bird.

"I'm not crazy," Ada shot back from her perch on her bird.

Oscar laid a calming hand on George's shoulder. "It's all right to be afraid to fly. I was, too. I watched Ada build the machine from scraps of metal and sticks of wood. I didn't think she could do it, but she did. She'll get you home safely. You can trust her."

"Trust her? I don't know her. Or you." George shrank back from Oscar. How could he trust anyone when he couldn't trust the world not to come crashing down around him at any moment? "You're friends with *her* and a monkey who eats rocks."

In a flash, Ada had jumped down from the bird and stood between George and Oscar, jabbing her finger at George's chest. Behind her, Ruthie the orangutan did the same thing. "Don't insult us because you're a coward. If it weren't for me, you wouldn't even have that map."

Ada's words hit George like a mallet. *The spine of a snail. The brains of a bowl of porridge.* "I am not a coward," he said.

"I have responsibilities. Besides, I'm sure that my bad luck would strike the moment I stepped into your mechanical bird and make it fall to pieces or burst into flames, burn Kensington Palace to the ground, and topple the entire British Empire."

"Responsibilities. Bad luck. Those are terrible excuses," she said plainly, a faint note of pity in her voice. "Come with me and we can find the Star together. That's what you want, isn't it? To find the Star?"

With a jerk of his arm, he yanked the glass door open. "Frobisher needs me. I have duties here, *Miss* Byron, unlike you," he said curtly.

Ada looked at him in her strange, unnerving way, as if she were assessing him. "Well, if you want to sell the map, would you accept a hundred pounds for it?"

"You have a buyer?" His heart suddenly turned to ice. He had made up his mind to sell it a few hours ago, but now that it was actually happening . . .

"Yes," she said. "Me."

Chapter Eight

George stared at Ada, stunned, as she reached into several of her many pockets, eventually producing a small scroll of parchment. He immediately recognized the Bank of England's official seal. One hundred pounds. That much money could solve his financial problems. His tongue turned dry before he realized his jaw had dropped.

"Do you accept?" Ada asked primly.

George could only nod.

"Excellent. It's settled. One hundred pounds for the map to the Star of Victory. You'd never have found the Star without me anyway," Ada said, her dark eyes blazing against her pale cheeks. "Perhaps it's for the best I won't be accompanied by an *intrepid* explorer such as the 3rd Lord of Devonshire, whose exciting exploits consist of climbing to the top of his staircase and crossing the street once every few years."

George recoiled, stung. He knew what the word *intrepid* meant, and that she had used it sarcastically. "I'll gladly stay inside my house forever if it means that I never see you or one of your confounded contraptions again. You're the rudest, most arrogant, smuggest person in the world, Ada Byron. Good day."

Before he could change his mind, he took the money and handed her the map. Then, without a backward glance, he turned away from Ada, the bird, the trees that shrouded Oscar and Ruthie—the entire wonderful, strange, infuriating spectacle.

And left.

And yet, with every step, a terrible feeling of dread expanded in his stomach. By the time he exited the palace gates, his heart was heavier than a sack of stones. His grandfather would have been disappointed in him for selling the map, and for throwing away any hope of ever finding the Star. But his grandfather was no longer alive to be disappointed, he told himself. This made George sad, but it was long past time he made the practical choice.

For once, his Revenues were going to do more than just cover his Expenses for the month. Now he possessed one hundred pounds to pay off his debts and to buy food and medicine for Frobisher. The money was enough to cover their expenses for a few years. Perhaps tomorrow he could even buy himself a whole new set of clothes and a set for Frobisher, too.

By the time George arrived back at the familiar green lawn of Dorset Square, he felt slightly better. He lingered outside the front door of No. 8, pausing to admire the way the glow of the streetlamps illuminated the house his grandfather had built. He remembered how his grandfather would often stop on the front steps, just as George was doing now, to gaze up at the house with pride. The mansion was slowly crumbling, but it belonged to him. Every brick, every window, every inch of No. 8.

Yes, this was where he belonged. Not on some harebrained scheme in a flying rust bucket.

Inside No. 8, George put a candle in an old burnished lantern to light his way upstairs, eager to tell Frobisher that he had solved their money problems. At least for a few years. Frobisher had long ago moved from his cramped servants' quarters in the attic to one of the empty bedrooms on the second floor. His room was so dark, George's candle hardly penetrated when he cracked the door open.

"Frobisher?" George strained his eyes to see in the dim light. Frobisher was sitting up on his bed with his back to the window, his gray head slumped onto his chin. A loud snore confirmed he was asleep.

George slipped his brand-new banknote into Frobisher's shirt pocket. It would be a wonderful surprise, he thought. A glint of light drew his eye downward, where he noticed the shine of a gold button. George brought his candle closer...

His grandfather's old seafarer's uniform lay across Frobisher's lap. George's heart swelled with surprise and gratitude—he barely cared that Frobisher had lied to him earlier about selling it. What had the manservant had to sell in the uniform's place? George hoped it wasn't Frobisher's beloved periscope, the only item he'd brought to No. 8, or the old wire cage he'd been fixing up as a home for Mrs. Daly.

Gingerly, George picked up the sailor's jacket, and it fell open in front of him. The suit was much smaller than he remembered; the stitches at the seams were a brighter blue, too, not dirty and worn like they had been before.

George started at a creaking noise. But it was only Frobisher, waking from his sleep. A long blue thread trailed from his left hand.

"Frobisher, did you..."

Frobisher drew his arm back and forth, miming sewing.

"You were tailoring this for me?"

The manservant gestured for George to put the uniform on. He did, and the fabric slipped over his body like a glove. George ran his hands over the rough blue sleeves. The fabric still smelled of salt and sweat and tobacco. It had warmed his grandfather on cold nights at sea. It had protected him from wind and rain and every kind of weather.

Frobisher knew George better than anyone, maybe even better than his grandfather had. He knew that George had been poring over the map for years, dreaming of the day when he might seek out the Star of Victory to carry on the Devonshire legacy. George swallowed his shame.

Ada.

The map was with Ada now.

George sneaked a glance out the window. Above the dark windows of No. 5, the night sky was so black, so empty. He couldn't help imagining what it would be like to become a shining speck in that sky. How would it feel to fly through the air like a bird, closer to the stars than anyone had ever been?

Fear dragged him back to earth. No. 8—its crumbling walls, its animal tenants, its Frobisher—needed him to stay.

George's shoulders sank and he opened his mouth to explain all this to Frobisher. But his manservant's moist gray eyes were opened wide, and his thin lips parted as though he wanted to say something.

Then, for the first time in two years, Frobisher spoke.

To say he spoke might have been a bit of an embellishment, but George was quite sure he heard the ailing man choke out a single word:

"Go."

George took off the sailing jacket and crumpled it under his arm. "Don't be silly. This place would fall apart if I weren't here."

71

Frobisher coughed insistently. He pointed at the window.

"I don't want to hear another word about it," declared George. "I've made up my mind and that's all there is to it. I'm going to take a bath now. I think you'll change your mind about me leaving after you check your pocket."

Downstairs, with water from one of the rainwater collection buckets, which Frobisher had left to warm in the sun, George scrubbed himself clean of the dust and grime and confusion that had settled into every pore of his skin, and began to feel more like himself. It wasn't cowardly to be reluctant to travel, he thought as he rinsed his hair. Far from it. It was practical. After all, he didn't need some outlandish journey of self-discovery to teach him life lessons he already knew. He was the 3rd Lord of Devonshire, king of his castle, protector of his domain. This was where he belonged. Right here.

With wet hair and a clean conscience, George slipped between his bedsheets. In the morning, he would tell Frobisher to go to the druggist straightaway and get himself some medicine. After that, he would put an advertisement in the newspaper to rent out rooms in the house. It was not ideal, but it was a much more practical way than treasure hunting. And the title *landlord* did have a nice ring to it. He could live in the attic, he reasoned, and come out only at night until he was too old to be sent to the orphanage.

George drifted off to sleep, his head swimming with rent sums, surcharges, and additional fees.

Chapter Nine

Early the next morning, before the sun had fully risen, George was startled awake by the sound of breaking glass, followed by a loud crash.

"Not again," he groaned. Today was supposed to be a fresh start. The last thing he wanted to deal with was another invasion from the mechanical bird. Whatever damage it had caused this time, he didn't want to know. It would be better to stay in bed.

The house settled back down into silence. There was no sound from Frobisher's room or downstairs. Deep in George's belly, a little worm of anxiety began to wriggle. Ada should have left with the map. If she was already gone, then whatever came through his window wasn't likely to be friendly.

George climbed out of bed and looked into the hallway.

"Frobisher? Are you all right?" he called out. There was no answer, and no noise.

Down the hall, he found Frobisher's door ajar. "Frobisher?" He stepped into the room, hoping to see the manservant's wrinkled, sniffly face, but found nothing other than an empty bed.

Well, not nothing. Curiously, the threadbare quilt sat in a heap on the floor. The mattress, too, looked as though it had been jostled to one side. Had Frobisher gotten up in a hurry?

George inspected the room further and found that Frobisher's coat, scarf, and hats were gone. Peeking out from under the mattress was the banknote he'd slipped into Frobisher's pocket only hours ago.

George's pulse quickened.

He raced downstairs, calling Frobisher's name. In the entryway, broken glass sparkled like diamonds.

"No. Not again," he breathed. Goose bumps prickled his arms as an icy current of fear washed over him.

In the middle of the glass shards was a large gray rock. A piece of blue-and-green cloth was wrapped around the rock like a bandage. George immediately recognized the hand-drawn squiggles on the fabric; it was Frobisher's neckerchief.

Careful not to step on any glass, George rushed over to pick up the rock. When he untied the neckerchief, a small piece of paper fluttered down like a falling leaf. The note was written in atrocious handwriting, and the spelling was not much better, but the message was clear.

We Hav takin yoR Mann.
BRinge the StaR To Venice
in ten days oR He Diyes.

George stared at the note in disbelief. This couldn't be happening, he told himself. But no matter how long he stood there, listening, the sound of coughing did not reach his ears. No heavy feet walloped the rotten floorboards.

He was alone. Truly alone.

Frobisher had been kidnapped.

Clutching the neckerchief, George paced back and forth across the marble entryway. All of his plans from the night before evaporated like a soap bubble popping on a blade of grass.

Because the thief (Roy, George remembered) had never delivered the map, the Organization must have decided to take the only thing in the world of any value to George, he reasoned. George had known it was only a matter of time before his bad-luck curse claimed its next victim. Poor Frobisher hadn't stood a chance.

George had to find the Star. According to the poorly scribbled instructions on the note, he couldn't save Frobisher without it. Which meant...

There was only one person who could help him: Ada Byron.

The realization hit George like a punch to his gut. He had hoped that yesterday would be the last time he ever laid eyes on that infuriating girl. Now he had no choice but to demand his map back. It was the least she could do. She'd had no business interfering with Roy. If she had left him alone, Roy might have taken the map, but at least Frobisher would be safe. Her meddling had made every-thing ten times worse.

With no time to lose, George quickly dressed himself, put on the sailing jacket Frobisher had altered for him, and tucked the hundred-pound banknote into his pocket. For luck (he could use all he could get), he tied Frobisher's neckerchief around his arm. Thus attired, George marched across the street to determine Ada's whereabouts so that she could return his map. There was no other way to save his manservant's life.

To George's surprise, when he knocked on the door, the butler informed him that Miss Byron was upstairs and that he was welcome to enter. Ada's workshop was even more cluttered this morning, if that was possible. Her puffy dresses and papers were half-packed, half-scattered across the floor. When George had finished explaining his situation and politely requested that she return his map in exchange for returning her one hundred pounds, she studied him with her keen eyes.

"My answer is no," she said.

"No? What do you mean, no?" George implored, his voice rising higher and higher. "A piece of paper means more to you than Frobisher's life? Please, Ada."

Ada raised her eyebrows. "Calm down, George. I didn't say I wouldn't help you. You said the ransom note didn't ask for the map to the Star of Victory. It asked for the Star."

"Yes, and . . ."

"Where are you going to start?"

"Well," he answered impatiently. Panic bubbled in his throat. The map was a map of the entire world. The Star could be anywhere. He would probably start in London, of course...but he couldn't search all of London in ten days, let alone the entire planet, and get to Venice in time.

"Where does your gut tell you to go?" she demanded.

"My...what?"

"What does your gut say?" she asked impatiently. "Mine says that the Star is near Geneva. Those *lambda*s I showed you earlier are the only Greek letters anywhere on the map. And, as I'm sure you're aware, since the *lambda* is a triangle, it is also the alchemical symbol for fire."

George stared at her blankly.

"Stars and fire, get it? Also, if you combine two triangles, they form a hexagram." She whipped a sketchbook out of her pocket and drew two triangles on top of each other to illustrate her point. It looked like this: ✳ "See, a hexagram is a six-pointed star. It's the only logical conclusion."

"Well, your gut is very good at reading symbols." The speed of Ada's interpretation of the map astounded him, as did her logic. But he could find no fault with it. It was

79

certainly better than his current plan, which was to search the entirety of Europe. "All I know is that I have to save Frobisher."

"Then it's settled. We have a better chance of finding the Star if we work together," Ada said.

"But..." An odd hot-and-cold feeling washed over him. Perhaps it was his gut trying to speak to him. "Why would you help me find the Star? It doesn't mean anything to you."

Ada brushed a dark curl from the side of her face. "Unlike you, I'm bored of hanging around Dorset Square for hours on end with nothing better to do than watch carriages roll past. I don't know why you're so suspicious. You came to me this time."

George felt as though he were trapped in a maze of locked doors and Ada was hiding the only key. "Very well, we can search for the Star together."

Ada clapped her hands, and her eyes lit up with delight. She extracted another, larger notebook from beneath a pile of canvas and began scribbling calculations on the paper. "I'll need to get some more fuel. How much do you weigh, Lord Devonshire? About eighty pounds, do you think? Will you be bringing any additional baggage with you?"

"Excuse me, I wasn't finished," George said. "We can search for the Star together *on one condition*: we are not taking that flying contraption of yours."

"Condition not accepted," Ada replied. "We have a long way to go and the sky is the quickest way to get there."

Chapter Ten

At the controls, Ada's face shone with determination. In the seat next to her, George watched the ground beneath them grow smaller, smaller, smaller, until the city below looked like a set of miniatures.

He squeezed his eyes shut, trying to convince his roiling stomach that he was in his bathtub, not flying in a giant tin bucket. At every bump, he had the urge to demand that Ada deliver him back to his doorstep. But he only had to think of Frobisher to bite his tongue.

If George didn't find the Star of Victory, Frobisher would die.

It was like the start of some fairy tale or adventure

story that his grandfather had once recited in front of the fireplace.

To Ada, that might have been exciting. But George didn't *like* living in a fairy tale or adventure. There was a reason fairy tales were not real. He was learning firsthand that living one was very, very unpleasant.

"What's our gyroscope reading, George?" Ada called out over the wind.

Begrudgingly, he forced his eyes open. The nose of the mechanical bird angled sickeningly toward the sun. His stomach dropped farther toward his toes, as if it were struggling to escape his body and flee straight back to earth.

They were still climbing. The rings of the gyroscope tilted in George's hands. "Sixty-one, no, sixty-two degrees," he said.

In the pilot's seat beside him, Ada's hair had escaped her leather cap. Strands of it whipped back and forth in the wind, flicking his face. The air stung his eyes, but he refused to wear the goggles Ada had given him. They were downright ridiculous.

"Take deep, slow breaths, George!" Ada said, glancing at him. He couldn't see her eyes clearly—they were obscured behind a whitish layer of condensation on her own preposterous goggles—but he was sure she was having the time of her life. "Are you all right? It looks as if you might be having an attack of nerves."

"All right? Of course I'm not all right. Everything is awful. With my luck, we'll drop out of the sky at any moment. Frobisher has been taken captive. And I forgot to feed his pet rat."

"Mrs. Daly will be fine, George. We'll find the Star, rescue Frobisher, and be back in time to join her for tea," Ada called merrily.

"Really?"

"Well, no, not really. You take everything so seriously! That would be impossible. I just meant that we'll be back very quickly. What are we at now?"

"Twenty-six degrees," he replied gloomily.

Ada popped a lever and leaned over the side of the bird. "We're leveling out. Look at the wonderful view. It might cheer you up."

George peered cautiously down over the city, which was spread out beneath him—a real-life map drawn in light and shadow. Tiny toy-sized carriages weaved among ant-sized people in the twisting streets. The Thames River appeared like a dark ribbon tossed carelessly among the gray buildings and roads. George watched as they flew over Old London Bridge, then the new London Bridge being built right next to it.

The view was indescribably beautiful. He was higher than the highest mountain, looking down at the city from the viewpoint of the birds. He couldn't have looked away now even if he'd wanted to. For a fleeting moment, George felt as if his grandfather would be proud of him for finally embracing his destiny, and he had a glimmer of hope that everything would turn out fine.

And, in that same brief moment, George had an even wilder thought: if he rescued Frobisher with Ada's help, his bad-luck curse might finally come to an end.

But then, just as suddenly, fog blurred the glowing city. Everything disappeared completely in a giant smudge of gray—including George's confidence.

"What's happening?" he shouted, hoping Ada couldn't hear the panic in his voice over the whir of the machine's engines and the wind.

"We've entered a cloud," Ada shouted back.

"Of course," George said. "A cloud." They were *inside a cloud*. A fluffy gray cloud.

Well, it didn't feel fluffy. In fact, drops of water had begun to cling to his face and drench his clothes. But a memory suddenly popped into his head. When he was very little, he had always imagined that clouds were soft and tasted sweet, like whipped cream. Maybe...

Slowly, he stuck out his tongue. He was disappointed when he tasted nothing but wet.

"Navigating these low stratus clouds is the best way to avoid being seen by the Organization," Ada went on. "They use spy balloons on cloudy days to watch all the comings and goings in the city."

It was an outlandish idea, and George opened his mouth to tell her so. But just then, the little airship shook from a sudden jolt. The machine began to rattle and clatter like a cart over cobblestones. George's grip on the gyroscope slipped as the rings spun wildly, and his stomach dipped back into his toes.

"Nothing to worry about," Ada said. "A few bumps while flying through turbulent air are perfectly normal."

"I wasn't worried," George mumbled. How could *air* be bumpy? "When will we get there?"

Ada tapped a glass compass embedded in the panel in front of her. "Soon," she replied.

Before George could ask her to clarify exactly how soon, an enormous dark gray bubble appeared straight ahead of them. "Look out!"

They swerved to the left, Ada steering to avoid the object in their path, and George's warning was lost in the groan and shudder of the little airship's motor. He gazed at the bubble that loomed mere inches from the mechanical bird's silver wings.

It was the top half of a giant gray balloon. The bottom half was hidden within the cloud.

"Saints alive!" George breathed.

Ada tossed her head. "I told you. Observation balloons. The basket hangs just below the clouds while the rest is hidden inside the cloud. Perfect for spying. The whole thing is powered by a—"

"I know what a balloon is," George said through gritted teeth. In fact, he'd loved perusing his grandfather's illustrations of flying objects (before selling them, of course). But the balloon they'd almost hit looked nothing like those colorful spheres he'd seen in his grandfather's books. It looked like a dirty gray monstrosity. He shivered.

"You're not afraid of a little thunder and lightning, are you?" Ada yelled back at him.

He was, but he wasn't about to admit that to Ada.

As if on cue, the clouds grew thicker. An icy gust of wind howled across the mechanical bird's wings, piercing George's jacket. Any lingering wonder he felt was replaced by utter terror. A bolt of lightning lit up the clouds ahead with an eerie spark. Every bump made his stomach drop to his toes. At any moment he could be jostled right out of his seat, *splat* onto the ground, and he would be no help to Frobisher at all.

Coiled behind his seat was a length of rope. Eagerly, George grabbed the rope and began to loop it around himself and his seat. (Sailors lashed themselves to the mast of a ship to survive a storm, George remembered hearing his grandfather say.) He pulled the rope tight and secured it with a carrick bend knot so that even if the flying machine turned upside down, he would not fall out.

"I like your resourcefulness, Lord Devonshire, but I feel it is my duty to inform you that, in the event of an emergency, bailing out will be your best chance of survival. After you jump, you should spread your arms and legs wide to minimize impact."

"I prefer to stay tied down, thank you!" George shouted over the shrieking wind.

The front of the airship dipped suddenly, and George

felt the ropes loosen around his body as he was tossed back against his seat. His heart leapt into his throat.

Were they falling?

They were falling.

"We're at negative fifteen degrees!" George shouted.

"Perfectly under control!" Ada cried.

In a flash, they dropped out of the cloud and into a downpour. Panic raced up George's spine. Water streamed into his eyes, and he could barely see an inch in front of him. He could still hear, though, and Ada's voice entered his ear as if through a long tunnel.

"Grab hold, George!"

A cold, wet hand pried his fingers from the ropes and guided his hands to a lever. He gripped it. He leaned so far forward that his forehead pressed against the instrument panel, and the loosened ropes pulled against his chest again. Before he could object, Ada was climbing out of her seat.

George watched in horror as she crawled slowly but determinedly onto the wing of the bird. Her brown curls were plastered to her pale face, and her skirts clung to her legs. She moved with grim determination, inching hand over hand farther onto the wing despite the forces of wind and water swirling around them. She braced herself with the toes of one foot, then reached out and jerked a flap on the wing. It came free with a screech of metal against metal. George sucked in a breath. He could hardly believe his eyes. Ada must be invincible.

When she slipped and lost her footing on the wing, he knew she would catch herself. And she did. When her skirts tangled in her legs, he knew she would untangle them. And she did. When her foot slipped again, he knew she would find a foothold.

But she didn't. Her dainty leather boots could not gain traction on the slick metal surface. She clutched the lip of the wing, her feet now dangling over the edge. At any moment, her grip could fail and she would fall to the earth. That is, if the unpiloted mechanical bird did not crash first.

"Lord Devonshire!" she called out. "A little help?"

He let go of the lever and scrambled to untie his carrick bend knot, but the ropes now looked like a tangle of vines. How foolish he had been to expose Ada to his curse. He never should have gotten into her airship.

"Lord Devonshire!" Ada's voice rang out, singing in his ears like a bell. It calmed him slightly. "Please don't give up."

"I—I—I'm coming!" George said through his chattering teeth.

The knot resisted, but with Ada's urging, George gave a mighty tug and finally released himself from the wet ropes. He sprang out of his seat, leaned over the wing, and grabbed her hand. When their fingertips connected, he gripped her hand tightly as she pulled herself toward him. Without thinking, he heaved her up, and they both fell backward with a moist *thwunk* into their seats.

Before he could cry out in relief, the propeller stopped turning. Ada didn't seem to notice.

"Thank you, George. That was very heroic," she said, giving him a wet slap on the back as she wriggled into the pilot's seat. "Though it would have been a great test of my new parachute. I've adapted it from da Vinci's original design, but with a few modifications to the frame, which was *far* too rigid and cumbersome, I—"

"Miss Byron! It appears your flying machine has stopped flying."

"Oh yes," she said. "We're going to crash now. We've run out of fuel."

As if in response, a loud knocking sound came from the compartment behind George.

Then everything went dark.

Chapter Eleven

Lord Devonshire. Lord Devonshire. *George,*" Ada's voice called from above him. A gloved hand pulled George's fingers from over his face, and Ada's begoggled eyes came into view again. Apparently, he had clamped his hands over his own eyes.

"We've landed?" he squeaked.

He could hardly believe it. They were on solid ground again. They had survived. They had *survived.* His bad luck was awful, but not fatal. He frantically touched his face and patted his legs. He whooped with joy as he ran his fingers through his hair and discovered that none of it had blown away.

Elated that all his vital parts were intact, he clutched

Ada's shoulders and shook her gleefully. "We're alive! Can you believe it?"

Ada watched him with a bemused smirk. "Do you want to check the map to make sure none of the ink blew away?"

The map! George plunged his hand into his chest pocket and breathed a deep sigh of relief when his fingers found its familiar smooth surface. If they had lost the map, then all hope of finding Frobisher would have been lost, too.

When he felt more like himself, George peered around. He could hear rushing water nearby. They were at the edge of a scrubby forest, surrounded on all sides by thin birch trees. Behind them, a row of the same saplings were flattened in a strip about the size of the mechanical bird.

"Good thing I installed the auxiliary wings last week. We glided all the way to the ground. I think you might have passed out from fear," Ada said.

He blushed, but she didn't seem to be making fun of him. "I was right. We should have taken a more reliable form of transportation. Your engine malfunctioned."

She sat back abruptly, fanning out her skirt like a peacock showing its feathers. "*No*. It wasn't my design. It's the strangest thing. We ran out of fuel. I calculated exactly how much we would need, down to the drop."

"Apparently not," George said.

"No, George," she said sharply. "You are so stubborn. It's important to look for other reasons. There *must* be another reason. Such as..."

A knock sounded, this time followed by a muffled voice coming from the compartment at the back of the airship. Someone was *inside* the mechanical bird.

"I think we have a stowaway," Ada whispered, pointing at the small hatch at the rear of the airship.

George climbed shakily out of the bird, looking for lurking shadows and tufts of red hair. "It's probably an agent of the Organization. We can't let them escape. They might know something about where Frobisher is being held. Go around to the other side so that we can cut them off."

"An ingenious plan, Lord Devonshire," Ada said dryly, but she went to the other side of the bird as he suggested.

Knees trembling, George found the shiny brass knob on the side of the rear compartment. He turned the knob. The door sprang open and—

Out popped a sleepy orangutan and a boy with green fingers.

"Hello, George," Oscar said, his brown eyes heavy with exhaustion but his voice still brimming with cheer.

"That's it! We were carrying more weight than I thought," Ada said, coming around to peer into the compartment as if there were nothing at all remarkable about a boy and his orangutan hiding inside her flying machine. "Is there anyone else in there?"

George peeked inside, half hoping Frobisher would climb out, too.

"Hello, Ada," Oscar said. "It's just me and Ruthie and my rock collection as far as I know. I hope you don't mind. When you sneaked into the menagerie and packed the bird this morning, I knew you'd forgotten your promise to take me on your next trip. I'll never get a true variety of minerals for my collection if I stay in one place my whole life. I know you said I'd have to wait, but . . ." He shrugged.

"But you endangered us all by coming anyway?" George said. Disbelief and rage battled in his voice.

"I didn't mean for anyone to get hurt. I was trying to help." Oscar turned to Ada. "Remember, you made me a promise? You're always telling me that a person is only as good as their word, so I made sure to come along so that you didn't break a promise to me, because that would mean your word wasn't good anymore." His face lit up with a smile. "I took out your parachutes to make some room. I hope you didn't need them for anything."

Ada opened her mouth, then shut it quickly as if she'd changed her mind about what she wanted to say. "How many minerals do you have in your collection?"

"Why on earth does *that* matter?" George muttered. (No one was listening to him.)

"Sixty-five, at the moment," Oscar replied. "Plus the glauconite and the pestle in Ruthie's stomach. Sixty-seven."

"Ah, that accounts for the rest of the added weight," Ada said. "You might as well come out. Without fuel, we'll have to camp here for the night."

"But Frobisher—"

"Remember what the note said, George. Ten days. That's plenty of time. You mustn't be worried. That's an order. My mother believes that worry and emotion clog your reasoning capabilities," Ada said.

Though frustration made his toes curl, George didn't protest further. If it hadn't been for her, Frobisher might not have been kidnapped. But now Ada was his only hope to save him. Her bird had nearly crashed, but it *had* brought them this far. George didn't like the idea of putting his future in her hands, but he liked the idea of Frobisher dying much less.

Plus, though he would never admit it to Ada, George couldn't shake the feeling that she was changing the effects of his bad-luck curse. The problem was that he still couldn't tell if she was making it better—or worse.

At the base of the largest tree they could find, near a burbling creek that fed into a shallow, brownish river, George, Ada, and Oscar set up camp. (Actually, Oscar spent his evening hours crushing blackberries into a dark red paste, and George complained that his back was too sore to lift things, so Ada did most of the setting up.) By the time the sun had set, the previously empty campsite held two snug tents, a fire pit, and an elaborate trap designed to catch any agents of the Organization who might have followed them.

George spread out the map carefully on the ground so that he and Ada could pinpoint their location. Ruthie produced a large banana leaf from a small canvas bag filled with an assortment of fruits and spread it on the ground next to them, chattering softly to herself. She learned by imitating people, Oscar explained.

Ada tapped a spot in the north of France along the narrow blue thread of the Vesle River. "We aren't far from an artillery in Reims. I can surely get fuel there, in some form. But their defenses will be strong to fend off pirate raids and the like, which means there will be quite a few guards to get past."

Oscar lifted a berry-stained finger, presumably to make a point about his pirate father or something else equally absurd, but George cut him off. "And after that, Miss Byron?"

"Then we go on to Lac Léman. It's what the local people in Switzerland call Lake Geneva."

George found the two triangle shapes in the middle of Switzerland: ΛΛ. Two pitched tents, two mountaintops, or two Greek *lambda*s: LL. A hexagram somehow, like Ada had said, that led them here. Could his grandfather's puzzle really be that easy?

"Are you sure that the Star of Victory is actually at Lake Geneva?" George asked. "My grandfather said he was being chased by pirates when he hid the Star. It hardly makes sense that it would be that far from the sea."

"I think a landlocked country would be *exactly* the

place you'd hide something from pirates," Oscar said. "They don't do well on land."

Ada laughed. "Oh *no*, George, it will not be that easy. Lake Geneva is still a large area to search. We'll need to find the next piece of the clue."

"The next piece?"

"Yes, of course. There might be several steps. You didn't think your grandfather would make it as straightforward as a few *lambdas*, did you?"

When George was silent, she tucked a strand of dark hair behind her ear and added, "I need your help reading the map. You have the answer locked away inside of you."

At Ada's assertion that he, the 3rd Lord of Devonshire, was going to help read the map, he felt an altogether different kind of panic than he'd felt when they were falling through the sky just a short time earlier. This panic made him fidget and experience the sudden urge to run back to Dorset Square.

He'd spent years trying to read the map, with absolutely no success.

"But you do know where the Star is?" George asked.

"Of course I know where it is. I'm the one who told you

all about the *lambdas* and the hexagrams, remember? I just don't know where *precisely*."

"How is that not the same thing?" George protested.

"It's a matter of scale, you see. If someone asked me where to find a turnip, for example, I might tell them to go to the greengrocer's shop at the end of Wimpole Street. Of course, standing outside the shop, you are unlikely to come across a turnip. You'd need to go inside the shop and ask the grocer where he keeps his turnips. As I said—you, George, are my grocer."

George grew hot and cold again, as if he were trying to solve a difficult equation while standing in front of a classroom. (Not that George had been in a classroom, but that was how he imagined he would feel if he could afford to attend boarding school like other young gentlemen of quality.) "Lake Geneva is not a greengrocer's, and the Star of Victory is not a turnip."

Ada sighed. "You said that your grandfather was supposed to pass along the knowledge of where to find the Star to you. He made the map for you, and you alone. I'm sure of it."

This should have made George feel better, but it only

made him feel worse. If Ada was right, then it was utterly and completely up to him.

Oscar smiled his gap-toothed smile and put a berry-tinted hand on George's shoulder, patting him gently. The gesture reminded George of Frobisher. A fresh wave of sadness and determination surged through him. He sucked in a deep breath and blurted out the truth: "I don't know how to read the map. I've never been able to understand it."

"Oh, I know that," Ada said. "What I mean is that I need to understand your grandfather in order to decipher the map. You understand him better than anyone, don't you?"

George twisted one of the gold buttons on his jacket and nodded. In many ways, his grandfather had been the complete opposite of George. He was loud and entertaining and friendly to everyone he met. Sometimes George thought he was embarrassingly improper, but he would have given anything to have him alive for one more day.

"What did he say about the Star?" Ada reached over for her sketchbook and poised her pencil above it to take notes.

"Well, he used to tell me stories about his adventures. My grandfather practiced oratory. I was his only audience." Listening to his grandfather shape his life into stories and speeches had been one of George's favorite activities. "I suppose I could try to recite his tale about the Star."

"Yes, tell the story," Oscar said. "Ruthie loves stories. She likes music even better. She adores the opera. We sneaked into every performance of *The Barber of Seville*. Can you sing it to us instead?" He burst out into a refrain, singing "Figaro, Figaro, Figaro."

"No, no, no," George said. "I'm not going to sing it or dance it or turn it into a puppet show. This is important. This is *history*. I'll tell you, but you have to promise not to laugh or chuckle or giggle."

"I promise," Ada said solemnly. Oscar agreed, then windmilled his arms at Ruthie. She grunted.

"That means she agrees, too," Oscar clarified. He pulled out a paintbrush, turned the handle side around, and poised it over the bare dirt in front of him. Ruthie picked up a twig and waved it over her banana leaf.

George cleared his throat the way his grandfather used to do when he told the story to young George.

And he began.

Chapter Twelve

*O**nce, many years ago—***

"How many years ago?" Oscar interrupted.

Five hundred. Once, five hundred years ago, Sir John Devonshire was sent on a secret mission by King Edward III. Sir John was a brave, loyal knight who would go to the ends of the earth for his King. And that's exactly what King Edward asked him to do. The King of England was very young, and—

"How young?" Oscar said. "I need to know how many wrinkles to draw on his face."

The King was eighteen. Or twenty. He was tired of other people telling him what to do all the time and interrupting him when he tried to tell important stories. And because he was a king, he could banish people who annoyed him.

The person who most annoyed him was the King of France. He didn't like that he was supposed to bow down before the King of France. The French made him very mad. He decided that he would teach the French a lesson. He would be the King of both England and France.

The English King's subjects thought that invading France was a terrible idea. He knew that he would need something extraordinary to convince his subjects to follow him into war. Something that would convince his subjects that they would be victorious against the French.

"Hmm, was it . . . a Star of Victory?" Ada said.

If you'll let me finish . . . Sir John set sail on a fine summer day. He traveled over land and sea, chasing clues and defeating his numerous foes. He faced untold dangers but saw many wonders. He—

"What wonders?" Oscar asked. "Rainbows?" He scratched a rainbow into the dirt with the handle of his paintbrush.

Better than rainbows! Men with eyes on their shoulders! A woman who turned into a dragon! A tribe who lived off the smell of apples alone.

"I highly doubt that," Ada interjected.

Finally, he found what he was looking for—a magical blue stone with a shining silver star inside. It guaranteed victory to its owner. Sir John brought the Star back to King Edward. The King went to war and all was going well—

"As well as any unnecessary, murderous campaign can go," Ada muttered.

All was going gloriously! The English fought nobly against the French forces. They were ready to march into Paris and storm the French palace, but then the Star went missing!

"What about the woman who turned into a dragon?" Oscar asked.

No more interruptions, please, this is the climax of the story. The Star went missing. Someone had stolen it. Lightning split the sky and a hailstorm rained down, killing a thousand English soldiers in their tents. It was a devastating blow that ended the war. Eventually, the King got the Star back, but from that day on, he did everything in his power to hold on to the Star. Sir John was given the duty of protecting it and getting it back if it was ever stolen again. He hid it somewhere safe and made a map for his children to find it if they ever needed it.

George took a deep breath and sat down. Oratory was exhausting.

"And then..." Ada prompted.

"And my ancestors have been protecting the Star ever since," George finished. His gaze fell to the ground in front of him, which Oscar had illustrated with all the wonders of his story, including an eerily accurate depiction of the 1st Lord of Devonshire. Even with only a paintbrush handle and dirt, Oscar was quite good.

"That's an interesting story, George, but...I don't think it helps us very much." Ada's sketchbook lay open in her lap, its crisp white page still perfectly white. Catching his stare, she quickly closed the book. "Are you sure you're remembering it correctly?"

"Of course I remember it, it was my grandfather's favorite," he snapped, though he wasn't angry at Ada. He was angry at himself. It had been two years since his grandfather died, even longer since he'd told George stories by the fire. What if George had remembered everything wrong?

"What about your grandfather?" Ada said slowly. "What was his part in it?"

George cleared his throat, eager to talk about something he *did* know for sure. "When it was my grandfather's turn to find the Star of Victory, he followed the map his own father had made for him. The Star was hidden in a remote fjord in Norway. This zero written here"—he pointed to the faded black 0 at Norway's northern tip—"is where my grandfather found it. On his way across the Atlantic Ocean, his ship was attacked by the fearsome pirate Bartholomy Bibble, and he had to hide it again."

"Bibble the Beastly, the Bane of Britain!" Oscar exclaimed, his tongue lisping slightly against his missing teeth.

"Yes, that's the one. My grandfather was forced to hide it until the next Devonshire could find it. He made the map for my father, but my father, he—he chose to follow other pursuits."

"Rock collecting?" Oscar asked.

George shook his head.

"Bird-watching?"

George shook his head again.

"Fly-fishing?"

"Honestly, Oscar. Not everyone likes fresh air as much as you do," George said sharply. He sat down again next to the fire and let Ruthie drape her banana leaf over his knee like a small blanket. He was thankful when Oscar fell quiet.

Silence was better than admitting the truth.

George's father's other pursuit was George. When George's mother died giving birth to him, everything had ground to a halt. With George to take care of, the 2nd Lord of Devonshire's desire for adventure had turned into a desire to gamble. A lot.

"Well...what about your story, George?" Oscar said in a soft voice. "Maybe the answer's there."

"I don't have a story. Just a string of bad luck."

"That's not true; everyone has a story."

George's gaze dropped to his lap. Ruthie had fallen fast asleep on the ground next to him, her head resting against his leg. For a few moments, the memory of his grandfather telling him about the Star of Victory had made a huge, warm bubble in his chest—but now it burst, leaving only a soggy, cold feeling in its place. Grandfather was dead and he was never coming back.

A ghostly white-and-black-spotted moth fluttered past the fire, then continued into the forest. Ada nodded after it. "Oscar, would you mind catching that moth? I don't think I've ever seen that species."

When Oscar had disappeared into the night, Ada turned back to George. "You don't really believe in all that mystical nonsense your grandfather told you, do you? About magic and fate and all that?" The reflected flames of the campfire danced in her dark eyes.

George swallowed a burning feeling in his throat. He wished he could lay his head down on his pillow back at No. 8 Dorset Square. The sheets on his bed were threadbare, but they were better than the cold, hard ground. "I'll add it to my list of shortcomings."

"I didn't mean...George, the world is wonderful enough; we don't need magic—"

But George had already turned away from her. He was so determined to ignore her that he hardly flinched when Ruthie—no doubt in a fit of dreaming—wrapped her long, hairy arms around his ankle.

At least her fur was soft and warm. And soon George slept.

Chapter Thirteen

George dreamed that his grandfather was a chicken. Of course, his grandfather was not a plain brown chicken, but a brilliantly speckled Hamburg rooster with a ruby comb atop his head. George was not sure how he knew that this handsome chicken was his grandfather, but regardless, he was very happy to see him.

"Grandfather, I am going to find the Star!" George told the chicken.

The chicken nodded and preened his long tail feathers.

Ada appeared out of nowhere and scooped the chicken into her arms. As she did, the chicken's feathers began to fall off, one by one.

"No, stop!" George yelled. "Make it stop!"

"I'm sorry, George, but you really *must* get up."

George's eyes snapped open and he sprang up, gasping. Ada stood over him. Her hair was carefully brushed and curled into dark ringlets framing her pale face. Thankfully, she was not holding a chicken. Above, the sky was bright blue.

"I've already fetched fuel and Oscar's helped me reignite the engine with a flint from his collection. Please be careful, Oscar," she called, pivoting away from George. "Put that stick down. You can't roast fruit over this fire. It's not the same as a campfire. The gas is highly combustible."

While Ada and Oscar continued to chat about different types of combustion and load items into the mechanical bird, George packed his things (which did not take very long, since he had so few things). He brushed a few short orange hairs from his blue jacket and retied Frobisher's neckerchief snugly around his arm. Where was Frobisher now? Had he managed to snatch the last of his cherry pastilles from beside his bed before he'd been dragged away by those ruffians? At least he was wearing his coat, scarf, and hats when he was taken. That was quite lucky. But even with proper clothes, could he survive long enough for George to find the Star of Victory, or would it be too late?

"Hurry up!" George began tossing Oscar's mineral collection (which had increased since last night with the addition of an orange chunk of clay and a glittery sheet of mica) into one of his canvas bags, which was woven from a pair of old pants. "Come on, come on, we don't have all the time in the world!"

To his surprise, Ada *did* hurry up, as did Oscar. Even Ruthie began chattering excitedly and windmilling her arms around. Soon they were in the mechanical bird again, buzzing along the flat banks of the river.

A few hours later, when the sun was high in the sky, Ada made a smooth, even pleasant, landing in a flat brown field. In the distance, white-topped mountains rose like a wall of whipped-cream peaks on the horizon. Together with Ada and Oscar, George helped to push the mechanical bird into a grove of trees at the edge of a farm while Ada informed them about all the foreign governments who'd like to steal her inventions in order to use them for their own advancement. Ruthie climbed up into a wild pear tree and munched on leaves and fruit.

They had done it. Even with George's bad luck, they had made it to Switzerland.

"How far is it to the lake?" George asked. He hoped

she would have another breakthrough about the map. He didn't know a *lambda* from a llama.

"Half a mile or so," Ada replied. "We're at the southern end, near the city of Geneva. I thought that would be a good place to start while you figure out the clue."

George's palms grew slick with sweat. Suddenly, he felt like crying. Frobisher was going to meet his doom.

"You'll figure it out, George," Oscar said cheerfully. "This walk will spark your inspiration. Last night while I was chasing the moth, I remembered the first book Ada let me borrow from her library. *American Entomology*. It had the loveliest illustrations of moths and butterflies. I would copy those pictures for hours and hours. That's why, as soon as I find some canvas, I'm going to paint a tiger moth." Oscar inhaled a deep breath of fresh air, a serene smile spreading across his face, as though he'd solved George's problem.

"I don't see how chasing insects is going to help me, Oscar," George grumbled.

"On the contrary, Oscar is bang on the mark. Walks are one of the best ways to stimulate the brain. Your grandfather probably would have told you something that didn't seem important at the time. Think of anything he told you about Geneva, no matter how insignificant. Anything at all."

George flipped through the pages of his memories. He couldn't recall his grandfather ever telling him anything about Switzerland. George's favorite stories had been his grandfather's tales of adventure on the high seas or faraway islands lush with coconut groves. There was nothing faraway about Switzerland.

And yet.

His grandfather's favorite book, one of the only two left in his library at No. 8, was *The History of the Rhône*. He told George every summer that he had never seen anything more beautiful than the lavender fields blooming in June on the banks of the Rhône River. The Rhône began in Switzerland, fed into Lake Geneva, then flowed south through France to the Mediterranean Sea.

"My grandfather had a book called *The History of the Rhône*," George said finally. He began to recite some facts he remembered from reading the book countless times. "The city of Geneva is divided by the Rhône River into three unequal parts."

"Of course," Ada said.

"The city has four bridges and six churches."

"Obviously."

"It was conquered by the Romans under Caesar and—"

"Yes, yes," Ada said, waving her hand to stop him. "That's all very good, but it doesn't help us to know the history or population density, et cetera, et cetera. What we need to know isn't the kind of thing you can find in a book. Tell me why your grandfather would have been here in Geneva. What was he doing?"

"My grandfather only told me that he liked the lavender fields he saw in France on the way to Geneva. He never said why he was here. But..." George stopped in his tracks, causing Ruthie to bump into the back of his legs and topple over onto a tuft of grass. An unpleasant recollection had latched on to George's memory like a mosquito.

"But what?" Ada prodded.

"Well... once, my father told me that my grandfather was thrown into prison. In Switzerland." When he drank too much brandy, George's father had had the unpleasant habit of saying very disparaging things about the 1st Lord of Devonshire. Though George had tried very, very hard to forget these unpleasant moments, they invaded his head once in a while. "Falsely imprisoned, of course. I'm sure of that. My grandfather was a good man. He wasn't a criminal."

Oscar cheerfully called out, "Not all criminals are bad."

"Yes, they are," George said. "They've committed a crime. Only bad people commit crimes."

"Good and bad are shades of things just as lavender and eggplant are shades of purple. People aren't just all one or the other," Oscar said, spreading his fingers wide as he spoke. "My father is a pirate. If he was ever caught, he'd go to prison. But that doesn't mean that he's a bad person."

"If he's a pirate, then he's a *terrible* person. Pirates have no regard for the law or for human decency. They'd sooner cut your throat than look at you. My grandfather never broke the law once in his life. He was a pillar of the community."

"So is my father," Oscar said matter-of-factly. "He is a pillar of the pirate community. I'm sure of it."

George clutched a handful of his hair and forcefully smoothed it down. "You don't understand what I'm saying, Oscar. If you did, you'd agree with me."

"Not agreeing with you isn't the same as not

understanding. I understand you just fine." Oscar's brown eyes narrowed. "My father isn't a bad person. When he remembers to come back and get me, you'll see."

George's jaw dropped. "Your father abandoned you? He should go to prison just for that!"

"It was an accident," Oscar said lightly. "It could happen to anyone."

George felt a tug of pity. Surely, Oscar was too young to admit that this was just a fantasy. Somewhere deep down, he had to know that his father, whoever he was, was neither a pirate nor a saint.

"My grandfather would never abandon his son. Not even if his son was a lazy, no-good, lying, cheating, stealing, disreputable cork-brain, or a failure like..." *Like me*, he finished in his head. There was that lump in his throat again. "Like some other sons. My grandfather went to church every Sunday. He donated money to the orphans' and widows' homes. His face was always freshly shaven, his clothes were always pressed. And he never, ever, would have done something illegal."

"Eureka! That's it!" Ada said. She stared at George with a look that shone dark and bright at the same time.

"That's *what*?" George asked.

George looked on while Ada fell to her knees and unrolled the map. "If you're right about your grandfather, then..." Her voice trailed off as she squinted closely at the parchment.

A strange, unfamiliar feeling rose in George's chest. Maybe he could figure this out and save Frobisher. Maybe he was right about Ada breaking his curse. She looked up at him, a smile tugging at one corner of her mouth.

"My grandfather *was* a good man," George said.

"Just like my father," Oscar said quickly.

George groaned. The spell was broken. "No, *not* like your father!"

"Boys, please stop arguing. I need to concentrate," Ada said. "What was that book you mentioned? *A Reliable Record of European Waterways*?"

"*The History of the Rhône*," George said, kneeling beside her to look at the map. Ruthie sat down next to them and unfurled her banana leaf on the ground, tilting her head at it in a perfect impression of Ada.

Ada ran her finger along the thick blue line of the map that George knew was supposed to be the Rhône River. At the point where the river met Lake Geneva, her finger stopped. Beneath the lake, there was a small string of letters, and the letters were underlined. She stared at the letters for a moment, then gasped and began to rummage through her leather satchel.

George leaned over the map. The small string of letters read <u>XXIV°</u>. In Roman numerals, George knew, that meant twenty-four degrees.

But he didn't see anything remarkable about the numbers. He had pored over that map time and time again. Ada placed a brass half-circle on top of the map at the point where the Rhône River flowed out of Lake Geneva on the west side, and aligned it with the line under the Roman numerals.

"What is that brass thing for?" Oscar asked, poking his shaggy head over George's shoulder.

"It's a protractor," George answered. "It measures angles."

"Yes, you see, at first I thought the markings must mark a latitude, but they don't," Ada said. "They mark an *angle*."

She took out a ruler and a pencil and marked a line that was twenty-four degrees from the line under the Roman numerals. The pencil line stretched beneath the lake, then crossed land again at the far end where the eastern shore of the crescent-shaped lake curved around.

"Just as I thought," Ada declared, tapping the spot at the east end of the lake with her pencil. "Chillon Castle. An old prison. If you are correct about your grandfather, George, and he was not a criminal, then perhaps he went to prison on purpose. To...what?" she asked, looking expectantly at George.

"To—to—" There was that feeling again, creeping into him like rainwater into the floorboards at No. 8. He stared into Ada's eyes but found nothing, no hidden answer or clue, to help him.

Then, in an instant, it all made sense and he understood. Of course.

"To hide the Star." George was so happy that he almost didn't mind Ada's pencil marks on his map.

"That's right!" Ada said. "We are going to prison."

Chapter Fourteen

With everything stowed safely back inside the mechanical bird, they marched out of the forest toward the city of Geneva—toward the Star of Victory. All around them, a cold mist rose up from the ground as the sun warmed the chilly earth. Ruthie, whose attachment to George seemed to be increasing by the second, insisted on riding on his back while they tramped through muddy fields. Oscar informed him that Ruthie could sense when people were unhappy. According to him, she was trying to squeeze George's sadness out.

Plunging through the fog, Ada and George traded their knowledge of the history of Chillon Castle. George knew the facts about the castle from his grandfather's book. The castle was built in the twelfth century to guard Lake Geneva. It had been a prison and a fortress and was now a tourist attraction.

Ada, however, told a different story....

THE INCREDIBLY SAD BUT POETIC TALE OF FRANÇOIS BONIVARD, ALSO KNOWN AS THE PRISONER OF CHILLON

There was once a fearsome soldier named Bonivard who was arrested and thrown into the dungeons of Chillon Castle.

"What for? What did he do?" George interrupted.

His crime was not belonging to the same religion as his enemies. There was no trial, no judge, no jury. Some of us would say that this was perfectly just, because all laws should be followed and all criminals are wicked no matter what.

"Like you, George," Oscar whispered.

Bonivard's two brothers were imprisoned, too. They were each chained by their ankles to a pillar and could walk no more than five paces in any direction. They waited and waited to be freed, but help never came.

Ruthie's furry arms gripped George's neck more tightly, but despite her warmth, a shiver zipped up and down his spine.

The oldest brother gave up first. He stopped eating or drinking, until he died. After he was gone, the younger brother lost his mind. He ranted and raved until he lay down and never got up again. Although Bonivard's brothers' souls had fled, their bodies remained. They stayed chained even in death.

Day in and day out, Bonivard paced up and down, up and down. He paced for weeks, for months, for years. He paced and paced, his chains rattling behind him until he wore a path in the stone floor. And still, to this very day, in the chilly dungeons of the castle, you can hear his chains rattle and—

"Weren't you the one lecturing me yesterday about believing in mystical forces?" George said all in one breath. He cleared his throat, trying to disguise that his voice was slightly higher and squeakier than usual. "No more oratory. You're butchering the art form. And honestly, I don't see how an old ghost story is going to help us find the Star. It's not as if a ghost is guarding it."

"Or is it?" countered Ada, raising her eyebrows.

Oscar scratched his chin thoughtfully. "Do you think ghosts are transparent or solid? Do they have rules they must follow? Do they have to knock before they come into a room even though they can most likely float through doors?"

"Can we please focus on coming up with a plan to find the Star? Frobisher's life *really* depends on it," George said. In the distance, the trees had thinned out to reveal signs of civilization in the fog. He knew it was Geneva, though from where he stood, the city looked like white bits of litter on the pretty countryside.

"A good plan takes all variables into account, including the existence of ghosts," Ada said.

"Are you telling me you think ghosts are real?" Of all the ridiculous things Ada had said since the day George met her, this was the most preposterous.

"Not at all. She's telling you to keep an open mind," Oscar said.

"An open mind about what?"

"I can't tell you," said Ada. "It would ruin the plan."

"What plan?"

"I can't tell you that, either."

George ran his hands through his hair in frustration. "Then how will I know what to keep an open mind about? Ruthie, stop that!" From her perch on his shoulders, the orangutan had begun to pull at her hair, too, so that a tiny shower of dirt, tufts of orange fur, and the occasional insect was raining down on George's head.

"You'll know," Ada said mysteriously. "Wouldn't you agree, Oscar?"

Oscar smiled his gap-toothed smile. "No doubt. You'll know it when you see it. Like that time at Covent Garden when the actor picked up the skull but we had put your giant hermit crab inside it while we..." His words trailed off into giggles.

"And everyone in the theater screamed, 'No, Hamlet, that's not a skull, it's a...'" Ada began to giggle, too, until her entire body shook with laughter so fiercely that she could not even finish her sentence. Soon they'd both doubled over, practically shrieking with breathless laughter.

George crossed his arms grouchily as he walked. "I hope for Frobisher's sake you two are having a good time. I doubt *he's* laughing very much right now." With one graceful leap, Ruthie hopped down from his back and stood next to him, arms crossed and chin angled toward the sky, which made Oscar and Ada erupt all over again.

Thankfully, by two o'clock their giggles finally died down, and the smooth gray stone walls surrounding the city of Geneva came into clear view. With Ruthie loping in front, they made their way to a gate in the wall that was closed off by two huge wooden doors with iron hinges.

George gulped. This was it. The gate to the city.

Once they were inside, Ada instructed them to wait at the top of a steep avenue that plunged sharply down toward the lake while she inquired with a local shopkeeper about boats to Chillon Castle. Oscar's head whipped in every direction, as if he didn't know where to look first. Finally, he set his eyes on the famously blue lake and gasped.

"I've never seen that color before." He gripped George's arm with his thin fingers, which were nevertheless very strong from grinding pigments. Next to them, Ruthie waved her fists in the air. "George, how would you describe it? Ruthie says it's royal blue, but I think it's more azure. . . . What do you think?"

"I think it's blue," George said stonily.

"You're right! It *is* all of the blues at once." Oscar's brown eyes grew suddenly round and wistful. "I wish Ruthie hadn't eaten my pestle so I could re-create the color. Nothing else crushes the pigments so fine. Did I tell you my father left it with me?"

"Mhm."

They stood in silence until Oscar, who seemed to be allergic to quiet, piped up again. "You still seem unhappy. The whole point of this trip is to cheer you up."

"*Oscar*," George practically hissed, "the point of this trip is. To. Save. Frobisher!"

Oscar continued as if George hadn't spoken. "I thought flying would cheer you up. But that didn't seem to work. Would you like to look at this fascinating piece of gravel I found?"

George sighed and did his best to nod interestedly at the bit of gravel. He even sprinkled in a few *ooh*s and *aah*s before saying, "Oscar, what kind of things have you learned with Miss Byron?"

Oscar blinked thoughtfully. "She's taught me all sorts of plummy things. I know why birds can fly and why a rainbow is half a circle."

George snorted. "If you ever want to make something of yourself, you need more of an education. If you're going to be an artist, you'll need to know history, bookkeeping, and chemistry in order to have stimulating conversations with your patrons."

"I suppose," Oscar said.

"This trip will be an excellent opportunity to study geography as well as social, economic, and political history. Let's begin with Geneva, where we are standing now. Understanding the context of this setting will be vital should you choose to paint a landscape of our current location," George lectured. He noticed that Oscar's normally bright eyes had glazed over with boredom, so he skipped his planned lesson about the Grand Council and the House of Savoy. "The chief industry in Geneva is jewelry. For example, my grandfather gave me his Swiss pocket watch, which was made in this very same city by the Jaquet Droz workshop."

Here, George would have held up his gold pocket watch for Oscar to admire, but he'd had Frobisher sell it months ago.

"Jewelry!" Oscar said, his eyes lighting up again. "Maybe I will find some lapis lazuli to add to my mineral collection. It's the only way to make ultramarine blue pigment."

George sighed. Rocks again.

"Ada, can we go see the minerals, please?" Oscar asked when Ada rejoined them.

"After we find the Star, of course," George added. Teaching Oscar, George had briefly forgotten the weight of the task in front of them. "A life depends on it."

"And I should like to see the hydraulic machine that powers the city's fountains, but George is right—we're on a rescue mission," Ada said. Her voice was uncharacteristically harsh, and George flashed Oscar a look of apology. He hadn't meant to get him in trouble. "We have to hurry. The steamboat for Chillon leaves at three thirty sharp."

"But—" George looked at the position of the sun in the sky. It was the only navigational skill he had acquired at No. 8. "It's not quite three o'clock. Are we far from the docks? Will we make it in time?"

"It's precisely three o'clock and no, we are not far from the docks. But we have materials to collect. For the plan."

They followed Ada through the city down the steep, narrow Avenue Rousseau. The *tick-tick-tick* of clocks spilled out into the avenue from watchmakers' shops. The smell of fresh-baked pastries wafted through the air along with clouds of fine dust; everywhere the shopkeepers were busy sweeping their floors or offering trays full of samples. George's stomach growled as they passed a bakery, but there was no time to pause. When they reached the bottom of the avenue, they found the lake and dozens of boats docked at the piers.

Ada gathered their small group into a close huddle. "We'll have to split up for the supplies, then meet back here before the ship leaves in half an hour. Oscar, you go to the soap maker and get as much lye as they have. I'll go to the cobbler for some rubber. Ruthie, you keep a lookout for any members of the Organization, and give us a warning cry if you see anyone suspicious." Oscar made his arm-wheeling motions at Ruthie.

"And me?" George asked.

"Oh, right. George...you keep an eye on the time. Got it?"

"Isn't there something more important..."

Before George could finish, Ada and Oscar took off like a shot into the streets, and George was left holding Ruthie's hand.

Chapter Fifteen

A small crowd of people had gathered to board the *Poulette*, the steamboat that would ferry them across the vast blue lake. And one by one, the group of waiting passengers turned to stare at the young English lord holding the hand of an ape.

George swallowed. The crowd whispered in French, a language George didn't understand a word of, because he'd had to dismiss all of his tutors, including his French tutor, after his grandfather died and his money troubles began. (As far as he knew, Monsieur Camembert was still alive, at least. Unlike George's mathematics tutor, who, he'd heard, was killed by a cricket ball while playing a match with his new pupil [Exhibit #13].) After a few moments passed and the murmurs didn't stop, George felt absolutely, utterly ridiculous.

For some reason, they'd left him behind.

Probably as some elaborate joke, or one of their pointless larks.

Or because Ada didn't believe in him, he thought. But he'd figured out the castle clue, hadn't he? At least the start of it.

Just then, Ruthie pointed at a woman with a parasol and bared her teeth. A worried mutter broke out among the crowd. Burning from his cheeks to his toes, George hoisted Ruthie into his arms, turned on his heel, and marched down the cobblestone streets near the waterfront, determined to do something, *anything* else.

He soon found himself in front of Jaquet Droz's workshop. If he was supposed to keep an eye on the time, he thought vengefully, then he might as well look at the best timepieces in the world. He set Ruthie down, clutched her hand, and gently tugged her inside.

The shop was more splendid than George could have imagined. The wooden shelves were filled with clocks of all different shapes and sizes. Some of the clocks had miniature mechanical animals, including birds that rivaled

Ada's little metal one for intricacy and fine workmanship. He wandered along the glass cases, admiring the sleek gold pocket watches that looked just like his grandfather's. His eyes pored over the intricate gears and delicate springs that cascaded down the walls like silver and brass lace. A sudden burst of sadness almost knocked him down. His grandfather might have walked these same aisles. Frobisher would have liked to come here.

Or would he have? With a pang, George realized that he'd been so preoccupied with paying off his father's debts for the last two years, he'd never asked Frobisher what he liked. As far as he knew, Frobisher's interests were limited to George, Mrs. Daly, and his small silver-and-brass periscope. Now George might never have the chance to find out.

He had dropped Ruthie's hand to wipe a tear from his eye when he caught sight of something extraordinary at the far end of the shop: a curling silver butterfly that looked so much like an enlarged version of one of the drawings on his grandfather's map, it stunned George speechless.

Everything shifted out of focus except for the butterfly. His feet guided him automatically across the room until he was close enough to see that the butterfly was not on the wall, like the other objects in the shop. It was on a chain around the neck of a young, pale-faced woman seated at an organ, playing a lively tune.

"Pardon me, miss," he said, looking up from her neck, cheeks hot with embarrassment.

The woman's head snapped sideways to face George with a click. Her white eyelids shut with another click. Then, all at once, she stopped playing the organ. She stopped breathing. With a lurch of surprise, George realized that she was *not* a flesh-and-blood woman. She was a mechanism, a machine, just like the clock birds. George was shocked. How could a person be a machine?

George reached out to grab Ruthie's hand, but she was no longer by his side. Panic flooded him in hot and cold waves. "Ruthie! Ruthie!"

He whipped around, eager to find Ruthie and leave the shop, the butterfly the least of his concerns. Unfortunately, he smacked right into another customer. "Pardon me," he said, then stopped short again.

A man towered over him. His face was painted like a clown's. He was mechanical, too.

George stumbled quickly out of the shop, his heart

racing. As he did, he saw a flash of orange disappearing around the corner: Ruthie.

"Come back, Ruthie, you silly ape!" George shouted, silently reprimanding himself for leaving the docks. They would probably miss the ferry altogether. Which meant they might never find the Star. Or save Frobisher.

Maybe Ada was right not to trust him with anything.

"Ruthie." People were now giving him a wide berth. "We'll be late for the ferry!"

To his immense relief, Ruthie appeared again, hopping from her left foot to her right. She wheeled her arms around in frantic circles. *"Owoomph!"* she screeched.

"Stop making a scene. I don't know what you're saying. Let's go!"

George took Ruthie's hand, but Ruthie did not want to go. She pulled away, flinging her spidery arms into the air. Her strange little back-and-forth dance became wilder.

"Owoomph!" Ruthie screeched again. She stepped backward, then forward, and pointed behind her.

"Ruthie, please come here," George coaxed, more gently this time. He reached his arms out, hoping for the first time that she would spring into them. But Ruthie lurched backward each time he took a step toward her.

Someone clutched his elbow. He shouted in surprise and spun around.

But it was only Oscar. His voluminous brown hair was damp, sticking to his forehead in clumps. He must have run to them.

"I heard her screeching all the way at the dock. Ruthie, what's wrong?" Oscar shifted the paper-wrapped package he was carrying under one arm so that he could beckon to Ruthie with his other hand.

But the danger was soon clear.

From the alley behind her, exactly where she had been pointing, a man lurched out into the street. Even from a distance, George caught sight of his stony, fixed glare.

The man's arms reached out to the walls to steady himself. He put one foot on the ground uncertainly, as though the cobblestones were moving beneath him—just the way Ruthie had, backward and forward, except that he was far more terrifying than a juvenile orangutan.

George froze. "Another mechanical man!" he shouted. "They're after us!"

"I think he's a regular man, but he *is* odd," Oscar said, a curious expression on his face. "Maybe his leg is broken and he needs help."

Staggering even closer, the man opened his lips to speak, revealing a mouth made entirely of flashing silver and gold. Wheezing, he staggered close enough to grab the front of Oscar's shirt. Ruthie screeched again.

With one swift lunge, George scooped her up into his arms and darted away from the terrifying metal monstrosity.

"What are you waiting for, Oscar?" he screamed. "Run!"

Chapter Sixteen

Ada was waiting for them on the *Poulette*. White steam billowed from the boat's slender chimney. Her eyes grew wide when George, Oscar, and Ruthie launched themselves onto the boat in one panting, sweating mass, just as the ferry was inching away from the dock.

"What happened? Was it the Organization? Are they following us?"

Not until the ship had pulled away from the dock could George finally calm his racing heart and tell Ada everything he had seen. She listened carefully, and when George finished, she took a deep, exaggerated breath. "Calm down, George. Breathe. Once you've gotten control of your emotions, I'm sure you'll be able to think more clearly. Pierre Jaquet-Droz had a shop in London, too. He made all kinds of clockwork dolls to amuse rich customers. That's the most likely explanation."

"How can you be sure?" George asked. "If the Organization is as clever as you say, couldn't they have sent an army of metal men to chase us down?"

"Did these mechanical people have weapons?" Ada asked.

"Not the man I saw," Oscar said. "His skin was a dark shade of umber and crinkly as leather. He wasn't a machine. I think he knew Ruthie. If you hadn't made us run away from him, maybe he could have explained."

"He was trying to kill us! Ask Ruthie, she'll tell you." George felt ridiculous as soon as he said it. Ruthie couldn't speak, even if Oscar had convinced himself otherwise. She was an animal.

Oscar frowned. "Ruthie only knows forty-two words and half of them are foods and colors. I saw him, too, and I think he was a sailor, probably a pirate."

"Maybe he was both," Ada said. "A mechanical pirate. He could be guarding the shop to keep thieves away. An automaton can be designed to perform any sequence of movements. If they can play an instrument and walk, why

139

not fight away intruders?" Ada drummed her fingertips against her cheeks. "Maybe I could keep one outside my room for protection against spies."

While Ada and Oscar continued to talk about the possibilities for mechanical people, George hung his head. He didn't like being chased by mechanical men, and the possibility of one living with Ada across Dorset Square did not thrill him.

The journey across Lake Geneva helped dispel thoughts of automatons. The prow of the boat cut through the stunning blue water, which was nothing at all like the muddy brown Thames of London. White sailboats skimmed the blue lake, and the snowcapped Alps surrounded the water like an amphitheater. George's grandfather had often told him how beautiful the deep blue sea was, especially the turquoise waters of a tropical isle. It was hard to imagine that they were more beautiful than this.

Eventually, they arrived at their destination on the opposite shore of the lake in the shadows of the snow-dusted mountain peaks. The tree-covered banks loomed like enormous waves ready to crash onto the narrow shore. The *Poulette* puttered past Chillon Castle, which jutted out into the lake, its reflection shimmering ghostly beneath it.

The oval castle's white stone walls rose straight up out of the blue water as if it were floating. Atop each of the round turrets, red flags snapped in the breeze. From the outside, it looked like something from a fairy tale, a castle fit for a princess (or a prince or a lord), but George knew that what really had been inside those walls was a prison.

His stomach dropped. The six-hundred-year-old castle was enormous. Even if they managed to get inside, how long would it take for them to find the Star? What if they were wrong and the Star wasn't in there at all? Or worse, what if they were caught and chained up inside those walls, and he couldn't save Frobisher? What if they died in there and their ghosts could never leave, just like in Ada's story about Bonivard?

When the boat docked in the shadow of the castle's high walls, George trudged off a few paces behind Oscar and Ruthie, his heart heavy with fear and doubt. Ahead of him, Ruthie hopped out of Oscar's mineral bag and loped over to George, patting her chest and whining softly. If George hadn't known better, he'd have said she was trying to comfort him. It was more likely that Oscar's pestle was giving her a stomachache.

He turned to Ada, who, as usual, was smiling as

though she didn't have a care in the world. "Now what? Do we just walk into the prison and ask them to give us the Star?"

She shook her head. "Don't be silly. Of course not. It's not a prison anymore. We're going to take a tour of the old castle, just like any other tourists. First, we need Bonivard."

"Bonivard? You mean the soldier whose brothers died in the castle and he kept pacing and pacing and never stopped? That Bonivard?"

Ada nodded, a devilish grin spreading over her face. "Just follow my lead, and this will all be over quickly."

George highly doubted that.

They followed a path along the lakeshore to a covered bridge, which was the only entrance into the castle. A guard in a red coat with yellow sleeves stood watch.

"*Bonjour, parlez-vous anglais?*" Ada smiled charmingly at the guard.

"*Oui.* Yes, I speak English," the man replied.

Ada clapped her hands excitedly. "Excellent. My friends and I would like a tour of the castle, please."

The guard glanced at the empty path behind them, arching one eyebrow in suspicion. "Where are your parents?"

"My mother is at the spa," Ada said, patting her cheeks with a pretend powder puff. "But she didn't want me or my two friends here to miss out on seeing the most haunted castle in all of Europe. Oh, how I adore ghosts!"

The guard laughed. His face crinkled in kindly wrinkles around his eyes. "You may be disappointed, *mademoiselle*. I have worked at the Château de Chillon for many years and have taken many people on tours, but never have I seen even one little ghost."

"Of course you haven't," Ada admonished. "You've been talking when you give your tours. The ghost I want to see, Bonivard"—George shivered, remembering Ada's story—"only appears if the castle is completely silent. When he was a prisoner, he spent his time alone, and so his ghost appears when he *thinks* he is alone. We need our tour to be completely silent. Then we will see the ghost. First we'll hear his footsteps. Then his chains will rattle. And then he will appear."

The guard laughed again, long and loud. "I will take you on the tour, *mademoiselle*. And I will be silent. But you must leave your pet outside."

"Our *pet*?" Ada said indignantly. "Ruthie is not our pet. And she hardly ever bites."

"Then I insist that you leave your animal *friend* outside," the guard said.

Lifting his nose at the officer, Oscar windmilled his arms at Ruthie, who scampered up into a tree next to the bridge. Ada, however, smiled mischievously.

The guard took them on a tour of the castle from top to bottom. Their footsteps echoed in the stone corridors as they walked, but they did not speak. First they climbed up a tall tower that overlooked the brilliant blue water of Lake Geneva.

"It's most likely in the dungeons," Ada whispered to George.

"The Star?" George whispered back. The guard shot him a glance.

Ada nodded. "And the ghost, of course."

After they climbed down from the tower, they walked through a little chapel with faded paintings on the walls. That was when George heard it.

Thump. Thump.

None of them were moving, but muffled bumps echoed through the chapel. The guard laughed nervously, and Ada quickly shushed him.

They moved on down another dimly lit stone corridor.

When they stopped at the end for the guard to unlock a large iron door, footsteps rang out behind them. They all looked at one another with frightened glances. Even Ada.

George's heart began to pound. Because they were closer to the Star, he told himself, *not* because he was afraid of Bonivard's ghost. He swallowed, reminding himself that it was all part of Ada's plan. It had to be. But even though he knew she was pulling some clever trick, he jumped at every sound as they descended into the lower levels of the castle. The guard, who'd grown pale, looked relieved when they came to the last stop: the dungeons.

The archway that led into the dungeons looked as if it had been carved out of a mountain. On the other side was a tunnel that extended into darkness as far as George could see. One by one, they stepped forward, into the shadows.

A cold wind blew through the room.

Without thinking, George reached out for Ruthie's hand, but grabbed only air. Silly, really. He didn't need reassurance from an ape. So instead, he and Oscar gripped each other's arms as they moved with the guard through the dungeon tunnels. Barrels and crates of gunpowder marked with symbols that looked like golden pineapples

145

were stacked all around. But although this place was being used as a storeroom, its true purpose was clear: rusted chains were still attached to each of the pillars. That sent a shiver up George's spine.

Clink. It sounded as if a chain had dropped to the floor.

Creak. A heavy door whined on its hinges.

George whirled around to look behind them. It was difficult to see anything in the dark dungeon, but he thought he saw a shadow race up a pillar, faster than any human. He yelped.

The guard searched the vast room, his wide eyes flitting to each dark, dusty corner. "Where is the girl?" he snapped.

"I'm right here!" Ada whispered, popping out from behind another stone pillar.

Again the chains clinked against the stone floor. This time, the noise didn't stop.

"Th-this is the end of the t-tour," the guard stuttered, frozen in place in the middle of the room. "Please to the exit. Out. Out. That way. *Allons-y.*"

A peculiar squeaking, stretching sound replaced the clinking chains, as if something were expanding out of thin air.

George's eyes adjusted to the dim shadows of the dungeon just in time to watch a strange shape, clothed in ancient rags, emerge from the shadows. There was the sound of fluttering fabric dancing on the wind as the apparition glided toward them.

"The ghost of Bonivard!" he shouted. "He's coming!"

Chapter Seventeen

The guard tore out of the dungeon screaming, *"Fantôme!"*

Before George could bolt after him, Ada clamped down on his collar. "Honestly, George. You're more excitable than a puppy. Calm down."

"But—but—the ghost," George blubbered, straining to get away from the apparition that was still gliding toward them.

With her free hand, Ada reached forward and undressed the ghost with a swift tug on its rags. Underneath was a pale yellow sphere suspended in the air as if by magic. "It's a rubber balloon," Ada explained.

"Oh, a balloon. Right." He had never seen one so small. To show he wasn't afraid, he poked the balloon with his finger.

"Careful!" Ada rushed to grab the balloon. She tucked it under her arm gently. "It's filled with hydrogen gas. Very flammable."

"But the chains and the footsteps," George said. "I heard them clear as day. And how did you get a balloon down here?"

"Don't worry about the balloon. You can come out now, Ruthie," Ada called loudly, and the orangutan emerged from behind a stack of barrels. She was wearing a pair of heavy boots on her feet and holding a chain, a huge grin smeared across her face.

"It was Ruthie the whole time?" George asked.

Ada tapped her forehead. "And your imagination filling in the rest. I didn't tell you, of course, because your reaction helped convince the guard."

"I'm glad I could be of use," George said icily.

Ada rolled her eyes. "Oh, don't be angry. We don't have time for it! The guard won't stay away for long. Once his pride recovers, he'll be back. We've got to find the Star quickly. Look for hollow spots, like this." Ada demonstrated by getting down on her hands and knees and knocking on the stone floor with her fist every few inches.

Luckily, George realized with a flutter of excitement, he was an expert at finding hollow spots in walls and floors. He'd spent two years patching up No. 8 Dorset Square, which had more holes than Swiss cheese. Methodically, his fists banged and knocked along the insides of the chilly stone castle. With each rap of his knuckles, his elation grew.

Knock. Ada's wild plans had gotten them here.

Knock. To the place where the Star of Victory could be hidden.

Knock. They would recue Frobisher.

Knock. If his grandfather could see him, he'd be so proud.

Knock. His bad-luck curse might finally be broken.

George felt as though an invisible wall around him was falling apart in huge pieces, letting in the sun for the first time.

Soon, despite the cool air in the dungeon, sweat dripped down George's back. Knocking all the while, he and Oscar moved every box, crate, and barrel of gunpowder in the vicinity, but found no sign of anything that could contain the gemstone they were seeking.

Just as George was about to give up hope entirely, there was a ground-shaking *boom*.

Oscar tumbled down from the top of a pillar, straight onto George, who crashed to his stomach with a walloping thud. Ruthie screeched and flung herself down on top of them, knocking what was left of his breath right out of him. By the time the two boys and the orangutan had untangled themselves, a foul black cloud of smoke was rolling toward them.

"Ada?" Oscar called out. But she didn't call back.

"Miss Byron! Ada!" George shouted. The black smoke stung his eyes and filled his mouth, making him cough. Was she alive? Had his curse claimed its next victim? He staggered to his feet and crashed into a barrel, sending it tipping wildly back and forth.

Finally, he heard her cry out, "Over here!"

Stumbling through the acrid smoke, he found Ada kneeling next to a massive hole in the stone floor. Her hair was wild, her face was covered in soot, and her dress was filthy, but she was unhurt. Pieces of shattered stone and rubber and clods of black dirt surrounded the hole.

"It was a trap," Ada explained. Her voice was raspy. "Someone must have gotten here first and set up this flagstone to explode."

No.

George could see the evidence with his own eyes, but his mind refused to believe it. Without the Star, Frobisher was as good as dead.

Then, to make matters worse, the door of the dungeon banged open and voices began to call out, *"Étalez-vous! Cherchez dans le donjon!"*

Guards.

"They're going to search the dungeon for us," Ada whispered. "We don't have time to answer their questions, so we can't get caught. I found a way out, but how will we avoid being seen?"

"Leave that to me," Oscar said. He sprinted to the entrance of the dungeon, pressing his back against the black rock wall so that the smoke would hide him from the guards. He found the barrels marked with golden pineapple-shaped bombs and, one by one, he toppled the barrels so that they rolled toward the guards' feet.

"La poudre noire!" they called to one another. They were so concerned about catching the barrels of explosive

gunpowder that they didn't notice a few children darting through the smoke.

Ada ran straight toward an outer wall and suddenly dropped out of sight. Oscar, carrying Ruthie, followed. George took a deep breath and ran to the spot where they had disappeared, finding a door that was only visible if you crouched down and looked through a small gap between the floor and the wall. George slid through the gap, out into the fresh air. With a splash, he dropped into the shallow waters near the lakeshore.

George half walked, half paddled to the shore, where Ada and Oscar lay panting on a flat rock. In the branches of a nearby tree, Ruthie sat shivering with her arms crossed.

"I failed," George said flatly. "I do not deserve the title of Lord Devonshire. In Frobisher's time of need, I failed him."

"George," Ada said sympathetically.

"You don't need to make me feel better," George continued. He sat up to look at the castle. Gray smoke billowed from the dungeon's narrow windows. How much time would he spend in prison for destruction of government property? Seventy years? Eighty years? It didn't matter. The Star was gone either way. Maybe Frobisher's kidnappers would accept something else as a ransom payment. Maybe—

"George!" Ada snapped, waving a wooden box in his face.

George sat up. "Is that...?"

Ada placed the wooden box in his hands. "That's what I was trying to tell you, if you had stopped moaning for a minute."

His heart caught in his throat. The box, carved with intricate swirls, was just the right size to hold the Star. There had once been a metal lock on the front of the box, but it was broken. No doubt the Organization's carefully planned explosion had blown it to smithereens. Hopefully, the gem inside was undamaged.

George lifted the lid with trembling hands. Rich blue velvet lined the inside. There were depressions in the fabric where an object had once rested.

But the box was empty.

Just as he had feared, the Star was gone.

Chapter Eighteen

At George's insistence, Ada searched the empty box carefully while they hid among the rocks until it was safe to leave, and found a small scroll of parchment yellowed with age. Unrolling it, George felt a sharp pang of anguish when he recognized his grandfather's loopy handwriting. The message written on the note was:

This is only the beginning.

But it wasn't the beginning of anything, because the Star was already missing.

To have come so close only to be taunted by his dead grandfather's words was the cruelest of jokes. Tamping down a groan of despair, George crumpled the infuriating, mysterious note and threw it into the lake at his feet. As soon as the paper had sunk below the water and disappeared, he instantly regretted losing a piece of his grandfather, but it was too late.

"Someone must have taken the Star, then set the trap in the dungeon, knowing we were in pursuit," Ada said.

"But who?" George's mind spun. After two years of resisting his bad luck, Frobisher was going to meet his doom in the most horrible way. George would never forgive himself. "Who would do this?"

"It was probably the Organization!" Oscar volunteered. "They must have just stolen the Star. Maybe only hours ago. We can't be far behind."

"That doesn't make sense, Oscar. They're the ones who took Frobisher. It must have been someone else. Someone who knew about it—"

"Maybe Oscar is right, George," Ada said, cutting him off. "Maybe the Organization is putting you through some kind of...trial. Or maybe they took the Star first in case you weren't planning on rescuing Frobisher once you found it."

"How could they think that?" George said.

"They're very sinister. Maybe..." Ada tilted her head, thinking. "Maybe they want something more from you than the Star."

"What else could they possibly want? My house is empty! I'm all alone in the world!" George said, throwing his hands in the air.

"That's not true, George. You aren't alone," Oscar said. Ruthie nodded in agreement. "You have us now." He motioned for Ruthie to come down from her tree and join them. "And we can bring some of the plants from the menagerie to fill up your house, and Ruthie and I will come stay with you."

George managed a small smile. He wanted to tell Oscar that stuffing his leaky old house with plants wouldn't fill up the emptiness caused by Frobisher's absence, but there was so much pity in Oscar's eyes that he couldn't. Instead, he threw the wooden box into the lake and shouted, "The Organization is a plague upon this earth!"

"Two days ago, you didn't believe they existed," Ada pointed out.

"How can I not believe in them? They've taken everything in the world that matters most to me," George continued.

How had the Organization known? Had George, Ada, and Oscar led them straight to the Star? Was the Organization really only one step ahead? Had they missed them by minutes? Was their conversation being overheard at this very moment?

"I have an idea. Maybe there's a rebel faction within the Organization," Ada said.

Oscar looked puzzled. "How much of a fraction? A half? A third?"

"No, Oscar, not a fraction, a faction—a small group of people with different plans than the rest. Now that I'm thinking about it, maybe Roy is part of this faction. He could have followed us to take the Star for himself, the same thing he tried to do with George's map."

"But you said—"

"Quiet, George, I'm thinking. Perhaps he got hold of one of Niépce's heliography plates and made an exposure of it. But he doesn't seem bright enough for that."

"Who? What?" George asked.

"One of my friends, Nicéphore Niépce, invented a camera that makes images of real things using sunlight and chemicals. It's quite amazing."

George buried his head in his hands. All was lost. He

could not outwit the Organization. He could not even outwit Roy.

But Ada could.

"We have to find him," George said quietly, lifting his head slightly to look at Ada.

"What?"

"We have to find Roy, or whoever stole the Star, and get it back. It's the only way to rescue Frobisher," George said.

Ada twisted her lips into a grimace. "At every turn, they tried to hinder us. They used explosives to stop us from leaving the dungeon alive. I think the man with the metal teeth *was* another part of their plan. It's too dangerous. We're lucky we're not dead already."

George stood up on the rock. His shoulders straightened with resolve. "I'm not giving up. I'll keep looking for the Star until time runs out and there's no hope left. As Oscar said, we can't be far behind. We can still do this."

Oscar cheered, his jack-o'-lantern grin lighting up his face. "Let's do it!"

"No. It's too dangerous," Ada said flatly. She grasped her wet skirts and firmly twisted them. Water splattered onto the gray rocks, painting them black. Her mouth was set in a thin, hard line. "I can handle this on my own. There's a train station just up the road in the city of Montreux. I will buy two tickets for you both. I'll take the ferry back to the bird to spare you any more trouble."

She was probably thrilled to be rid of him, George thought, and felt a rush of heat to his cheeks. Maybe she even thought he would be a hindrance to whatever plan she was hatching.

"Absolutely not," he said. "It is *not* time for this adventure to end. Frobisher is kidnapped because of me. I'm not going home without him, Star or no Star. You said earlier that I didn't believe in the Organization. Well, you were right. But I believe now. How can I not believe? The world Out Here isn't what I thought it would be, but running and hiding isn't the answer. My bad luck could catch up to me at any moment. Until then, I've got to keep going. Yesterday I flew through the clouds. Today I saw people who were machines. I invaded a castle. Who's to say we won't find Frobisher tomorrow?"

Tumbling out of his mouth, the speech sounded distant to George, as if a stranger were talking instead of him. But he needed to believe that the words were true. A happy ending was possible. His eyes lingered on Ada, who was observing him with her keen gaze as if he had a broken mechanism that needed to be fixed.

"I can't go home. Not yet. I won't."

For one more second, Ada examined him. Then she smiled. "It's working. I can hardly believe it."

"Believe what? What's working?" George asked.

She clapped. "Come on, boys, let's go to Venice!"

"Go together?" George put down his hands. "But you said it was dangerous!"

"I was just testing you. I needed to see if you were really ready," Ada said.

He blinked at her. "Venice?" he repeated. According to the ransom note thrown through George's window, that was where they were supposed to go—but only with the Star.

"Yes, Venice. If Roy did steal the Star, he most likely went to Venice as well. There's a black market for all kinds of illegal or stolen items there. It's a hub of criminal activity. That's probably why the Organization instructed you to bring the Star to Venice in the first place, because that's where they were going to sell it for the highest price. No doubt Roy is greedy and wants the highest price for himself. Ergo, we may find our foe in Venice. In fact..."

Bunching up her skirts around her knees with one hand, she waded into the water to where the empty box that George had hurled into the lake was still floating. (Her skirts were in no danger of getting wet again. George's throwing arm was not very impressive.) She bent over to inspect the box, and pinched something invisible between her fingers. When she straightened up, she held a single red strand of hair up to the sun. "Look, George. A miracle! I must have missed it the first time."

So strongly did George want to believe in the miracle that he didn't ask to look more closely at the hair. He wasn't about to question it or Ada. She had been right about everything else so far. As long as George continued to believe, he would get his happy ending.

"All roads lead to Venice, it seems," George said. "How soon can we get there?"

Chapter Nineteen

After George, Ada, Oscar, and Ruthie had eaten dinner (a stew made from nuts and mushrooms that Ada picked with Ruthie's help), George sat in front of the bonfire, which Oscar had brought to life with a flint stone from his collection. Unable to sleep, George stayed awake, poring over his grandfather's map long after everyone else had crawled into their makeshift tents. Since the map was no more use to them in the search for the Star, George had reclaimed it from Ada.

When the fire died down into embers, he craned his neck to look up into the black void above him, his chest aching with sadness. He touched Frobisher's neckerchief, which was still tied firmly around his arm, and traced its familiar green squiggles with the tip of his finger. Was Frobisher staying warm wherever he was? Had his kidnappers stashed him in Venice?

Two days had passed since they'd taken off from Dorset Square, which meant they only had eight days left to find and rescue him. Ada kept insisting that it was plenty of time, that everything would be all right. But as the fire turned the logs into ashes, George's fears pushed in again alongside the growing darkness. Every time he closed his eyes, doubts slithered through his brain, and taunts hissed in his ears in the voice of his father:

What if Oscar hadn't stowed away and you'd reached the castle a day sooner?

What if you never find the Star and Frobisher dies, regretting the day he ever laid eyes on the cursed 3rd Lord of Devonshire?

A sudden crunching of leaves made George start upright. After a moment, all was silent except for the soft pop and crackle of the fire's embers.

Then—was that a flash of red hair in the woods?

"Ruthie?" George shivered and wrapped his arms around himself. "Oscar?"

Quietly, he got up to peek into Oscar's tent, but it was empty.

A twig snapped, this time near Ada's tent. George almost swallowed his tongue.

Had Oscar been taken? Would Roy, the redheaded thief, appear like an ogre and steal the map again? Or would he kidnap Ada next as a part of his twisted plan?

Fear coursed through George. He could *not* let his curse take one more person away from him. He gritted his teeth to keep them from chattering and tiptoed around the fire, toward Ada's tent. The campsite appeared undisturbed, and Ada's traps were unsprung, but he heard the rustling again. Then George had to stifle a scream.

A monstrous hand had just pushed the tent flap aside.

Without a second glance, George tumbled backward and grabbed for the half-empty pot of stew. As a figure emerged fully from Ada's tent, George tossed the liquid at the intruder. He missed.

"George, what are you doing up?" Oscar crawled out after the mysterious figure, who was actually just Ruthie in Ada's pilot jacket.

George hastily put down the pot. "I was throwing out the stew. Didn't want to attract any wild animals." He cleared his throat. "What were you doing in Miss Byron's tent, anyway?"

Oscar sheepishly pulled a notebook from behind his back. It was Ada's. George recognized it from her satchel.

George took the notebook from Oscar and flipped through the pages filled with her windswept handwriting. Her words were spaced far apart, as if she were leaving room for things unsaid. "Why do you have her notebook?"

Oscar hung his head. "I just wanted a bit of paper. I didn't think to bring any of my sketchbooks with me when Ruthie and I got into the mechanical bird," he said. To George's horror, Oscar sniffed back a tear.

"It's only paper, Oscar. After we find Frobisher, or the Star, we can find you some paper."

"No, it's not that. It's just . . . well, you'll say I'm foolish."

"I won't," George replied, resolving to say something nice, no matter what Oscar came up with next.

"Well . . . ever since I could hold a pencil, I've been drawing pictures and sending them to my father. Now that Ada has taught me how to read and write a little bit, I've been writing letters to my father, too."

"The pirate? But you said he abandon—that you, erm, got separated."

"It's all right, George. I said he *accidentally* abandoned me," Oscar clarified. "I tell him where I am and what I'm

166

doing. If he is ever going to find me again, he needs some help. I put my letters into bottles and throw them off the docks into the Thames River so that he will get them. He's a pirate, so he's always moving around. But all rivers run into the sea, don't they? That's what Ada said."

George quickly swallowed a smile when he saw that Oscar was serious.

"Ada says the currents in the river aren't a penny post. She says the odds are infinite. No, that wasn't the right word."

"Infinitesimal?" George corrected.

"Yes, really, really small. But really small isn't the same as nothing."

George's mind attempted the calculation. The chances of one of Oscar's messages reaching anyone, let alone his father, pirate or not, were almost zero. But *almost zero* was about the same chance as finding a mystical gem by following a treasure map in a flying contraption.

In other words, almost zero was not the same as zero zero.

Maybe, just this once, he could indulge Oscar. It *would* make their trip go more smoothly if they weren't bickering all the time. George flipped to the end of the notebook, tore out a page, and handed both to Oscar. "Well . . . go on, then."

Beaming, Oscar reached into his pocket and pulled out a pencil (which looked as if it had been chewed by powerful orangutan teeth) and bent over the paper. As he began to draw, Ruthie climbed up into the space between George's crossed legs and he absentmindedly stroked her furry head. She shifted contentedly under his palm and, after a few moments, fell soundly asleep.

To George's amazement, an image of Ada, Oscar, George, and Ruthie flying in the mechanical bird emerged from the tip of Oscar's pencil. Clouds fluffier than those George had glimpsed from the mechanical bird took shape with only a few swipes of lead. Again, Ada had been right: Oscar was a gifted artist.

But then, as Oscar began to compose his letter on the bottom half of the page, the confidence slipped from his face. After two minutes, he had managed to write only *Deer father its oscar* in shaky script.

Watching Oscar earnestly laboring over his letter, George felt a surge of usefulness. "Oscar, why don't you tell me what you'd like to say, and I'll write it out for you?"

Oscar handed over the pencil and paper eagerly. "It would be nice to take a break. Writing is hard work."

George licked the tip of the pencil and began.

Dear Father,

It's Oscar. I hope this letter finds you well. If you are looking for me, I am not in London. Ada and I have gone on a trip in her bird. Ruthie ate my pestle, my favorite rock that you gave me when I was a baby! But Ada assures me it's safe in Ruthie's belly and it will come out soon enough. We are in Switzerland near Geneva today. We went to a castle. I met a new friend named George, 3rd Lord of Devonshire, who is a very noble gentleman.

If you are near Switzerland, come find me. If you are in London, wait for me. I miss you.

> *Love from your faithful son,*
> *Oscar*

"Would you like a portrait?" Oscar asked once they had stuck the note into the bottle. "As payment, for helping me write my letter?"

George was so surprised by Oscar's offer, all he could

say was "Oh." Once, he'd had oil portraits of his entire family, including his mother. Now they belonged to someone else, sold a year ago. (George sometimes wondered who would want portraits of someone *else's* family, though he tried very hard not to think about the fact that they were hanging over a stranger's fireplace.)

"Or not," Oscar said quickly. "I just thought you might like it. And I have some yellow ochre that is the same color as your hair."

George measured out his words carefully so that he wouldn't choke on the lump in his throat. "Thank you, Oscar. It's just—I'd rather have a portrait of someone else. My grandfather or my mother, maybe. But I don't quite remember how they looked."

"I know how Frobisher looks," Oscar said brightly.

"You do?" Apparently, Frobisher had quite the social life outside of No. 8. After spending two years with him, George had assumed he knew everything there was to know about his manservant.

Oscar poised his pencil over the paper. "He taught me the hand signals I use to speak with Ruthie. It's a language called semaphore. I can try to draw him from memory, and you can help me fill in the details."

In the flickering firelight, George watched Frobisher come to life on the page in layers of gray. "I wish I were an artist like you," he said suddenly, surprising himself. He hadn't meant to say it.

"Why?"

"Well..." Why *had* he said that? "I'd draw my whole family so that I could look at them and never forget their faces. It must be nice."

"I draw my mother all the time," Oscar said. "Or what I imagine she looked like. My father met her when his ship docked in Tahiti. When he comes back for me, I hope he'll take me there so I can see her again and meet her family. The beaches there are black as coal and the forests are full of flowers. Ada told me."

A comfortable quiet fell over them. Oscar expertly smudged lines into shadow with the side of his thumb, and George marveled at how many shades of gray could come out of something so simple as lead. Finally, with George's guidance, Oscar added a few more lines on Frobisher's sagging jowls. "There," he said. "What do you think?"

"It's perfect." Just seeing Frobisher's dear, wrinkly face made George feel better. "I don't know what else to say."

Oscar closed Ada's notebook and tucked it under his arm. He glanced at Ruthie, who was still snoring gently between George's feet. "I understand. Sometimes words aren't the best way to say something anyway."

Fearing he wouldn't be able to hold back tears any longer, George folded the portrait of Frobisher and slid it into his pocket until it was flush against the map. "Perhaps if I were an artist like you, I could have sold portraits in Kensington Park and paid off my father's debts already. I could keep the house, and Frobisher could stay as long as he wanted."

Oscar stared at him blankly. Ruthie stirred, nuzzling herself against George's ankle. "George, do you think Frobisher would abandon you if you didn't have a house?"

George blinked. "Well...there'd be no reason for him to stay without a house." At a loss for words, he flattened his hair. "Why? Has he told you he would?"

Oscar laughed, shaking his head. "We'll find the Star soon, don't worry. Frobisher will be all right, and then you can ask him yourself. I'm sure of it."

"How are you always so hopeful?" George asked.

Oscar tilted his head, frowning slightly as if he didn't quite understand the question. "I don't know. Hope doesn't cost anything, so you might as well have lots of it, I guess." He smiled then, and his face glowed more than usual in the light of the fire. "Good night, George."

"Good night, Oscar."

For a second, George considered going back to his tent. But stirring might wake Ruthie, who was still curled around his legs. Instead, he bent over, scooping up every soft thing within reach—leaves, his jacket, a tarpaulin Ada had discarded by the fire—and piled one on top of another until he made a passable mattress underneath him.

Comfortably on his back, he looked up again at the dark sky. The stars twinkled, winking back at him from a blanket of black. Was it his imagination, or did they sparkle a little more than they did in the sky above Dorset Square? Perhaps he had never looked at them closely enough, he thought, just before drifting into a dreamless sleep.

Chapter Twenty

When they left Switzerland the next day, they soared through white clouds into a blue sky. George couldn't help but notice that the sky was the same sapphire blue as the Star of Victory they hoped to find. Perhaps that was a good sign.

"Away, away, my steed and I. We speed like meteors through the sky," Ada remarked poetically, then fell silent. Her silence struck George as odd, but he quickly dismissed the feeling. She was most likely occupied with the plan brewing in her swirling, incomprehensible brain.

Their path wasn't clear to George, but they had a clue. The missing Star of Victory. The red hair. No doubt as soon as they landed in Venice, Ada would execute her ingenious method of destroying the Organization's whole operation in addition to rescuing Frobisher and regaining the Star from Roy, George thought. Today would be better. It had to be.

The ride grew rougher as they passed over the snowy peaks of the Alps. George was not worried, though. They had weathered a worse storm on the way to Geneva. When Ada laughed as the airship dipped and swelled on the invisible waves of the wind, George did, too (although his laugh came out more like a scream).

As they passed over another peak, the clouds parted and George watched patches of sunlight sweep over the mountainsides. Thin streams sparkled like strings of diamonds that trickled down the slopes before intertwining in the valleys to form rushing rivers. Maybe Oscar's bottles really would reach the sea after all.

The shadow of the bird far below raced up and over the mountain behind them. But something curious was chasing its dark tail. Another shadow.

Shading his eyes, George looked back and spotted another bird above them. A rather large one.

"What kind of bird is that, Miss Byron?" George cried, pointing up.

Just then the clouds thickened, so when everyone else looked, there was nothing to see.

"I think you're imagining things, Lord Devonshire," Ada said. "Birds tend to keep their distance from the airship. I have a theory that they think it's a predator."

George didn't argue but watched vigilantly until the clouds parted again. "There it is! Look!"

Indeed, a shadowy shape could be seen directly above their heads for a moment. George thought it was a large bird—until it glinted in the sun.

"It looks a lot like ours," Oscar said, squinting. Whimpering, Ruthie climbed onto George's lap and wrapped her arms around his neck. "It's the same color as the bird you made last year that you crashed in Trafalgar Sq—"

The airship plunged sharply downward right in the middle of Oscar's sentence. Oscar yelled in shock, but George's stomach jumped into his throat, blocking his voice.

When he was brave enough to open his eyes, he saw that Ada had jammed the throttle down as far as it could go. But she was already pulling it back toward her, and soon the mechanical bird evened out with a *putt-putt-putter*ing shudder.

George glanced over the edge as far as he dared. They had dropped considerably closer to the mountain peaks, so close that he heard the sound of the rivers. He looked up again, straining to see the other bird, but it had disappeared.

"It *is* the Organization! They're still following us!" He had to yell, because in the lower atmosphere, the wind was chaotic. His hair whipped into his face.

"It was probably just a mirage or an atmospheric refraction that mirrored our own image!" Ada shouted back. A sharp gust of wind picked up the airship, then dropped it with a jolt. Ruthie's fingers dug into his shoulders. "No need for alarm."

"It had its own shadow. Can a mirage do that?"

"Well, no," Ada admitted.

George was too panicked to feel smug that he was right. "What are we going to do?"

"We could turn around in circles to confuse them," Oscar suggested in a shaky voice.

Ada pulled down on the steering controls again, and the engine quieted to a soft, purring rumble. "There's nothing we can do but keep going unless we want to run out of fuel again. We're all going to the same place, anyway." Her familiar, slightly devious grin had returned. "If the Organization thinks we'll give up now, they're in for a surprise."

A memory surfaced in his mind, something she'd said in her room in Dorset Square. "Miss Byron...do you think the Organization stole your inventions?"

"Lord Devonshire, do you think I would *ever* let that happen?"

He settled back in his seat to keep an eye out for the other bird, or whatever it was, in case it returned. It only occurred to him later, when they were skimming an even lower set of stringy, cream-colored clouds, that she hadn't really answered his question.

When they finally dropped out of the clouds again, George glimpsed a cluster of scattered islands in the roiling sea below. Venice. He felt a tug of triumph in his stomach. It seemed to float on the water, breaking through the slate-gray surface where the mouth of a river fed into the sea. As they sank lower in the sky, he saw that every bit of dry earth was bristling with red-roofed buildings and the spires of churches, which poked up like sharpened spears ready to impale them.

Nowhere was there a flat, open field to land in.

"Hang on tight, George," Oscar whispered in his ear. "This is the same thing that happened when Ada and I crashed in Trafalgar Square. If you hadn't noticed, she is very good at flying, but not so good at landing."

And before George could respond, Ada jammed the steering column as far forward as it would go, plunging the mechanical bird straight for the spiky skyline.

Ada navigated toward an open plaza ahead—a flat *but very small* plaza. At the end of it was the tallest spire in the whole city, a brick tower with a steep green roof. Perched on the very top of the tower's roof was a golden angel. Its golden wings were spread wide in welcome, its arm raised in a blessing.

"Ada, we're going to crash!" George yelled, pointing wildly as they plummeted toward the tower.

"I'm trying to turn!" Ada cried. "It's not working." George gripped her shoulder in fear. "Don't worry, everything will be fine!"

And for a moment, because Ada sounded so confident, he really did believe everything would be fine. He believed it up until the very moment they crashed into the angel.

The crash seemed to happen in slow motion. There

was an awful crunch when the tip of the bird's left wing hit the gold statue. Though Ada jerked the steering column in a desperate attempt to turn, one of the airship's huge rubber wheels struck the hem of the angel's robe, making it crumple like paper. George turned around just in time to see the angel statue tip, tip, tip, and fall, plummeting from the tall tower onto the stone pavement below.

The airship was falling, too, but George was so distraught that he hardly realized Ada was gliding the bird onto the rooftop of a nearby church. Colors flashed by as if they were flying through an oil painting—white marble, red brick, green copper. Massive stone pillars hid them from view, allowing the battered bird to skid to a halt unseen next to a giant golden dome on the long, flat roof of the cathedral.

With a jerk of his legs, George scrambled out of his seat as soon as he could. Next to him, Ada, Oscar, and Ruthie wriggled free and tumbled onto the roof in a single squirming mass. Hooting, Ruthie gingerly cradled her banana-leaf map, rocking it back and forth in her arms like an infant.

George breathed a sigh of relief. Other than a few bruises and scrapes, they were all unharmed.

The same could not be said of the mechanical bird.

One of the wings was nearly split in two. A giant gash blazed across the left side, almost severing the nose where it was bolted to the rest of the bird. A strangled moan escaped from Ada's throat as she inspected the damage with her palm covering her mouth.

"Ada," George started, reaching his hand out to comfort her.

Her eyes, round with devastation, snapped to him. "Not now."

George drew his hand back, swallowing the threat of his own tears. Why did failure follow him everywhere? His curse was relentless. This time, the only casualties had been the airship and the statue. Next time, Oscar or Ada or Ruthie could be the ones who got hurt or worse. He was foolish, foolish, foolish to have forgotten that. The sooner he found the Star and could retreat home with Frobisher, the better.

A series of excited grunts broke into George's thoughts. Ruthie was leaning over the lip of the roof, frantically gesturing to something below.

"What is it, Ruthie?" Oscar asked. He and George followed her finger to see the fallen angel lying in the middle of a crowd, flattened and mangled into a golden pancake in the open plaza.

"Police," Oscar said.

The crowd murmured as smartly dressed officers clip-clopped through the plaza on horseback. George felt beads of cold sweat spring out of the back of his neck. They couldn't get caught. If they were caught, they would be thrown in prison. Italian prison, where George's cries for help would not even be understood.

"Ada—" She had slumped over the mechanical bird, her eyes hidden in the bend of her elbow, her shoulders shaking. The thought of Ada crying unnerved him more than anything, even the prospect of being thrown into prison, but he tried to steel his voice. "I'm sorry, but we have to leave."

He knew how much her heart must be hurting right now. The mechanical bird was her prized possession. She had invented it from her imagination, had built it with her own hands, cared for it, fueled it, and loved it. It was her Mrs. Daly. Her mineral collection. Maybe even her Star of Victory. And George had absolutely no idea what to say to comfort her. Other than Oscar's words the night before, nothing anyone had said thus far in his life had been able to comfort him.

"Ada—" Oscar tried.

Her head jerked up. She cleared her throat and briskly rubbed her face. "We have to save it. Help me with this, please. Quickly," she said, beckoning George, Oscar, and Ruthie.

Though she occasionally stopped to wipe her eyes and nose, her hands were a blur as they worked over the bird, loosening bolts to disassemble it into seven pieces. In a clipped voice, she instructed Oscar and George to store each part in a large, shaded cupola. When they were done, Ruthie loped to the far corner on her knuckles, gesturing to a ladder that led all the way down to a shaded alley. The alley led to the plaza, where the police had begun to circle like hawks.

"Just act normal. Blend into the crowd," Ada said, pulling her dark curls over her grease- and tear-streaked face.

A cart carrying a mountain of oranges rumbled past them. Ruthie, who had been riding on Oscar's back, leapt onto the cart, landing with a dull thud on the pile of ripe fruit.

"Ruthie!" George broke away from Oscar and Ada to whisk Ruthie off before she drew any more attention to them. The cart's driver, an old woman wrapped in a brightly colored shawl, chided George loudly in Italian. With Ruthie tucked under one arm, he fled.

But the crowd had closed in around them. There was no sign of Ada's bouncing brown curls or Oscar's fluttering stained fingers anywhere he looked. Soon George and Ruthie were adrift in the swirling sea of people, pushed this way and that by bread vendors, confused tourists, and children in patchwork clothes, until they were practically underneath the hooves of the police horses next to the fallen statue. Ruthie whimpered.

One of the officers—the one with the tallest and whitest horse—dismounted from his gleaming brown saddle. He was dressed in an ink-black military uniform with a silken black cape. On his head was a black bicorn hat with a furiously red plume. His black mustache, which bristled this way and that as he swept his eyes over the crowd, was the same shape as his hat.

"Il Naso," someone murmured fearfully.

The policeman threw back his shoulders and sniffed the air. Swiftly, as if the sniff bore a secret message that George did not understand, the crowd of Venetians and tourists thinned out until only George and a few other curious onlookers remained. Still, George did not see Ada or Oscar anywhere in the plaza.

George watched as the man called Il Naso knelt down next to the angel. The officer lowered his face so close to the golden statue that the hairs of his mustache brushed against it. Then a sinister, gleeful smile spread over his face. The look reminded George of a cat that had a mouse pressed underneath its paw.

Using his index and middle fingers like tweezers, the officer reached into the wreckage and pulled out a long, gleaming shard of silver metal.

Then Il Naso's gaze fixed on George. George blinked in fear. Il Naso did not.

With a swish of his cape, he sprang to his feet and began to cross the square—directly for George and Ruthie.

Lord Devonshire turned his back to the angel and ran.

Chapter Twenty-One

Still throwing glances behind him to search for Il Naso, George finally found Ada and Oscar near a stack of warm bread on the edge of the plaza. Or rather, they found *him*. He would never have recognized them in their new, preposterous disguises, which Ada had procured in the twenty minutes they'd been separated. She'd put on a white porcelain mask that covered the top half of her face and had twisted her hair up into intricate knots; Oscar now wore a towering plumed hat bursting with what appeared to be parrot feathers.

"It's a pirate hat," he said happily.

"I thought the point of a disguise was *not* to attract attention."

In response, Ada draped Ruthie in a shawl and Oscar gathered her in his arms like a baby. The baker's smock they had stolen ("borrowed," according to Ada) for George was much too big, but Ada made him wear it anyway.

She led them through winding alleyways and over yellow- and gray-stoned bridges until they came to a wide canal the color of an overcast sky. Black gondolas shaped like peapods crowded the churning water. To Oscar's delight (and Ruthie's dismay, based on her grunting), Ada directed them into a boat. She whispered their destination to the gondolier and, with a long pole, he steered them away.

While George told them about Il Naso, Oscar gawked at all the people they passed. "Don't you think this is the sort of place a pirate would live? Everything is next to the water. Maybe I can find someone who knows my father."

"The Adriatic Sea used to be a nest of pirates. But I believe they were all beheaded," George replied tersely. Once again, the urgency of the situation seemed to fly right over Oscar's head. Ada's bird had been wrecked. Despite what Ada repeated over and over, Frobisher was still in danger. They'd lost the Star. And now the police knew George's face. His nerves felt as frayed as the rough, wiry hair that poked up from Ruthie's head.

"Ada, where are we going?" George asked. "Have you visited Venice before? Are we going to find out where Roy might be hiding?"

"No, George, my mother won't let me come here," she said quickly. "But I have a lead."

"A lead?" George's heart thumped. "What is it? A secret message? A symbol? A clue?"

"Well, no. It's more like an idea. If the Organization has been spying on me, it follows that they are spying on other brilliant scientists. I suspect that a few scientists may even be working *for* the Organization. I happen to know that a brilliant young scientist is in Venice on holiday. We might find a clue to the Organization's whereabouts in his apartment. But be careful what you say around him." She narrowed her eyes. "I don't know whose side he's on yet. And keep an eye out for Roy. He'll probably be disguised."

"Right," George said, his head spinning with the speed of her thoughts. The mystery of the Organization continued to deepen.

"Stop here." Ada pointed at a faded pink house with a green door. As they disembarked, she took Ruthie from Oscar's arms and unbundled her with one tug, mimed knocking, then pointed at the top-floor window. Ruthie scampered up to the fourth story of the house, skipping from window frames to balconies to the drainpipe. Then she rapped on the closed shutters of an attic window.

A second later, the shutters opened with a creak. A gawky young man with a large forehead and brown sideburns leaned out of the window. Seeing Ruthie, he cocked his head to the side but didn't shout or run away as George might have done if an orangutan had knocked on his shutters.

"Hello there," said the young man in a deep, slow voice with a familiar English accent, extending his hand to Ruthie. "Goodness, you are a fine-looking *Pongo pygmaeus*!"

"Hello, Mr. Darwin?" Ada called out. She took off her mask. "Charles?"

The young man looked down at her, shading his eyes so that he could see her face. "It can't be. Ada Byron! So this must be Ruthie?" Ruthie flashed a toothy grin.

"Yes, Mr. Darwin. This is Oscar and George." ("Lord Devonshire," George muttered halfheartedly.) "My friends and I were wondering if we might stop for a brief visit."

"Ah, on holiday as well?" The young man laughed. "How convenient. Are you sure you're not here to spy on my mollusk collection? I'm catching up to you!"

"Ha! Did you hear that? Classic spy deflection technique.

We're not sp—" George said, but Ada elbowed him, causing him to choke on his words.

"*Not speleologists*," she continued, aiming a pointed look at George, "because we don't study cave snails. Only freshwater ones."

But Mr. Darwin wasn't listening to Ada's flimsy cover-up, nor did he seem to notice George's outburst. He was too busy examining Ruthie from nose to toes. "The door is open," he finally called down, disappearing inside with a bang of the shutters.

"How do you know this fellow?" George kept his voice low as they climbed the stairs. "What if he really is a spy for the Organization?"

"I highly doubt he is. I just thought it was fair that you knew there was a possibility and to be watchful. I've been corresponding with him every day for months," Ada replied. "He's studying to be a naturalist. Or rather, he would be if his father didn't want him to be a doctor. At any rate, he's been most helpful in answering my questions about beetle wings."

George frowned. Could a man who studied beetle wings be of any interest to the Organization?

"You have that *are you sure* look on your face, George, and yes—I'm *sure* this is the right thing to do. Do you have any bright ideas you'd like to propose?"

"Well, no." He cast his gaze to the ground, embarrassed. He really didn't have any ideas.

"Then you can be sure to be on the lookout for any clues that might lead us to the Organization. And Frobisher's whereabouts," she said in a kinder voice. "Oh, and Oscar, keep an eye on Ruthie so she doesn't eat anything. He has an extensive mineral collection. Like you."

Upstairs, Ada and Mr. Darwin began to talk immediately about scientific things. George picked out a few Latinate words in their conversation (*ossicle, vestigial, reticulate*), which he recognized from his studies, but trying to remember all their meanings gave him a headache. While Ada questioned Darwin, he decided, he would make himself useful and look for clues.

Mr. Darwin's rented attic room reminded George of Ada's bedroom. Yellowed papers ripped from books were pinned to every wall, each with a picture of a different creature. Scribbled notes surrounded each illustration like dark clouds. Looking from one to the next, George spotted a wide-winged butterfly, a dark beetle with the antlers of a stag, and several different renderings of a colorful squat-billed bird.

But unlike Ada's room, this one wasn't alive with ticking inventions. It was alive with actual living things. A box on the table quivered slightly. Freshly picked plants and flowers were piled on the counters. Two enormous, striped tarantulas waved their hairy legs from inside a glass case. Specks moved inside a glass tube full of dirt. (George found this *very* suspicious, but he couldn't see how it was a clue.)

A page with a picture of an insect playing with a round ball fluttered to the ground next to the open window. George picked it up and brought his nose close to the page....

"Dung beetles!" Darwin cried out, clapping his hand on George's back.

George flushed. "Excuse me, sir, but that is a rather rude thing to say in front of a lady."

Ada laughed, and George flushed even hotter.

"No, George, he's referring to the illustration. They're dung beetles. They roll animal excrement into a ball and eat it."

"More specifically," Darwin added, "this particular

species are in the phylum Arthropoda, composing the suborder Polyphaga, in the superfamily Scarabaeoidea."

"Y-yes, yes, I know what sub-supergenealogy they are in," George stammered. He put the page down next to the glass tube filled with dirt and moving reddish-brown specks. Surely, this young man was hiding something. "And what is this?" George said accusatorily, jabbing a finger at the tube.

"Those are a previously unidentified species of stinging ant, from the genus Solenopsis. Be very careful. They sting."

"Perfectly normal, Lord Devonshire," Ada said politely, but she narrowed her eyes at George before she and Darwin started to talk again.

George grew sulkier by the minute. Roy could be using the Star of Victory to help the Organization take over the world right now, and Ada was wasting time discussing—

"—varus angulation of the knees—"

Whatever *that* meant. He scraped his fingers through his tangled hair.

"Miss Byron!" George finally snapped. By the looks of shock on his companions' faces (even Ruthie's), he'd raised his voice more than he meant to. "May we return to our business?"

Ada blinked. "Charles, perhaps you can take Oscar to the lagoon and show him some of the rock formations you wrote me about? He could sketch some of them for you. He is an excellent artist and an aspiring geologist."

"It would be my pleasure," Darwin said with a wink.

As soon as the door shut behind Oscar, Ruthie, and Mr. Darwin, George let his questions fly. "What clever way will you use to find Roy? Can you speak Italian? We'll be able to track them down in seven days, won't we?"

Ada furrowed her brow. "Let's not rush," she said.

"How can you say that?" George demanded, dismayed. "Of course we need to move quickly. Frobisher is counting on us."

Ada stood up straighter. "The Organization is dangerous and they're smart. If we keep rushing after them, they'll always stay one step ahead. Remember, we have the element of surprise. Now, I'm going out for a bit."

"So you do have a plan," George said slowly.

Ada scoffed. "Of course I have a plan. It's a brilliant plan. Better than my last one."

"And..."

"And," Ada said, "if you're captured by the Organization, the less you know, the better. We'll have to split up."

Nervously, George ran his fingers through his hair. Splitting up meant he would be alone in a foreign city where an olfactorily gifted policeman might be hunting him this very second. "If you think it's best."

"I do," Ada said firmly.

"But what about Il Naso?"

"George," she said, arching her eyebrow in disbelief. "Are you telling me that you're worried a police officer is going to track you down by *smelling* you, using only the scent of a metal scrap from the mechanical bird?"

George bit his lip. It *did* sound silly. "You said to follow my gut."

"In that case, you should be careful, Lord Devonshire," Ada said. She then scooped out a handful of soil from one of Darwin's many potted plants and began to smear it over George's face and neck.

"Ada! What—what do you think you're doing!" he cried, pushing her hand away. A sizable chunk of dirt fell from his hair and broke apart when it hit the floor.

"It'll mask your scent. I've a theory that—"

George frantically brushed his face clean. "I'll take my chances without the dirt. What am I supposed to do?"

Ada scribbled a few words on a piece of paper. The

sound of her pencil scratching over the page filled him with courage, with purpose. When she finished, she handed him a bag of Venetian coins that she'd packed, an empty sack, and the paper. The paper said:

1. Go to the nearest market
2. Find one pound of each in this order:
   Salt
   Sugar
   Flour
   Butter
   Eggs
   Rhubarb
3. Buy them at the best price
4. Come back

George had never been shopping in his life. That was Frobisher's job. "How is this going to help us find the Organization?"

Ada raised one finger to silence him. "The less you know, the better, remember?"

Chapter Twenty-Two

Picking his way through women in brightly colored dresses and clusters of children playing marbles or bocce, George walked down Darwin's street, over the bridge to the other side of the canal, and down a bustling thoroughfare, just as Ada had instructed.

Truly, he was an explorer now. If Marco Polo could find his way from Venice to China and back, surely the 3rd Lord of Devonshire could handle a trip to the local market by himself. Steeled by the thought of the ancient explorers who had launched their epic journeys from this very island, George trekked through the winding footpaths of Venice, his chin held high.

He quickly learned that Venice was a city better suited

for fish than for people. It was impossible to escape the water, which was everywhere. (Everything also stank of fish, and every surface was hazy as if covered in a layer of scum.) Between the canals that threaded through the city and the pale buildings that rose up from the water's edge, there was no room for horses or carts. There was scarcely room to walk.

Despite the difficulties of navigating an unfamiliar, half-submerged maze of streets, George persisted until he found an outdoor market in a courtyard.

Buying the ingredients from the list proved to be more challenging than getting to the market. Sugar and salt looked identical, but he quickly discovered that it was not polite to taste them to discover which was which. His hand smarted from the slap he received from the dry goods seller. And who knew that there were so many different varieties of flour? Wheat flour, barley flour, rye flour, almond flour, chestnut flour; some was farina, some was semolina. He bought all of them, just in case (for the lowest possible price, of course).

As George recorded his purchases on the list with a pencil borrowed from Oscar's bag, he had the distinct feeling that he was being watched. His gut kicked, telling him that somewhere near, a threat was circling him. Every unfamiliar noise made him flinch.

The policeman could show up at any moment.

The Organization could be anywhere.

No one could be ruled out as a possible Roy in disguise: men, women, children, babies. Or they could all be agents of his pursuers.

Without Ruthie, Ada, and Oscar, he felt more scared with every step, but he couldn't go home without completing his mission. Only after several wrong turns did he find a vegetable stand. He asked the tiny, wizened old woman behind the stand for rhubarb, and she replied, *"Non capisco."*

"No, I don't want a piece of scone. Rhubarb. Do you have any roo-barb?"

The old woman wrinkled her nose. *"Vai, vai, bambino stupido."*

"How rude! I'll take my money elsewhere. You're the one who is *stupido*." George turned away in a huff. At least now he knew one word that he could use in Italian.

Then, like the breeze itself, a quiet swept through the market crowd. He felt that strong, leaden kick in his gut again. And again. Unfortunately, his mind was now so attuned to his gut that he had absolutely no idea where the threat was coming from.

Until he heard the swish of a cape followed by a familiar sniff. Before he saw the man, George knew who it was.

"Il Naso," the old woman murmured.

The crowd in the marketplace parted just as it had earlier that day in the plaza. Mustache bristling, Il Naso sauntered toward George, who had frozen in place despite the sudden urge to run. The policeman's shiny boots squeaked with each step.

When he was only a few steps away, Il Naso plucked a handful of ruffled green leaves with red stalks from the vegetable stand and offered the colorful plant to George. "I believe this is what you are looking for. *Rabarbaro*," Il Naso said.

Managing a nod, George stuffed the rhubarb into his sack. "Thank you, Officer."

Il Naso waited while George, trembling, paid the old woman for the colorful vegetable. "What's for dinner?" he asked. His tone was amiable, but his stare was as cold as ice, and the smile on his face was as slick as olive oil.

George licked his dry lips. "Food" was all he could muster.

"Looks as though you are cooking for many people, yes?" Il Naso peered into George's bag. "Maybe you are cooking for some other people who have been busy today making trouble in Venice."

"I'm not sure what you mean," George said, backing away slowly. His heart was racing now. He would give anything to be covered in dirt, if it made him invisible to Il Naso.

The police officer picked up a tomato, inhaling its scent deeply. "Did you know that a mother can recognize her child from scent alone? It's true. The nose is a powerful organ. And my nose can smell a man's feelings from fifty paces. Do you know what I smell on you?"

George shook his head, cowering back against the onions and turnips.

Il Naso leaned forward. George flinched, anticipating that Il Naso was going to grab him and cart him away to prison. "I smell guilt with a trace of deceit. It's not an unusual smell for the accomplice to a crime. But what is unusual is that I caught a whiff of just that smell earlier today at the piazza, after the statue of the archangel Gabriel fell from the campanile."

George's heart skipped a beat. "I—I don't know what you're talking about."

"But I'm not interested in you, little rabbit," said Il Naso, leaning in close. "I'm interested in the Byron girl. Where is your master?"

"My *master*?" George exclaimed. "I can assure you that I have no master. In fact, I come from a long line of English nobles who have been the benevolent employers of a number of servants. My man Frobisher would tell you." George stopped, emotion clogging his throat. Then he looked into Il Naso's eyes and remembered who he was yelling at. "I mean—what girl?" he bluffed.

"The English poet's daughter," Il Naso said.

"I'm afraid I don't know to whom you are referring," George said. How could Il Naso possibly know Ada? She had said she'd never been to Venice. "It's not as if all English people know each other."

Il Naso waved the tomato in George's face. "I think you are lying. You and your companion have much in common."

A tingle crept up George's back, raising the hairs on his neck. Had Il Naso mistaken Ada for someone else? Did she have a secret sister she hadn't told him about?

Il Naso studied George, then laughed cruelly. "Ah, so you do not know. You will find out soon enough, of that I am sure," he said, shaking his head. "Today, you are lucky. I cannot throw you in the workhouse for a lie. Your companion is another story, however. She is worse than the worst thieves in San Marco!"

A flood of terror washed over George. Il Naso was talking about throwing Ada into a prison workhouse. George had dragged her into this. He had already failed to keep Frobisher safe. Would he fail to protect Ada, too?

Il Naso squeezed the tomato just enough to leave shallow dents on its smooth red skin where his fingers had been. "Now, have you changed your mind? Are you ready to bring me to her?"

George's gut was screaming: *Get away, get away, get away*, but he couldn't outrun this man. Therefore, he needed a distraction. If Ada were here, she'd turn a turnip into a missile or a bag of flour into a—

A bag of flour.

Remembering the flour-bomb that had fallen from the ceiling in Ada's home only days before, he grabbed the paper bag of almond flour from his sack. He raised the bag over his head and slammed it to the ground in one quick motion, with as much strength as he could muster from his already-aching arms.

A white plume of flour exploded into the air, swirling between him and Il Naso like a frosty-white blizzard. The old woman behind the vegetable stand howled as the flour blanketed her vibrant vegetables with white dust. On the other side of the chalky cloud, Il Naso had begun to cough and wipe his eyes.

Joy surged through George, ungluing his feet from the ground. While Il Naso was temporarily blinded, he ran and didn't look back.

"Stay away from the poet's daughter," Il Naso called after him, between coughs. "She has a debt to pay. If I find you with her, you'll pay, too."

Chapter Twenty-Three

By the time George fled back to the pink house and vaulted up the three flights of stairs to the attic, his arms were screaming in pain from the weight of his purchases, which he didn't dare abandon. To make matters worse, an afternoon rain shower had soaked him thoroughly. Even the rain smelled of fish.

Throwing open the door, he found Ada sitting at a small round table in front of a large stack of letters. Her hair was damp and her mud-splattered boots dripped water where she had left them by the door, as if she'd only just beat him home. George slammed the door behind him, and the force of the slam caused her tower of letters to collapse.

"I followed your instructions," George said breathlessly. He took out the items from his sack and laid them on the small table. All but two of the eggs had broken, covering the inside of the canvas sack in a thick layer of pale yellow goo. The packages of flour had split open to reveal lumps of whitish paste where the fine powder had mixed with rain, and the rhubarb looked as if it had been stomped by a giant boot.

A dismal feeling came over George. He had even failed to get her ingredients. Now the plan was probably ruined. "I'm sorry, Miss Byron."

Ada gave the pile of crushed and soggy food a cursory glance before lighting the wood stove. She rummaged through the apartment's cupboards and found a round pan, then tied an overlarge apron around her waist and proceeded to pour the only semidry bag of flour into a bowl.

"This city is a stinking, festering cesspool of rotten sludge," George continued, emboldened by the fact that she didn't seem upset with him. He'd had quite the adventure, now that he considered it. In fact, it reminded him of his grandfather's harrowing tales. "Every surface is slimy with mold and algae. Why, even the police force is manned with the lowest of the low."

"Why do you say that?"

"I'll tell you," George said. He cleared his throat to begin, in a voice that would make his grandfather proud.

A FACTUAL AND ACCURATE CHRONICLE OF GEORGE'S AFTERNOON IN VENICE

There I was, minding my own business, helping an old lady learn English, when a battalion of police officers came and grabbed me. Of course, they were led by Il Naso, that nasty fellow.

He said, "Tell me where the girl is. Now, you bambino stupido! If you refuse, I'll put you in chains and send you to the workhouse."

"Are you all right, Miss Byron?"

Ada had stopped vigorously mashing pieces of butter into the bowl of flour. Yellow chunks fell from her fingers. She looked at George with wide, fearful eyes. "Yes, of course. I'm fine. I was just enthralled by your oratory. Go on," she said quickly.

This is the best part. I broke away from the police officers like this. Ha! With a chop and a kick, I escaped their grasp. I said, "I will never betray Ada Byron!"

Il Naso charged me like a bull. I stepped aside and he crashed

207

into a tower of turnips. He lay senseless on the ground. His bat-
talion fled. The entire market cheered. I put my boot on Il Naso's
chest and said, "That will teach you to threaten an English lord
and his friends." And then . . .

George stopped. Ada had rolled out the flour mixture
with a rolling pin and was pressing the dough roughly into
the pan. It didn't look like an experiment at all. It looked
like . . . a pie.

"Miss Byron, what are you doing?"

Ada glanced up, her eyes now wide and innocent.
"Baking."

"Are you telling me that I risked life and limb for a
pie? A rhubarb pie?" He picked up the empty flour bag
and shook it furiously. "This isn't going to help us find the
Organization!"

"We can't launch a proper investigation on an empty
stomach," Ada said weakly.

"But you said you had a plan. You said we had to split
up so that if one of us was . . ." George trailed off as he
remembered the way they had all split up in Geneva so
that Ada could exclude him from her plan. No matter how
big or small, how harebrained or brilliant, she always had
a plan, even if she didn't explain it to him. Maybe it was

the same kind of plan she'd had in Chillon Castle: George had been the unsuspecting distraction from a trap that Ada and Oscar were setting. If the Organization was the mouse and Ada had set out the mousetrap, then what was George? Was he a soggy piece of bread for the mouse to nibble on until the cheese was ready?

"You *do* have a plan, you just don't think I can handle it," he said miserably.

For once, maybe for the first time since he'd met her less than a week ago, he wanted Ada to contradict him. But the look on her face told him everything he needed to know.

He sank back into a chair, knees wobbling with shame.

"You sent me away on some useless errand because you think I'm a gutless milksop. *Send George off to get the groceries. He can't mess up a trip to the market.* That's what you were thinking, wasn't it?" He glanced at the pile of letters on the floor, one of which had an intricate drawing of a star on it. "You kept me out of the way so that you could work on a plan without me."

"George—"

"I'm a coward. You said I was a coward. Back in the menagerie."

"George, I—"

"Well, you were right." A sharp feeling coursed through him, like a physical crack in his chest. "I'm not the person I pretend to be."

Ada sighed. "Please stop. You're overreacting."

But George couldn't stop. His emotions poured out in an uncontrollable flood. "My father told me I had the spine of a snail and porridge for brains. He knew I was worthless. And you knew it all along, too."

"Your father was wrong. Snails are invertebrates, so none of them have spines." She wiped her hands on her apron, smearing oatmeal-colored dough across the pale pink fabric, and joined George at the table. "You're not worthless."

"I am. *You're* wrong."

"Wrong? *Me?*" Ada patted his arm with her flour-caked hand. George managed a weak smile. "Worth is subjective, George. Which means it's in the eye of the beholder. So you've had a few rough years. It's not your circumstances that define you, it's how you tackle them. You're as stubborn as a mule. You defended the map and Frobisher from attacks in your home. That doesn't sound like a coward to me. That sounds like a brave person."

George lifted his head a little. "Brave? Now you're just saying things to try to make me feel better."

"I am not," Ada argued. "I called you a coward back in London and I meant it then. But you changed the moment you came to me looking to save Frobisher. From one state to the next, like matter. Solid to liquid, liquid to . . . well, never mind. You saved Ruthie from the mechanical man in Geneva. And you braved the market and faced down an entire legion of policemen."

"I wasn't trying to be brave. *You* make me brave." The words came out in a rush, but he realized he meant it. So far, his bad-luck curse was being kept at bay. The flood of bad feelings in his chest began to drain away. A warm feeling of gratitude to Ada rushed into its place. "I wouldn't even have come close to saving Frobisher without you."

Ada smiled. "Now that you're done feeling sorry for yourself, there's something I need to—"

A loud banging interrupted her. Someone was at the front door, four stories below.

"Probably Ruthie . . ." George trailed off when he saw the blank expression on Ada's face. She was staring at something behind him, her face pale with fright. He turned to follow her gaze.

Smears of white powder trailed under the door, leading right to George's feet. Downstairs, the banging came again, so forcefully that the wooden shutters seemed to rattle.

George's stomach did a somersault. The flour he'd thrown when he was fleeing Il Naso had gotten everywhere. Even on his shoes. Which meant...

"Il Naso. He followed me!" George cried. "Hide!"

Chapter Twenty-Four

Ada whirled around, searching for somewhere to hide in the tiny apartment. Alas, there was no bedskirt on the bed, so they could not hide underneath it. Because Ada was rather small, she was able to squeeze behind the sofa, but the only piece of furniture George could find to hide behind was a coatrack.

The stairs were already creaking under Il Naso's weight.

"Ada, what do we do?" Of course he expected Ada to have a plan—a brilliant plan that involved jumping out the window and sprouting a pair of linen wings. But she said nothing. Why wasn't she doing something? From behind the sofa, she peeked up at him, her eyes glassy with fear.

"I don't know, George. I'm sorry. For everything."

"How about dirt? I should have listened to you the first time." He ran to the nearest potted plant and began smearing dirt on his arms. "Il Naso can smell our *feelings*. Think innocent thoughts."

On the other side of the door, the footsteps climbed closer and closer.

Suddenly, one of Darwin's other specimens caught his eye. An idea sprouted in his mind. It was just the sort of thing that Ada would have used in one of her bizarre, breathless plans if she hadn't been cowering behind the couch.

"Stay where you are." George carried the potted plant across the room to the large glass tube with the ants before he could change his mind. Gently, George removed the cover of the glass container and carefully tipped the squirming reddish-brown ants into the dirt of the potted plant, rearranging the leaves to hide them from view.

"George," Ada gasped. "That is brilliant."

Stay hidden, George mouthed.

The footsteps stopped just outside the attic apartment. George heard the policeman sniffing like a bloodhound.

Good.

George exhaled, pulse thrumming, and threw open the door with his free hand.

"Mr. Naso. What a delightful surprise! I'm so glad to see you," he said gallantly. "I'm sorry for my boorish behavior earlier. I feel absolutely wretched about it. You were only trying to do your job, and I assaulted you with powdered almonds."

Il Naso's thick black mustache twitched in surprise. "No apology is necessary, little rabbit. You have already given me exactly what I want." He glanced over George's shoulder. "Come out, *signorina*. I know you're hiding in there. I can smell your trickery."

George opened the door wider to allow Il Naso inside. "Please come in and take this gift as a token of my apology. It's an English tradition. Not accepting it would be very, very rude."

Il Naso brushed away the potted plant. "I cannot accept gifts from you."

"That's too bad," George said. "It has a very unusual fragrance. I thought that someone with your discerning olfactory capabilities would appreciate its delicate smell." He lifted the plant up to Il Naso's face so that the policeman had no choice but to take it.

Just as George had hoped, Il Naso inclined his nose to the plant, inhaling deeply . . .

And bolted upright with a yelp.

Red specks scurried over his prominent nose, leaving angry red bumps behind. Several climbed into his nostrils. He dropped the plant at his feet. The ceramic pot broke in two, spilling dirt—and ants—across his polished shoes. Immediately, the ants flowed up his legs like a raging river (with many legs).

As Il Naso frantically beat the reddish-brown specks off his face and clothes, George felt a thrill of triumph course through him, followed quickly by the tug of Ada's hand on his elbow. "Come on!"

In a flurry of skirts, dirt, ants, and flour, they ran past Il Naso, down the stairs, and into the light of day.

Other than his daily calisthenics chasing Mrs. Daly out of the cupboards and up and down the stairs with a broom, George did not get very much exercise in No. 8 Dorset Square. They were only able to run a few blocks until they were forced to rest behind an ivy-covered wall. When it no longer felt as if his lungs were on fire, he turned to Ada. "I'm sorry for leading Il Naso to your friend's apartment."

Ada dismissed him with a wave of her hand. "That was *very* clever, George. But you need to be more careful. You're going to get us caught."

He paused, remembering what Il Naso had called Ada in the marketplace. "How did that policeman know that your father was a poet? I thought you'd never been to Venice before."

"My father is a famous poet. I daresay, one of the best known in the world. If I had to guess, I'd say the policeman is an admirer. I resemble my father quite strongly. We have the same chin," Ada said breezily. "If you ever meet him, you'll see."

George tried to imagine Il Naso with his nose in a book of poetry and failed. "If you say so."

"As I was saying before we were interrupted, I sent you on that errand to distract the Organization from what I was doing. From now on, you must follow my instructions to the letter. Do you trust me?"

"Absolutely," George replied. "But I was thinking. Il Naso mentioned a place called San Marco. He said it's a thieves' den."

"And?" Ada raised her eyebrows.

"Well." George stopped, feeling rather silly. Was he really going to suggest they charge into a den of thieves, who were probably armed to the teeth? And do what? Demand the whereabouts of Roy, who was surely working under a pseudonym by now? "Just thought it might be important, that's all," he said quickly.

Thankfully, they managed to intercept Oscar, Ruthie, and Mr. Darwin before the trio returned to the apartment to find an angry, ant-ridden policeman. Mr. Darwin assured Ada that if Il Naso was still upstairs, he would keep him occupied as long as possible to allow the children and Ruthie time to get away.

"I thought the police were supposed to protect people from bad things. None of us did anything wrong," Oscar said as they slunk along the canal once more. Swaddled in his arms, Ruthie groaned softly in agreement. "Maybe if we stopped running from him and explained that he's made a mistake, he would leave us alone."

"I'm afraid we can't take that chance, Oscar. We'll have to find some other place to sleep. If we haven't found the Organization by then, of course," Ada said. "But there's something urgent we need to take care of tonight. And it can't wait. George has given me an idea."

"I have?"

"Yes. I need a part to fix the mechanical bird's engine and can only find it in a certain shop in San Marco. Without it, we're likely to crash midflight."

Oscar's face lit up. "We're fixing the bird?" Ada nodded. He whooped. "I can't wait to fly again. The wind in my hair, the world at my feet, nothing holding me down."

George shot Oscar a pointed glance. He was ready to fly again, too, but straight home and not until they had the Star. "I thought we were going to look for Roy, Ada. If we don't find the Star soon, Frobisher is going to die."

"Lord Devonshire, if we don't go to San Marco to get the part for the mechanical bird in order to fix it so that it's in tip-top shape, we won't be able to escape with Frobisher properly when we do find him, in the event we are chased," she said sternly. "And as I've already told you, I would never let anything happen to your man."

"And ... maybe we'll find a clue to the Organization in San Marco?" George asked.

"Of course. Thank you for finally suggesting it. You're beginning to catch on," Ada said, giving him a small smile. "I'm proud of you."

A smile burst onto his own face. It felt like the first in years. He coughed to cover up the blush that was overcoming his cheeks. "Catching on? To what?"

"You're starting to realize that anything's possible, Lord Devonshire."

Chapter Twenty-Five

This time, Ada made George and Oscar wear her dresses and tie silk kerchiefs over their hair. The Organization was looking for a young lady and two boys, so the disguises would be even more effective. Plus, she pointed out, girls were often overlooked, even by criminals. It was Frobisher's neckerchief that he fixed over his stubborn blond locks to perfect his disguise.

Ada had also made them promise to wait on the outskirts of the open plaza, Piazza San Marco, while she completed her simple errand, so that they were far away from any dangers that might lie in wait. From a distance, she argued, they could better catch a glimpse of any suspicious Organizational activity, in case she was followed.

George had promised to wait there.

But by his count—which was confirmed by the enormous blue-and-gold clock that hung on the face of a nearby building—she had been gone exactly thirty-seven minutes, which seemed like a very, very long time. Too long, he thought, though she hadn't told them exactly when she'd return to the arched portico that was their designated meeting point. Beneath the billowing linen sleeves of his dress, his skin was starting to prickle with worry.

It was evening now, but with gas lamps glowing on every corner and shop windows blazing with yellow light, it was nearly as bright as day. George paced back and forth near the gondola they'd "borrowed" to get there, occasionally swiping at his hair. Oscar busied himself inspecting the nub of charcoal that Darwin had given him during their outing. In her white lace-trimmed bonnet, Ruthie chirped happily over her banana-leaf map.

From where George was standing (or rather pacing), he could see across the wide-open square of the Piazza San Marco. Hung on the face of a building across the square, tucked into a shady corner underneath the blue clock, was the small blue door through which Ada had disappeared forty-two minutes ago now, insisting she'd be back before either Oscar or George could bat an eye.

As the hour grew later, the piazza grew busier. Patrons set up chairs outside the small cafés to sip their coffee in the cool evening air. Tables with card games or lottery wheels enticed people to spend money in the hope of striking it rich. (Oscar desperately wanted to try, and George had to keep pulling him back. Every gentleman knew that gambling by betting money on games of chance like cards or dice would lead to a life of vice and poverty.) But amid the crowd of people and the flurry of evening attractions, George kept his eyes fixed on only one doorway, watching for Ada's small, pale face to appear again.

Because George was staring so intently at the door, he hardly noticed when a tall figure wearing a black top hat and a long overcoat walked by the first time. The second time, though, the swish of the figure's overcoat caught George's eye. The third time the same figure walked by, something about him seemed eerily familiar. When the light from a lamppost illuminated the figure, George saw something that made him gasp.

A black hat.

A flash of bright red curls.

Roy.

"Oscar—it's the thief who broke into my house." George glanced back at Roy, who was still pacing in front of the small blue door. "He's probably waiting for Ada!"

"Are you sure, George?" Oscar squinted.

Fear crawled up George's spine. He hadn't seen the person's face, but it had to be him. "Of course I'm sure! Look, there he goes again."

"Well, we'll have to go after him, then!"

"Dressed like this?" George asked, gesturing at his ruffled gown. Oscar's white dress was already stained with dark streaks of charcoal.

"It's never stopped Ada. Stay here and watch the gondola, Ruthie." Oscar wheeled his arms. He lifted up his skirts and sprinted away.

"Not so fast!" George cried. "We have to blend in. Ladies don't run!"

"Ladies do all sorts of things!" Oscar called back. "It takes you so long to catch on, George."

But as he tried to daintily slip through the throngs of people gathered around dice games, George lost track of both Oscar and Roy. He walked quickly toward the last place he had seen the flash of red hair, fear climbing into his throat with every step. Could he stop the thief without Ada's help? He swallowed. He'd barely escaped the first time, at No. 8.

Finally, George spotted Roy's dark hat bobbing above the crowd. The closer he got, the harder his heart thudded in his chest. He felt split down the middle; half of him wanted to run away, half of him wanted to strike Roy in his sneering face.

Roy, too, seemed nervous. His face was hidden by the brim of his hat, and his collar was pulled up around his chin, but every few seconds, his eyes shot to the blue-and-gold clock to check the time. He hoisted over his shoulder the strap of a heavy leather case, which was closed by an enormous silver lock the size and shape of one of Darwin's tarantulas. It looked as though it held something important and valuable.

The Star.

It had to be.

Before George could find Oscar to formulate a plan, the clock struck the half hour in a long, crisp chime. Roy pulled the brim of his hat lower. He marched directly toward the door—right to the shop where Ada was buying the part for the bird.

That was all George needed.

With a cry, he catapulted forward into Roy's path, wrapping his fingers around the case. With a mighty tug, he yanked until the strap came free from Roy's shoulder—but the case tugged back. It was attached with a silver chain to a bracelet encircling Roy's rather delicate wrist.

"Oi! Let go," said Roy, in a lilting voice that was definitely not Roy's.

George looked up into the face of the tall person and saw immediately that he had been mistaken. This figure was not Roy. Not-Roy was also not a man. She was a tall, broad-shouldered woman with bundles of curly red hair. Her long coat had hidden her skirts and cinched waist.

"Sorry, ma'am." George sheepishly handed the case to her. Not-Roy said nothing, but her light blue eyes were full of disdain. She brushed herself off and marched ahead through the door, nodding curtly at two large men standing guard just inside. Oscar trailed close behind her.

George scratched at his hair underneath his kerchief, willing the blush in his cheeks to go away. But...

Why were there two men guarding the entrance to a shop? And why had the woman had that case strapped to her wrist with a chain?

Torn and confused, George felt as if his feet were rooted to the spot. Finally, after he heard the distant clip-clop of police horses' hooves across the square, he decided to find Oscar and return to Ruthie before they got into any more trouble. The last thing they needed was Il Naso on their trail again.

But Oscar had not given up the chase yet.

He had continued to follow Not-Roy, walking straight into the path of the two behemoth, muscly men on the other side of the shop door. Their huge arms, each the approximate width of George, were crossed over their chests, showing off forearms covered in tattoos. An enormous hand grabbed Oscar underneath the armpits and hoisted him in the air like a puppy dog.

Chapter Twenty-Six

"No!" George cried out, closing the distance between himself and the giant men before he could think twice. "He's—she's—just let him go!"

To George's surprise, the man holding Oscar lowered him to the ground. George watched Oscar windmill his limbs in the same language he used to talk to Ruthie, ending in a position with his arms crossed at the elbow to make an X.

"Don't worry, George. See their tattoos? They're buccaneers like my father! I spoke to them in semaphore to tell them we're friends. It's a traditional pirate greeting!" Oscar said reassuringly.

"Right," George said, his heart rate slowing. He cast

a glance up at the behemoth men. One of them had also crossed his arms in an X and, with a crooked smile, moved to let them aside. As they passed into a dark room, the other patted Oscar on the head fondly. Sweet, innocent Oscar, George thought—they'd probably taken pity on him.

"You need to be careful, Oscar. Don't talk to anyone else." George straightened Oscar's dress with a sharp tug. "Not every giant with a tattoo is a pirate. It's cute because you're young and charming, but if you don't grow up, you'll get yourself into trouble one of these days."

Oscar wasn't listening to George's lecture. He had wandered away into the dimly lit shop, eyes round with curiosity. George soon saw why.

This wasn't a shop at all. It was a casino. The air was thick with cigar smoke that drifted over the bent heads of the card players sitting at tables scattered throughout the room. Each table was dotted with piles of coins and jewels, fortunes to be won—or lost. It was a strange place for Not-Roy to enter, especially with a case locked more securely than a prison. But he didn't see a flash of Not-Roy's red hair anywhere—just gruff-looking men with unshaved faces. It occurred to George suddenly that there were no mechanical parts for sale that he could see. So why had Ada come here? And where was she?

All at once, he felt as though he could hardly breathe, and it wasn't because of the cigar smoke. Dread squeezed his chest like a vise. His father had gambled away the family's fortune in rooms just like this one, and it brought back memories that he'd tried very hard to forget. His head spun.

"Let's find Ada quickly," George whispered to Oscar.

Oscar's big brown eyes searched the room. "I don't see her anywhere."

In a nearby corner, a loud cheer erupted, followed by a chorus of fists slamming the table, which was just two apple barrels turned upside down. A group of people crowded around two seated card players. Money and jewelry were piled high between them in the center of the table. One of the men showed a pair of queens, then reached out to sweep the glittering pile into his lap.

"Don' feel sorry f' me," the other man said with a glance at his former possessions. George was surprised to hear him speak English. "My losing streak en's today. The Star of Victory is in Venice, and tonight it will be mine."

George inhaled sharply, taking a step toward the table.

The man's opponent scoffed. "The Star of Victory? I have never heard of this. What is it?" His Italian accent was thick, but George detected scorn in his voice.

"It's—it's—!" The first man hiccupped, then slammed his fist down on the table. His eyes, glassy with drink, began to search the crowd over the heads of his companions. "Harold! Harold, where's you at? Tell 'em!"

"Did you hear that?" George whispered to Oscar, not sure whether he was overjoyed or afraid or both. "Ada was right! Roy is somewhere close, and he has the Star. Or—" He stopped. "Someone called Harold. Maybe that's part of Roy's disguise. I have to talk to that man."

"Lord *Devonshire*! Oscar!" a voice behind them hissed. George turned to see Ada, her hair tucked into a cap. "I told you not to follow me in here. You're putting us all in danger."

Something behind George's shoulder caught her eye, and a look of fear washed over her face. George turned to follow her gaze, but she dropped to the floor and tugged Oscar and George down with her by the fronts of their dresses. With George and Oscar in tow, she crawled through the legs of the crowd until they were all stuffed knees to chin underneath a table. "We have to leave. *Now*."

"But, Ada—"

"Shhh." Ada reached up and grabbed a pitcher of sloshing golden liquid from the table above them.

"What are you doing?"

His words were lost in a shower of liquid as Ada dumped the pitcher over his head. She did the same to her own head, then Oscar's. "He has our scents," she whispered. "Follow me."

Just as they crawled out from underneath the table, still dripping, cries and shouted oaths filled the room in a sudden, swelling roar. The legs around them began to scatter. Chairs overturned with violent clatters. Even in the chaos, George's ears picked out a familiar voice.

"I knew I would find you here sooner or later, little one. Criminals always seek out other criminals." Il Naso swept his hands to one side of the room, motioning to a skinny, gap-toothed man who was frantically piling silver coins into his pockets. "Didn't I tell you this the last time we met?"

Il Naso was less than ten paces away—and so, George saw, was the man who had spoken of the Star of Victory. He'd dropped to the floor just as they had. Now he was crawling toward them through a tangle of chair legs, his red-rimmed eyes locked onto Ada.

His eyes were the last thing George saw before the room was thrown into darkness.

Il Naso let out a strangled cry of frustration. George felt a tug on his sleeve as Ada dragged him across the cramped space. He felt Oscar jostling at his side. "Come on," she whispered.

"But that man mentioned the Star. We have to go back for him," George said, desperately trying to dig his heels into the sticky ground.

Ada tugged on him harder. "We can find him later, George. Il Naso could relight the gas lamps any second."

Groping in the inky blackness, George's hands found a set of thick velvet drapes, which Ada pulled aside to reveal a rough wooden wall. When the wall gave way, George realized it was not a wall, but a door. They tumbled into the dim light of an alleyway. George caught a glimpse of a very angry Il Naso behind him before the door slammed shut again.

"There's a shortcut here," Ada said, guiding them through a shaded alleyway that led them back to the other side of the piazza, not far from where they'd left Ruthie.

As soon as they watched Il Naso burst into the square, mount his police horse, and gallop away in the other direction, George's breathing slowed. But his pulse still drummed in his ears. Something was not right. It wiggled back and forth in his gut, waving like a hand trying to get his attention.

"Miss Byron," he said slowly. "Why did Il Naso say you'd met before?"

A trace of fear flared in Ada's eyes like a spark, but the expression quickly vanished in favor of the face she always wore: slightly exasperated, mildly amused, brilliant. Maybe George had imagined the fear.

"Why did you barge into the middle of my plan, even though I specifically asked you not to?" she said, taking off toward Ruthie and their empty gondola, as if she were trying to run away from his question. George had no choice but to follow. Eyes darting between them, Oscar followed at a distance.

"Why are you changing the subject?"

"You said you trusted me, George," she said, whirling on him.

"I do. I was trying to help. I *did* help. Tonight I heard a man say he'd been promised the Star of Victory. He said someone named Harold knew about it."

"I told you, I have it all under control. Don't you remember we discussed the plan already?"

"I don't know anything about the plan!" George's voice echoed too loudly under the portico. He couldn't help but release the frustration gathering in his throat. "Is there something I should know about Il Naso and your father? Sometimes I feel as if I don't know anything about you at all."

"What more do you need to know?"

A memory surfaced in his mind. What had she said about her father, back in her room in Dorset Square? That her father was gone. George knew that *gone* was a polite way of saying *dead*, but it occurred to him that he'd never thought to ask her. "Is your father...dead?"

Ada wheeled again, curls bouncing around her angry face. "My father is not dead," she snapped.

George stepped back instinctively. "Then why are you so upset?"

"I—I'm not—" Her face grew a mottled red and her expression twisted, like she was waging a battle inside her head. "If you must know, my mother refuses to let me see him because she says he's not a good influence. She's afraid I'll pick up his bad habits. Unless something changes, we'll remain apart." Ada puffed up her cheeks, then exhaled her anger in a short burst of air. "Of all people, I should think you would understand, because your family—"

George's breath caught in his chest. He swallowed once, twice, three times, then smoothed down his hair. "Because my family *what*?"

"Nothing. Forget it."

But it was too late for George to forget, or to tame the beast that was now roaring in his chest. Which was why he said, "You're just jealous."

Ada scoffed. "Of what, exactly?"

"Of the Star of Victory!" he blurted out. "Of Frobisher! That I have a family legacy I'm proud of and you don't."

With that, Ada turned away from him, walking resolutely toward the gondola, where Ruthie and Oscar were already waiting. Though they both had cast their eyes down at the sloshing canal below, George knew they'd listened to every word.

George followed reluctantly, plunking down into the gondola with a thud and a splash. Behind him, Oscar had taken up the oar. Instinctively, George looked for Ruthie's dark, glowing eyes staring back at him, but she had already curled up in Ada's lap and didn't glance at him. Not even once.

Chapter Twenty-Seven

To say that George now trusted Ada more than he trusted anyone else in the whole world would be true. But it would also not be saying much. With the exception of his grandfather, George had never trusted anyone or anything before. Each dawn, he was pleasantly surprised when the sun did its job. Every day that Frobisher did not leave was a marvel. After all, everyone in George's life left eventually because of his curse. Sooner or later, George expected to find himself alone.

So when he awoke the next morning to find Ada's makeshift bed rumpled and empty, he was more upset at himself than at her.

After they'd returned from the disastrous trip to the

Piazza San Marco, Oscar had found them a nest of unused gondolas to sleep in for the night. Now, in the orange-gray light of the rising sun, he and Ruthie were still snoozing peacefully, rocking gently back and forth with the movement of the canal below.

But Ada was gone.

As were her notebook, her scarf, and even her goggles. George ran his fingers over his hair. He'd told her he trusted her. If nothing else, he tried to be a man of his word. She was probably just getting some breakfast.

Or, more likely, she wanted to be away from him.

George's moping quietly turned into worry. He tapped his fingers against his knee, which was bouncing up and down faster and faster with each passing second. Ruthie stirred. What if Ada had not left willingly? What if the Organization had stolen her in the middle of the night? What if she had gone out as part of her secret mission and finally been arrested by Il Naso?

A much more likely possibility floated into his head: what if he'd driven her away with his childishness?

The worry exploded into panic.

"Wake up! We have to find Ada!" George yelled, shaking Oscar and Ruthie's gondola to rouse them.

Oscar awoke instantly, though his smile was less bright than usual. "Good morning, George." He leaned over and peered into Ada's gondola. His forehead crinkled with concern. "Yes. That is worrisome."

Worrisome. George nearly swallowed his tongue. The only time he'd ever seen Oscar worried was when Ruthie ate his pestle, and he had been convinced then that she was going to die. If *Oscar* was concerned... "I knew it! She's been kidnapped."

"Kidnapped?" Oscar laughed. "Ada hasn't been kidnapped. She never gets kidnapped. She's escaped kidnapping..." He looked to the sky while counting on his fingers. "Twenty-seven times now. No, I'm worried because Ruthie was hanging on to her last night in the gondola. She only does that when she knows someone's sad. That's why she's been clinging to you this whole time. What do you think could have made Ada sad? She's hardly ever sad."

"Oh. Well." Out of the corner of his eye, George felt Ruthie's sleepy gaze on him. How could Ruthie detect that Ada was sad, when he hadn't? "She didn't seem very sad to me. And being sad is not an emergency. We can worry about her emotional state once we establish her physical state. If that red-haired oaf laid a hand on her, I'll..."

George didn't know exactly what he'd do. Something devastating, that was for sure.

After they put on new disguises (George wore the baker's smock, but Oscar preferred wearing Ada's skirts for comfort and the roomy pockets), they gathered their things and began to walk the streets in search of Ada. Throbbing peals of church bells filled the air. They weaved through a procession of priests in white robes and tall hats who were heading into a church. It must be Sunday, George realized. He'd lost all track of the calendar on their adventure.

"Let's split up. You go right; I'll go left," George told Oscar.

They parted ways, and George scoured the streets alone. With each turn, his nerves crumbled like a cookie. He even tried to sniff for Ada, like Il Naso, but all *that* led him to was a pile of goat dung.

After what seemed like hours, he ended up at the cathedral where they'd first arrived. It was practically the only place he hadn't looked. When he climbed to the roof, he found Ada kneeling next to the spread-out, semi-shattered wing of the mechanical bird, which now looked as if it had been stitched together by thick golden thread. Ada's sketchbook was open on the ground, her head bent over it as her pen made quick, sharp marks on the paper.

"There you are! I thought you'd been kidnapped!" George said. His voice came out gruff and angry, even though he was light-headed with relief.

She was safe.

He hadn't driven her away or caused her to be caught.

His curse hadn't claimed her (yet).

It wasn't his fault at all.

"Are you all right?" he asked.

She nodded without meeting his eye. "I said I wanted to work on the bird yesterday. I thought you'd heard me." She sat back, knees folded under her, and finally met George's eyes. "I took my notebook, my bag, my hat. Tell me, do kidnapping victims usually have time to pack?"

"That's—I didn't—" Was everything so obvious to her? So easy? The light-headed feeling vanished like a puff of smoke, replaced by what felt like a swarm of angry wasps. "I looked in every filthy corner of this city for you!"

"I can take care of myself." She turned away from him to resume scratching in her sketchbook.

His relief cascaded into a flood of anger. "*This* is what you've been doing?"

"It's part of the plan," Ada said, angling her body away from George.

"You should have just left a note," George countered. "It's the least you could do." He mimicked writing a note. *"Gone out. Back soon.* Four words."

Ada put down her pen and fixed her piercing gaze on him. "You're right," she said, her words dripping with scorn. "I'm so sorry. How thoughtless of me. Of course I should have followed the rules of decorum on the slight chance that my friends would wake up and not know where I was. Really, I *do* apologize."

"I was trying to protect you," George said through gritted teeth.

"Well, as you can see, I am perfectly safe and well. Run back to Oscar and I'll be there later," Ada said.

Any warmth he had felt for her was now rapidly turning cold. It swirled and condensed in his chest and climbed into his throat: "No."

Ada turned toward him again. For a moment, when her eyes caught the light of the sun, George could have sworn he saw tears—but a cloud passed overhead, darkening the sky, and the illusion was gone.

"Tell me what the plan is," he said.

"For the thousandth time, we talked about this yesterday. Trust me."

"No," George said. "From now on, you have to tell me everything."

"I do not," Ada said.

"Yes, you do," George said.

Ada stood up and brushed off her skirts. "We wouldn't even be here if it weren't for me. I don't owe you anything."

George crossed his arms stubbornly. "What's taking so long? Why haven't you mentioned Frobisher once during the whole time we've been here? Why are you ignoring what I overheard in San Marco? I told you, I saw Roy."

"Who turned out to be a perfectly normal woman with red hair. Everything can be explained away. Always."

Ada's voice grew low, and oddly pathetic. Something was different. Wrong, even. But how was he supposed to know what was transpiring in her incomprehensible mind?

Doubt coursed through him, and he steeled himself to keep his voice from quavering. "But her case. It looked... important. And I know for sure that a man in San Marco mentioned the Star of Victory. I heard it with my own ears."

"You found her! Good job, George," Oscar's cheerful voice called out from over the edge of the cathedral roof.

Ada jammed her ridiculous goggles into place over her eyes, shutting George out completely.

"Apparently she didn't need to be found," George said bitterly.

"I knew she wasn't lost," Oscar said. "Ada never gets lost. At least not directionally."

"See? Oscar trusts me. He knows I can follow a map. Unlike some people."

George's mouth twitched. Her words were sharp, barbed with hurt. "Why doesn't your *real* friend help you with your plan, then? Considering your mother approves of him and not me," George said sulkily, and turned to leave.

"George, wait. If you'll stop being so stubborn, we can work this out. Please, just be patient," Ada called after him, but he kept climbing down the ladder, not stopping even when her head appeared over him, shouting down from the roof. He climbed lower, lower, and lower still, until the churning of the canal below had drowned out her voice completely.

Chapter Twenty-Eight

But, as usual, George had nowhere to go. So he sat on the edge of the canal to stew in his frustration. He missed Frobisher. He missed the molding smell of No. 8. He missed having a purpose, even if it was to keep Mrs. Daly from chewing another hole in the floorboards. He desperately missed Revenues and Expenses.

Closing his eyes, he took account of every clue that had yet to be explained in the course of their adventure. The red hair at the castle. The woman with the locked case outside the casino last night. The man waiting to buy the Star from Harold *inside* the casino. Even the ornate metal butterfly from the shop in Geneva fluttered through his thoughts again, batting its wings as if it were trying to relay a secret message.

Did all of these coincidences really amount to nothing, as Ada had said? Surely it all meant *something*.

He slid the yellowing map out of his chest pocket and spread it over his lap. With his fingertip, he traced the edges of the drawn butterfly wing, which curved over the western edge of South America. It looked like the butterfly he'd seen in the shop. But perhaps any depiction of a butterfly would look the same to him. He wasn't an entomologist or a lepidopterist, or even a naturalist, so what did he know about butterflies?

Just as George decided that the butterfly was most certainly a coincidence that should be added to his list, he saw something that did not seem like a coincidence at all.

A few yards from where his feet were dangling over the edge of the canal, an unusual instrument emerged from the water, swiveling like the antenna of some underwater creature. With each turn, it glinted and flashed in the sun. George would have recognized that slim silver tube with its brass couplings and round lens anywhere.

It looked exactly like Frobisher's silver-and-brass periscope.

George sprang to his feet, alive with the sudden thought that the Organization had somehow trapped poor Frobisher under the murky canal water. Dodging several women with parasols, he ran to where the periscope had pierced the surface. At a closer distance, he saw that instead of extending in a straight line, the stalk bent over at the very end. When George dropped to his hands and knees to look even closer, ripples disturbed the flat surface of the water. The periscope began to speed away, shrinking down underwater until it was out of sight.

He inhaled sharply. Frobisher's periscope could not do *that*.

"Stop!" George cried. Then he caught a glimpse of a black shadow beneath the water shaped like an overturned gondola with a few small protrusions that looked like spikes jutting out of its side. On its back was a large fin, flapping slowly back and forth to propel it away.

It was an enormous mechanical fish.

He began to chase it, but the sidewalk abruptly ended where the narrow canal intersected with a much wider one. If he didn't find a boat, he'd never be able to keep up with the fish.

Luckily, a small gondola was moored on the other side of the canal. If George had been very athletic (he was not), he would have been able to take a flying leap and land in it. Instead, with no time to waste, he grabbed the loose end of a clothesline that dangled from a window above him. He pulled hard, ripping the clothesline from its pulleys and dropping bleached undergarments all over the cobblestone street. Twirling the clothesline overhead like a lasso, he aimed the rope at the prow of the gondola. It missed and splashed into the water.

"Drat!" George shouted. He watched hopelessly as the black shadow disappeared into the wide canal, leaving nothing but a few ripples to show it had ever been there at all.

Ada would know what to do, George thought, even if he was still angry at her. Yes, he had to run back to the cathedral and tell her what he'd seen. Who else could have a mechanical fish other than the Organization? The spikes he'd seen were most likely miniature cannons or an equally devious weapon. Before he could get very far, a rough, hairy hand grabbed his finger.

"Unhand me—*Ruthie*," George breathed, turning to

spot the ape. She released him, grabbing on to his pant leg instead. Behind her, Oscar was only a few paces away. His cheeks were rosy from running.

"George, we...we...need...your help," Oscar panted. Ruthie grunted and mimed pulling out her hair, as if she was frustrated.

"Oscar, we don't have time for whatever sadness- or mineral-related emergency you're dealing with," George said, lowering his voice on the last words. He took off again in the direction of the cathedral with Oscar and Ruthie trailing behind. "The Organization was here. Right *here*. I think I know where they're keeping Frobisher! Yes, it must be an underwater prison. Probably brimming with weapons. We have to tell Ada."

"But this *is* about Ada," Oscar insisted. "I took another piece of paper from her notebook to write a letter for my father, and I think I ripped out a drawing of the Star by mistake." Oscar said this between breaths as he jogged to keep up with George. "Maybe if you describe it, I can draw her a new one? Then she won't be so upset that I ruined one of her sketches. You know how much she cares about her inventions and her notebooks. It's the only thing she gets fussy about, and she's already sad because you argued. Please, George?"

Oscar pressed the scrap of paper into George's hand so that he had no choice but to take it. "This isn't important, Oscar, I—"

George stopped so suddenly that Oscar and Ruthie rammed into him from behind. The parchment, which looked to be the torn-off top half of a single page of note-book paper, fit neatly in his palm. He saw what Oscar was talking about: two dark, blunt prongs that looked to be part of a larger star. Oscar was wrong—it wasn't *his* Star—but it wasn't the drawing that had caught George's eye.

It was the fragment of the end of a letter written above the Star in Ada's windswept, wide-spaced handwriting.

> on Lord Byron, the esteemed poet
> and adventurer, last seen in Venice.
> In return for his location, I can
> offer the Star of Victory, a rare
> object never before available for
> purchase.
>
> Criminally yours,
> C. Harold

At first, the enormity of what he had read took his breath away. His chest squeezed so tight that he could hardly breathe. He stared into the ink on the parchment until it danced and swirled in front of his eyes, losing all meaning.

All of a sudden, his trance broke. He reversed direction. Up, down, up, down, he paced from one dock to the next as Oscar and Ruthie watched. He aimed a swift kick at a lamppost. The brass pole tolled like a bell.

The empty box from Chillon Castle.

The thief who'd been promised the Star by someone named Harold.

Ada was Harold.

George blinked several times to keep angry tears from falling. How could he have been so foolish?

"Are you all right, George?" Oscar said softly.

Ada had played him for a fool from the first moment she had laid eyes on his map. Ada had betrayed George in the worst way he could imagine.

Roy hadn't stolen the Star of Victory. Ada had.

Chapter Twenty-Nine

The note was like a burning coal in George's pocket.

Ada was a liar.

Ada was a thief.

Ada was an enemy.

"George!" Oscar cried out, but George ignored him.

The morning air was cool and damp, but he had to unbutton his collar as he climbed back up the ladder to the cupola. Oscar and Ruthie chased after him, though he couldn't hear their pleas and whines through the anger thrumming in his ears.

When he reached the roof, he threw the letter at Ada's feet. Ada snatched up the note, and her eyes grew wide.

"Are you Harold? Did you take the Star?" he demanded.

Ada pressed her lips together. "Don't jump to conclusions."

He refused to let her ignore his question. Not this time. "Tell me. Are. You. Harold?"

More than anything else in the world, he realized, he wanted her to say no. She only continued to stare at him, silent and steadfast.

Eventually, she said, "Yes."

He blinked. "Where is it? Where's the Star?" he asked through gritted teeth.

"George, please let me explain."

"You wouldn't even have known about the Star if not for me," he exploded.

"You would have still been in your crumbling mansion, living your small life, if it weren't for me. I bought that map from you because you were never going to follow it by yourself."

"George—Ada—please don't fight," Oscar said.

"I should have listened to Il Naso and never trusted you," George fumed. "He said you weren't my friend."

"And how would you know? You didn't *have* any friends before us."

"I—I have Frobisher!" George sputtered.

"Oh, really? I'm surprised you'd consider someone who's not *nobility* to be worthy of your friendship. It probably helps that he never talks back."

"Oh, what do you care about Frobisher?" George spat. "You'd rather he *die* so you can have the Star. You're putting his life in danger!"

Ada stared at him, unspoken words swirling in her eyes. "You know I would never let anything happen to Frobisher," she said quietly.

George opened his mouth to unleash a string of nasty words, but something Ada had said earlier surfaced violently in his mind. *Tell me, do kidnapping victims usually have time to pack?* Frobisher had taken his coat, his scarf, and every single one of his hats.

Suddenly, it felt as if a sack of flour had walloped George in the chest.

"Frobisher hasn't been kidnapped, has he?" he asked weakly.

Ada's shoulders sank. "He's been at my house the whole time."

George closed his eyes. Frobisher was safe. His heart

seemed to mend before cracking all over again. Because Frobisher, too, had lied to George. He'd faked his disappearance, then left his neckerchief with a pretend ransom note as part of the hoax. Why? Why had he tricked George so cruelly? Had he wanted George out of his life that badly?

"It was just a ruse to get you to leave, George. Frobisher wanted you to be happy. He wanted you to go on an adventure," Ada said gently.

"But why *you*, Ada? Why did you lie?"

Unmistakable tears shone in her eyes. She stood up straight and inhaled deeply, bracing herself to speak. "I wanted to trade the Star for information to find my father," she said. "He last wrote from Venice, before he stopped writing altogether. I had to save him from whatever trouble had kept him away for so long. But he—" A small sob escaped her throat, but she held back tears. "He's dead. He died four years ago. That hideous policeman told me this morning, and I finally believe it."

George's hand flicked as if to reach out and grab hers—but he didn't. Instead, he snapped, "I don't understand."

"I took a grain of truth and invented something."

"You made up the Organization?" George asked. "None of it was real?"

Ada nodded. "For a while my mother told me stories about a nameless, faceless enemy to explain my father's absence—and why he couldn't come back. She told me she asked him to stay away to keep me safe. I thought the Organization was real for years. I only started to question it—to realize how many improbable things I had made myself believe—after you started believing them, too." She wiped away a tear. "But I still thought that maybe, with the Star, I could find him, save him, and bring him home. I know now that he could have come home. He just didn't care enough about me to try."

The rage in George's chest cooled to a simmer. He remembered what Ada had confessed last night: that her mother refused to let Ada see her father because he was too dangerous. But that didn't change the fact that Ada had lied. "If the Organization doesn't exist, then why did the red-headed man steal my grandfather's map in the first place?"

"You had Frobisher trying to sell your grandfather's things all over town. He probably thought it was worth something," Ada said.

"The flying machine that looked like yours?"

"That was probably a regular bird. Our minds were filling in the rest."

"Like Bonivard," George said. "And Frobisher wrote the kidnapping note?"

She nodded. "I needed to get to Venice. That's where my father last wrote from. I thought we could find the Star, barter it for his release, or sell it to pay off whatever debts he owed. Then steal it back for you, of course."

"The red hair on the box?"

"Ruthie's."

"And the mechanical fish I saw in the canal?"

"What mechanical fish?" Ada stepped toward him, and without thinking, he stepped back, feeling hopelessly foolish.

"Never mind. You let me believe everything," he said. *Even that I was brave*, he thought bitterly. His cheeks burned with anger and embarrassment. "The Star is mine. Give it back."

Oscar strode calmly in front of Ada. "Pirates share everything with each other," he said with a smile, as if that would fix everything. "Whenever my father's ship gets something, they have to split it equally among the crew. We're shipmates, aren't we? So we should share the map and the Star."

Pressure rushed across George's temples, then bloomed into a throbbing headache. "How dare you suggest I share anything with her! We're not pirates, Oscar. And neither is your father. He's not a famous pirate captain. He's a worthless vagabond who abandoned his infant son to die."

"George!" Ada gasped.

Oscar's chin trembled. Huge, shining tears spilled over onto his cheeks. But George felt as though he were a spool of yarn unraveling. He couldn't stop.

"Don't take this out on Oscar. It's my fault," Ada said. "We wouldn't be here if I had just accepted that my father abandoned me."

"Can you blame him?" he snapped.

George didn't have time to see the devastated look that crossed her face; Ruthie launched herself at him, ripping the map from his hand. She stuffed the parchment right into her mouth.

"Keep your stupid monkey away from my map!" George shouted. He snatched the map out from between her teeth, but not before Ruthie tore a chunk off its edge. "This isn't how it's supposed to go! This is my legacy!"

Ada wiped away her tears with both hands. She reached into her pocket, pulled out a white cloth wrapped around a lumpy object a little larger than her fist, and threw it at George's feet. "Take it."

Carefully, George picked up the object and lifted the edge of the cloth. Inside was a spray of silver rods with hints of iridescent rainbows on its surface. The shiny rock was like nothing George had ever seen before. It was shaped like a flower made of knives, but the edges were not sharp.

"What is this? Another trick? One of Oscar's minerals?"

"It's what you wanted, Lord Devonshire," she said. "The Star of Victory. Your legacy. That's what was in the box I found at the castle."

He stared at the strange silver thing. It was nothing like what his grandfather had described. "But the Star of Victory is a priceless jewel. This is a piece of worthless, broken—"

"Junk."

"It can't be junk," George whispered under his breath. Then he added in a soft, hopeful voice, "Maybe it's another clue."

"It's junk. I couldn't even give it away to the thieves

in San Marco," she said. "I wasn't only being selfish. I was trying to protect you, too. I knew how heartbroken you would be when you saw it. I didn't want to tell you until I could figure out a way to fix how you'd feel. I thought going back home to Frobisher would help. Or going..."

"Going where?" George said grimly.

"Going home with us," she finished. "You had us."

Had. Past tense. George squeezed the Star in his fist. "Just—just—get away from me."

Ruthie climbed onto Ada's back, nestling her face into Ada's hair. Ada took Oscar's hand in her own and, with a gentle tug, led him away from George. "With pleasure, Lord Devonshire."

Chapter Thirty

Dear Frobisher,
You are hereby dismissed.

Snap. The tip of the pencil broke. George let out a frustrated grunt and chucked it into the canal. It *ping*ed off a gondola.

Frobisher had probably never wanted to go back to No. 8 anyway, he thought miserably, and began to walk. He walked past churches and shops and houses that blurred into the background. He walked around and around until the soles of his feet ached and throbbed, until he didn't know where he was.

But no matter how far he walked, he couldn't escape his thoughts.

Ada had lied to him so many times during the past few days that he wondered if she was even capable of telling the truth. First she had tricked him into selling his map by spinning a tale about the Organization, which was a figment of her imagination. Then she and Frobisher had faked his kidnapping so that George would join her in fulfilling his family obligation to find the Star of Victory, which turned out to be worthless. Worst of all, she had covered up her true purpose for wanting the Star, which was . . .

To help her father—who, she'd learned only today, was dead.

George felt a tug of shame but pushed it away. It didn't change the fact that she had lied to him. He began to tally up the lies in his head, calculating how many pounds he was owed in damages from her falsehoods.

Damages Caused by Ada	*Amount Owed to George*
Frobisher's lost wages and productivity during fake kidnapping	*+ £2*

Emotional pain and suffering from believing Frobisher was kidnapped	+ £1
Possession of Star of Victory with intent to sell	+ £0 (item is worthless)
Possession of the map to the Star of Victory obtained under false pretenses (but later returned without question)	- £100
Total:	97 pounds owed to Ada Byron

To his dismay, any way George tried to calculate the damages he had suffered from Ada, he still found himself in debt to her. Remarkably, Ada had not yet asked him to repay the money she'd given him in the menagerie when she'd originally purchased the map. His few bruises and scrapes would heal. All of his suffering was emotional. No amount of money would fix that kind of damage.

It certainly wouldn't fix Ada's.

Shame tugged at him again, harder this time. A sincere apology might not completely offset his emotions, but it would be a good place to start. And then, maybe, just maybe—well, it wouldn't cost him anything to apologize for his own harsh words. The terrible insults he'd hurled at them crashed upon him like a wave. He recalculated and determined that he owed Oscar, Ada, and Ruthie several apologies.

George stopped walking, realizing that his feet had led him to Darwin's pink house. It was some kind of sign. It had to be.

Was Ada upstairs? Oscar? Ruthie?

George resisted the urge to run up the steps. Instead, he adjusted his jacket and politely knocked on the door. If they were there, he could apologize and start to mend the awful tear between them.

But they were not there. However, the cheerful naturalist student Darwin admitted him without question, though he was clearly not as interested in the 3rd Lord of Devonshire as he had been in Ruthie.

"Would you like some tea?" Darwin asked.

George nodded wearily, then sat to rest his throbbing feet. "With some milk if you have it, please."

While Darwin counted out the teacups, he looked at the empty chairs around the table as if suddenly realizing that George had come alone. "Will your friends be along soon?"

"I'm not sure," George said truthfully.

Darwin sipped his tea. "I was hoping for young Oscar's assistance with a project. I was even going to pay him a small sum he could spend on paints or some such thing. He's brilliant."

"He is," George agreed, and felt a new wave of regret wash over him.

"Since Oscar isn't here, might you be willing to assist me?"

"Oh." George put down his tea. "Yes, I suppose I could."

Darwin picked up a large box with holes drilled into the top. Inside, the scrabbling, scratching sound of many tiny claws made George rethink his decision.

"Are you familiar with *Rattus norvegicus*?" Darwin asked. He raised the lid of the box to reveal dozens of enormous black and brown rats, who lifted their pointy faces to the light. Their little pink ears reminded George of all the times he'd woken up in his bed at No. 8 to find Mrs. Daly nibbling on his bedpost.

"Yes, I am very familiar with one rat in particular."

Darwin reached in to grasp a squirming rat by the belly. "Excellent. You'll make a fine assistant. Hold them this way, please, and I'll measure."

George held the rat firmly with two hands while Darwin measured and recorded the length of every feature of the rat's body: whiskers, nose, teeth, claws, toes, ears, and so on.

"If you don't mind me asking, why exactly are we doing this?"

Darwin marked down the length of the rat's tail. "To provide research for a theory I have about animals, and plants—all living things, actually. If I'm right, it explains everything about why the world is the way it is and why we are the way we are."

"Everything about the world? That's ambitious." Ada would approve, George thought. She probably already had.

"My theory is that little by little, a species can change over time. Organisms can become stronger and better adapted to their environments if their parents pass along certain traits to them. For example, this rat's teeth are approximately one percent longer than the others'. If that trait helps him survive longer, then he'll have more children. His children will have longer teeth, and so will his children's children. Eventually, *Rattus norvegicus* will become another species entirely."

"Another species?" George asked, looking down at the wriggling rat in his hands. He couldn't imagine how it would become anything else.

"Well, the change would take place over a very, very long time. As I said, it's just a theory."

"But what if the rat parent has a bad trait?" George asked. "What if he eats too much cheese and racks up a huge bill at the cheese shop or accidentally falls out of a window while he's roller-skating? Do those traits get passed on, too?"

Darwin wrinkled his large forehead as he considered George's question. "I don't think there are any 'bad' traits or 'good' ones. Just ones that help you survive or ones that don't. Mother Nature isn't a judge of character."

George pressed. "But what if the rat children don't want to be like their rat parents? What if they want to be good, honest rats who don't drive their friends away?"

"Well..."

"And what if the rat is cursed with bad luck? Is it fair that he passes the curse on to his children? Or should he never have children and live alone forever so that his terrible curse dies with him?" George caught his breath. He hadn't meant for the whirlwind of his thoughts to come out.

Darwin put down his ruler. "The one difference between humans and all other animals is that humans are infinitely more intelligent. If we were speaking of a rat, I would say that his children had no choice but to inherit his traits—the advantageous and the disadvantageous alike. But if we are speaking of a *Homo sapiens*, the wisest and most intuitive of all species, then I see no reason why his children could not forge their own path and decide for themselves what kind of life they wanted to lead—if they only tried." Darwin picked up his ruler again and smiled knowingly at George. "Does that answer your question?"

George nodded and stroked the rat's trembling head before placing it in the box and picking up another. Ada hadn't lied to George to be cruel to him, he realized. Mostly she had been lying to herself. With her mother's help, she had crafted a story about her father and the Organization with her imagination, just the way she created birds out of scrap metal and bolts. Just as he and his grandfather had made up stories by the fire. Oscar, too, had invented a story about his pirate father coming back for him.

With a wriggling rat in one hand, George felt as if he'd

ripped the mask off the ugliness of his life with the other. The truth that he'd been trying to deny slowly took shape in his mind. He couldn't ignore it any longer. He was lying to himself, too.

The Star of Victory wasn't real. What was hidden in Chillon Castle was just an odd coincidence, or another twisted, meaningless puzzle.

It was just a fairy tale.

George let out a deep breath. Maybe he had always known that his family's legacy was a fantasy, but every time he got close to the truth, it was too painful to admit.

Perhaps George was more like Ada than he'd thought. He had been blaming bad luck for driving everyone out of his life. But just as there was no Organization, there was no such thing as bad luck. It was an invention of his own making.

The 3rd Lord of Devonshire was alone because he'd chosen to be.

After the rat measuring was done and Darwin had left to fetch dinner, the small seed of George's wish to see Ada and Oscar again grew until his chest ached with it. The insults he'd hurled at them echoed over and over in his mind, and the images of their faces swirled in his imagination—so much so that when Ada appeared in Darwin's doorway, George thought she was a mirage.

Dark shadows curved under her eyes. Her curls were frizzy and unkempt, as though she had been tugging on them in frustration.

"Oscar and Ruthie have been kidnapped," she blurted out.

Instantly, the mirage was ruined. Maybe, unlike Darwin's rats, she would never, ever, ever change. "You think I'm foolish enough to fall for *that*? Come back when you're ready to stop pretending."

"George, I know how it sounds, but we don't have time for that. You need to put all that aside, because your friends need you," Ada said.

"You're not my friend. Friends don't keep lying. Friends don't betray each other." George swallowed.

Ada winced. It gave George a strange, mixed-up feeling of pleasure and regret.

"I can prove it. Look!" she insisted. In her outstretched hands, she held a limp green bundle with ragged edges.

"That's Ruthie's banana leaf," he said, trying to ignore Ada's pleading gaze.

She forced the folded banana leaf into his hands. "Yes,

obviously, it's Ruthie's banana leaf. Look what's written on it. It's a clue. Ruthie would never leave it behind and Oscar would never leave Ruthie behind. I told you, they've been kidnapped! We have to figure out who's behind this and go after them. I might have been inventing the Organization, but we're still in danger. I need your help."

"The way you needed my help before when Frobisher was kidnapped? You're not even putting effort into deceiving me anymore. Come up with some new tricks. Please leave, Ada."

"But look at the leaf. Someone wrote *Levrnaka* on it. It must be a place or a town. If you don't want to help me, then fine. Let me look at your map and I'll—"

"I said leave!" George shouted.

Her lips sealed shut in a familiar thin white-and-pink line before she spoke again. "George, please listen."

"I'm done playing games. No more clues. No more crumbs to follow," George said, stuffing the leaf into his pocket.

"Coward," Ada jeered.

"Liar," he spat back. "Say hello to Oscar and Ruthie for me," he added, but she had already disappeared down the stairs.

Chapter Thirty-One

George grasped the small white ticket in his hand: a one-way passage to London. Darwin had insisted on paying George for his rat-measuring assistance yesterday. The money had been enough to pay for the ticket with a few coins to spare. Now all George needed to do was get on the boat that would carry him home, where he would be rid of Ada Byron forever.

But first, he had to speak with the captain to make sure that the boat was seaworthy. Then he had no choice but to run to the market to barter for a hat to protect himself from the harsh afternoon sun. Then he needed to find a privy to, erm, relieve himself. After that, when he had walked halfway up the boarding plank, he was forced to return to the dock to search for a button that had fallen off his coat.

Finally, just as the whistle was screaming its last call and his foot was once again about to step onto the boarding plank, something caught his eye. Or rather, something caught his nose.

A whiff of triumph, mixed with linen bandages and potted plant soil.

A heavy hand came down on George's shoulder. He looked behind him and saw a bristly black mustache. Just above the mustache, a thick white bandage obscured a protruding nose. George gulped. Il Naso had found him. He should have boarded the boat when he had the chance.

But to his utter bewilderment, Il Naso clapped George on the shoulders, tipped his head back, and laughed.

"Little rabbit! Leaving Venice so soon? Or are you going on vacation like me?" He glanced at the ticket in George's hand. "*Uffa!* London is so boring. Go to Spain! That is where I spend my summers. It is much nicer there."

Was this a trap?

"You're not going to arrest me?" George asked carefully.

"Arrest you? No! In fact, I should congratulate you for ridding yourself of that infernal little Byron."

George's smile faltered. He was furious with Ada, but he didn't care for the way Il Naso spoke of her.

"Any damage you caused," Il Naso continued, pointing to his bandaged nose, "was under her direction, no doubt."

George mumbled, "Mhm." The boat whistle screeched behind him. "I really must be going," he said, turning around.

But Il Naso grabbed him and turned him back again. "I had her in my clutches this morning, you know. Finally, she could not slip away."

His clutches? George's heart squeezed. He did not like Il Naso's smug grin. Was Ada all right? Her affairs were no longer his concern, but ... He cleared his throat. "Have you imprisoned her?"

Il Naso straightened up. "No. I am fair, little rabbit. I simply banished her. She must leave and never again return to Venice. This is enough. Now I can go on my vacation in peace. I think you have learned your lesson and will obey the law. I can smell the regret." He sniffed, and for once, George thought it had nothing to do with the scents of others. "My own son did not learn this lesson in time. But I will not make this mistake again. Miss Byron must learn that, in the end, her crimes will always catch up to her."

George winced. Il Naso's unforgiving words sounded

an awful lot like the voice in his own head, with an added Italian accent. "And her father—he really passed away?"

"Yes. She looks just like him. The same big chin," Il Naso sneered. "And she sounds like him, too." He waved his meaty hand in the air, putting on a mock British accent. "'Oh, *signor*. I will pay the rent money to my landlord next month. Oh, *signor*, those are not even my dogs. I do not know why they are chewing on your boots.' *Che schifo!* Disgusting!"

"She's not like him," George said. "She's not like anyone."

He thought of what Oscar had told him: that there were as many shades of good and bad as colors themselves. Maybe Il Naso was wrong about Lord Byron. Sadly, Lord Byron was dead, so George would never know for sure.

The policeman narrowed his eyes, then sighed. "Well, we will see. But she finally paid his debts and paid for the damage to the statue, so I closed the case."

"She paid? Her father's debts?"

"Yes! I had to chase her all over Venice, but she finally paid me. When at last I cornered her so that she couldn't escape, she tried to pay with a check from the Bank of England. She was desperate to leave. 'My friends need me,' she said. I knew it was a forgery. I have seen all kinds of fake checks. I said, 'I will not be tricked by another Byron.

Next you will offer me a tin cup, telling me it is the—how do you say *Santo Graal*?—Holy Grail. I am no fool.'"

"But...what did she give you instead? How did she pay?" Behind George, the boat whistled twice.

"She paid with her flying contraption. It has many gold parts, enough to cover the cost of melting them down," Il Naso said, his eyes gleaming.

The policeman kept talking, but George had stopped listening. Il Naso's words had clogged his ears and turned his stomach to lead.

Ada would never part with her mechanical bird. Not for a story. Not for a lie.

He swayed on his feet. Ada had been telling the truth about Oscar being kidnapped, and he hadn't believed her. He'd sent her away. With a sickening lurch of his stomach, he realized that he hadn't even told her in detail about the mechanical fish he'd seen in the canal. What had she said in Darwin's apartment? That there was no Organization, but they were still in danger. What if the mechanical fish was part of an even bigger danger?

"Little rabbit, are you seasick already?" Il Naso asked.

The memory of Ruthie's poor, wilted banana leaf hit George the hardest of all. He took the wadded-up piece of foliage that he'd stuffed in his pocket and inspected it as if it would reveal another truth.

And it did.

Il Naso began sniffing wildly. "Put that thing away! I can smell it through my bandages."

"What? What is it?" George asked.

"Macassar oil. I've never been able to stand the scent," Il Naso said, his voice full of disgust.

George held the leaf up to his nose and breathed in the familiar scent. *Roy.*

No. *No no no no no.*

"Oscar's really been kidnapped! Ada's in trouble. She's gone after them!" he shouted. Why had he let her go? Why hadn't he listened? "You're the police! You have to do something! They've been taken somewhere called Levrnaka."

A group of old women with baskets full of fish had stopped to stare, clucking their tongues disapprovingly, but George didn't care.

"I am off duty. I do not work on my vacations. You can make a report at the police station. They will help you write to the police in Dalmatia if your friends are in trouble over in Levrnaka, across the Adriatic Sea," Il Naso said, taking a long, deep sniff of the sea breeze.

"Well—" George turned his mind inside out trying to think of a plan to get to Levrnaka fast. "How much for the bird? The contraption?"

"A lot," Il Naso said. "You could not afford it."

"How about a treasure map? It leads to a precious gemstone worth far more than the contraption. And you wouldn't have to melt it down," George said, inventing wildly. Never mind that it didn't lead to treasure. He pulled the map from his pocket, unfolding it to show Il Naso.

He expected the policeman to argue that the map wasn't real or that it had been damaged (a piece of it was in Ruthie's stomach, along with Oscar's pestle and countless other indigestible things that were not food). Instead, Il Naso eagerly snatched the map from George and said, "The contraption is next to the jail."

And with that, Il Naso turned his back to George and boarded the ship to Spain.

A single word popped into George's mind:

Run.

Then some more words.

Go. Leave them. It's not your fault. Not really.

Then, the worst of all—

Spine of a snail.

Brains of a bowl of porridge.

But his father was wrong.

As Ada had pointed out, snails do not have spines.

George had the spine . . . of a lion. No—of himself. He had the spine of a Lord of Devonshire. That would have to be good enough. And he might have the brains of a bowl of porridge, but he knew that he couldn't leave his friends, not after all they had been through.

Now all Lord Devonshire needed was a little luck.

Chapter Thirty-Two

It was not long before George realized that, unlike bad luck, his good luck wouldn't get him very far.

But before he found out how far his good luck would take him, Lord Devonshire became the captain of an airship. And it made him feel like a new person.

With maniacal glee and a great deal of newfound courage, he pulled the cord to the airship's engine until it purred like a cat. His fingers ached with the effort of gripping the steering column, but in a good way. A courageous way.

Old George would have trembled at the mere sight of the land growing smaller and smaller underneath him, until the Venetian islands below looked like pebbles flung into the sea. His knees would have buckled when he got so high that a spiderweb of ice formed over Ada's goggles, which he wore proudly. But New George was not scared. New George could see things clearly. New George had a purpose. He had a mission. His knees weren't shaking. Not at all.

If he started to tremble when the engine sputtered, then stopped whirring completely—that was out of pure excitement, not fear.

If he screamed when the airship began to plummet toward the sea—

Well, that was a cry of bravery.

Because if he was going to crash, he was going to crash *properly*.

Like a Greek hero, George flew into the air, spreading his arms as wide as wings, just the way Ada had instructed him to do, so long ago, should he ever crash. He trusted her now more than ever.

The next moment, cold seawater rushed over his head, and everything went dark.

Chapter Thirty-Three

George coughed up a lungful of salty water onto the hard wooden surface where he lay. He did not want to open his eyes.

As he lay on his stomach, eyes still pressed shut, he gradually became aware that the ground was moving. For a brief, terrifying second, he wondered if he had been swallowed by the mechanical fish he had seen swimming in the canal. Creaks and groans of wood rubbing on wood filled the air around him. A bell clanged. Seagulls screeched.

A stick poked at George's side.

"He dead?" a deep, rough voice asked.

George swatted the stick weakly. "Yes, I'm dead. Go away and let me be dead in peace."

"You ain't dead. You're on the *Kylling*," another voice answered in a thick accent.

Cautiously, George opened one eye. He hadn't been poked by a stick at all, he saw—it was a wooden leg. The wooden leg belonged to a small, scruffy man in faded sailor's clothes. Next to him stood a large, bald man in similar clothes, with scars layering his face like sheets of white lace. The bare arms and hands of both sailors were peppered with black tattoos of daggers and skulls.

George tried to stand up but immediately stumbled to his knees as the floor pitched beneath him. With frantic glances, he took in his surroundings: he was in a small, dark cabin lit only by a lantern swinging from the ceiling and a round window that looked out over the moonlit sea. The floor pitched again.

He was on a ship. A ship with men who had tattoos and wooden legs.

"Pirates!" George whispered to himself.

The two pirates howled with laughter, their mouths glittering with gold teeth.

"I demand to be released at once," George tried, finally

standing. "I am the 3rd Lord of Devonshire, citizen of the British Empire and peer of the realm."

The two pirates conferred with each other in a language full of the kinds of sounds uttered when choking to death. One of the pirates tugged on a lock of George's hair, then began to yell loudly at the other.

"D-don't kill me, p-please. I can pay a ransom. The— the Star of Victory," George sputtered. His hand flew to his chest pocket where he normally kept the map. If he hadn't given the paper map to Il Naso, it would have been ruined by seawater, he thought. But the Star was there in its place, safe and sound, still wrapped in its white cloth.

To his surprise, the pirates rushed out of the room as soon as he said the words "Star of Victory."

Assuming that the pirates had seen through his ruse, George leaned his head against the wall in despair. Another sudden rush of seasickness churned his stomach. He wondered if Ada, Oscar, and Ruthie were still alive and if they were safe. He clung to the thought of them as if it were a pocket of air and took a deep breath. He would figure out a way to get off this ship and get to his friends before something terrible happened. And if he didn't—

Sour bile prickled George's throat.

The pirate with the scars threw open the door, alone. He plucked the Star out of George's hand, then grabbed him by the wrists.

"I'm a noble citizen of the British Empire," George pleaded again as the pirate dragged him out of the cabin. "I demand to speak with the captain!"

On the top deck, chilly blasts of night air gusted around the ship's tall masts. George shivered in his wet clothes. When he saw what awaited him there, the last of his bravery disappeared like the spray of an ocean wave.

Standing before him was the most fearsome man George had ever seen.

The imposing man was dressed head to toe in gold. He had a gold feather in his hat, a long waistcoat and pants made of gold damask, a golden buckle on his belt, and a golden scabbard at his waist. But beneath his dazzling clothes, the parts of the pirate's body that weren't covered in gold were battle-scarred and occasionally missing. His left leg was an oar that had been painted gold and carved with mermaids.

He took the Star of Victory from his man and held it up in the moonlight.

"FAKE!" he yelled in a booming voice. His crew,

which had gathered around them in a circle, jeered and booed. "What's your name, boy?"

"George." His voice quaked.

Silence fell.

"Are you *the* George, 3rd LORD of Devonshire?" the captain asked, alternately shouting and speaking at a normal volume.

George's mouth dropped open. He had always expected to be recognized for his noble heritage, but...not by a pirate. Just barely, he managed a nod.

The captain took off his hat and swept back into a grand bow. "Bartholomy Bibble JUNIOR, captain of the *Kylling*," he said. "You might've heard of my FATHER, Bartholomy Bibble."

George gasped, then threw back his shoulders valiantly. "Your father tried to murder my grandfather. If you're here to finish the job, go ahead. But please wait until I rescue my friends from the jaws of death."

"Are you Ada Byron's companion?" Bibble asked eagerly. "My men said a DEMON from the sky crashed into the SEA while I was sleeping. Was it her AIRSHIP?"

"Yes." George's heart hammered in his chest. It hardly surprised him that the captain knew Ada, too. She had probably promised the Star of Victory to every thief, scala-wag, and ne'er-do-well in Europe. "She's not the one who tried to pass off a fake jewel. I am."

Bibble put his hat back on his head and turned to one of the other pirates. "Why does everyone always assume the WORST about me? It makes it AWFULLY difficult to have a civilized conversation." He balanced the Star on his fingertips lightly while moonbeams danced on its silver sprays. "I don't care about a silly TREASURE. Well, I do. OBVIOUSLY, I care about treasure. But not THIS one. My FATHER already found the Star of Victory. I have more IMPORTANT things to worry about."

Captain Bibble tossed the Star in George's direction. After George fumbled, then dropped it, he put it in his pocket. "I don't know what your father found, but this *is* the Star of Victory. If you don't want it and you don't want to kill me, then what do you want?"

The captain sniffed. If George hadn't known better, he would have thought Bibble was trying not to cry. "I want to find my SON, OSCAR."

George's mouth dropped open.

Impossible.

But...

Captain Bibble reached into a hidden pocket sewn into the sleeve that hung loosely over his missing arm and produced a packet of letters tied together with a string. "Oscar has been WRITING me letters since he could hold a PENCIL. He even sent me a sketch of PEANUTS, my beloved parrot, who died only days before I lost Oscar as a BABY. But I could never track him down. Every time I sent one of my MEN to London to retrieve him, they were CAPTURED. Not long ago, his HANDWRITING improved DRAMATICALLY. One of his last letters said he was going to GENEVA with the 3rd Lord of DEVONSHIRE. I sent my BEST MAN to get him, but he FAILED to bring back my SON."

"The man with the gold and silver teeth." The one Ruthie had followed outside the clockmaker's workshop in Geneva, George thought. His shoulders sagged with regret. Oscar had been right. "He was one of your pirates? I thought he was an automaton!"

"PIRATES don't do well on LAND," Bibble said. "Once we get our SEA LEGS, we can't WALK or BREATHE properly unless we're on a SHIP." Bibble squinted his one eye at George. "Then one of my men reported seeing an ORANG-UTAN in Venice. I sailed to the ADRIATIC at once to troll the waters around Venice looking for any sign of him."

"Incredible," George said. "I can't believe it."

"BELIEVE IT!" Captain Bibble cried. His eye opened wide, and George saw it light up, just like Oscar's. "Now, tell me. Where IS my SON?"

The wonder curdled to dread. "I think he's somewhere called Levrnaka."

Captain Bibble squinted. "The ONLY Levrnaka I know is an ABANDONED island in the Adriatic SEA. WHAT is he doing THERE?"

"He's been kidnapped," George answered.

All at once, a hundred swords slashed through the air as Captain Bibble tipped his head back and roared in anger. "KIDNAPPED!"

A hundred raspy voices shouted back, "KIDNAPPED!"

"Yes, KIDNAPPED!" George said.

Bibble grabbed George by the arm to draw him close and picked him up so that his feet were dangling above the floor. Bibble's breath was hot on George's cheek, but he didn't yell at him again. Instead, his one eye fell on the neckerchief tied around George's upper arm, then widened in alarm. "Where did you get this?" he growled through clenched gold teeth.

"My neckerchief? It belongs to my manservant, Frobisher."

Bibble let go of George, who clattered onto the deck. "Jon the Gardener is your manservant?"

The crew went eerily silent all at once, as if the name had cemented their lips shut.

"Jon the Gardener?" George laughed. "Jon *Frobisher* is my manservant."

With a rough tug, Bibble ripped the green- and blue-striped neckerchief off George's arm, then thrust the fabric into the sky. A hundred gasps rippled throughout the ship. "The neckerchief of Jon the Gardener, who watered the SEAWEED with BLOOD, who turned his ENEMIES to FERTILIZER!"

"But he's dead!" a gruff voice shouted.

"No—the rumors must be TRUE." Bibble Junior stared at the fabric with terror in his eye. "He abandoned his SHIP and his CREW two years ago for the life of a LANDLUBBER. He calls himself Frobisher, after his parrot!" Bibble's gaze fell back to George. His expression had shifted to a hard, murderous stare. "And this boy just admitted to KNOWING him."

"I—I think there's been some mistake," George stammered. "We can't possibly be talking about the same person. My Frobisher isn't a pirate. He can hardly—"

Breathe, George thought. Which was exactly what Bibble—and Oscar—had said happened to pirates who'd lost their sea legs. To George's horror, he realized that the hand-drawn squiggly green stripes on the background of blue were indeed seaweed, and not the result of poor artistry as he'd always thought.

"No friend of the GARDENER can be trusted. LOCK him up until my SON is found!" Bibble ordered.

Four pirates grabbed George roughly by the arms and legs. They hoisted him into the air like a rag doll and carried him away from Bibble.

"Captain, I had nothing to do with your son being kidnapped, I swear," he pleaded to Bibble's retreating back. "I don't know who has him, but they're very clever and dangerous!"

Bibble glanced back over his shoulder at George, a smile curling his lips. "The crew of the *Kylling* fears NO ONE. This ship is packed to the GILLS with EXPLOSIVES."

"They have machines the likes of which you've never seen!" George shouted. Desperation made his voice crack.

He wasn't certain that the mechanical fish *was* dangerous, but he *was* certain that he didn't want to risk leading Oscar's father straight into danger.

But no one paid attention to his warnings in the flurry of whistles and stomping and Bibble's shouted oaths. With a *whomp* of sails unfurling to catch the wind, the pirate crew set course for Levrnaka. George was carted belowdecks once more, then unceremoniously dumped back into the same small cabin he'd woken up in earlier.

They barred the door from the outside, sealing his fate with a heavy *clink*.

George was trapped.

Chapter Thirty-Four

Every half hour, a bell rang out in a pattern to mark the time. At five bells, a hint of golden light appeared through George's small porthole, just over the eastern horizon. Then, high in the crow's nest at the top of the mast, the lookout yelled, "Island ho, Captain!"

Through the porthole, George saw a low strip of land shimmering in the distance. Levrnaka. White beaches gently sloped upward into green, flat-topped forests. When the ship rounded a wide bay, the lookout called down again. "A bonfire, Captain!"

Sure enough, at the far end of the bay, George spotted a large bonfire flickering. The pirates celebrated by singing a rowdy song about slashing throats.

Smooth as a swan, the *Kylling* glided into the dark bay, until they were only a short distance from the shore. Were Oscar and Ruthie there? Had Ada already reached them? George strained to see any sign of his friends, but there was absolutely no sign of life.

Suddenly, the ship's timbers groaned around him, and George was thrown against the wall. The stern of the ship spun around—the bow must have struck something in the water. But when George regained his footing and looked out the porthole again, all he saw was the calm, dusky waters of the bay and a slice of the island.

Silence fell over the ship. The pirates were no longer celebrating. They, too, were staring down at the surface of the water below them.

Then an odd ripple in the water beneath George's porthole caught his attention. Peering down from his vantage point high above the sea, he spotted a shadow drifting underwater next to the ship. Then another near the bow. And another near the stern. Sweat began to bead on his brow. He counted at least five strange shadows coming closer and closer.

The shadows broke the surface of the water without making a sound. Except they weren't shadows at all. They were giant mechanical fish.

The *Kylling* had sailed into an ambush.

Confused shouts arose all over the ship as more metal submarines surfaced from under the water. George couldn't tear his eyes away from the menacing machines or their sharp, terrifying weapons, which were now rising from the ocean depths. Soon the sea was glittering with metal fins, bronze pincers, and harpoons shaped like narwhal tusks.

George sucked in a breath. A square hatch on one of the submarines opened to reveal a gaping black hole and two tiny red lights burning in the darkness. Hatch after hatch popped open, each filled with an identical pair of blinking red lights. Abruptly, as if on cue, the red lights swarmed out of the hatches. The lights were actually pairs of red eyes belonging to flying metal bats, whose flapping wings darkened the dawn as they rose into the sky.

"BEHEAD the DEVILS!" yelled Captain Bibble to his crew.

Howling bloodthirsty curses, the pirates set upon the bats with glee. They shot at them with muskets, swiped at them with knives, and slashed at them with rapiers. A few bats dropped into the sea, sinking as soon as they hit the water. But no matter how many bats were felled by the pirates, still more filled the skies.

It was terrifying.

Squinting against the rising sun, George scoured the shore again for a sign of his friends. Something on one of the rocks near the shore was moving. Two small Oscar- and Ruthie-shaped silhouettes were huddled on a boulder jutting out of the sea. The Oscar-shaped lump was making an X with his arms.

His heart leapt. George yelled until his throat was raw, which wasn't helpful to Oscar in the least. He needed to find a way out of the cabin and off the ship. Somebody had to save them. That was what Ada would do if she were here, he thought. Or if she was here, and already captured...

George shook his head to dispel the thought. He needed to rescue Oscar. The door of the cabin was barred, but the porthole was not locked. He had only to unfasten the screws and the window swung open. Gingerly, George eased his head and shoulders out of the opening. The rigging ropes attached to the hull were within reach. If no one was looking, he could easily climb them to the top deck.

But the coast was not clear. Above, the pirates crowded against the railing, brandishing sharp swords, knives, and other blades of every form and fashion, and several of the pirates toted miniature catapults made out of mop handles.

George had never seen so many weapons in his life. In the sea, the pilots of the mechanical fish had begun to board the pirate ship, too, each with a dagger clenched in his teeth. Each wore a familiar red coat, though George didn't have time to dwell on what that meant. He had to find his friends.

While bats continued to attack the pirates from the skies, mechanical fish rammed into the *Kylling* with their sharp fins below. The view from the porthole shifted lower a fraction at a time. The ship was tilting, sinking. It was only a matter of time before the ship flooded and wrecked alongside the beach. George reached for the rigging. It was the only way he could escape.

He climbed out of the porthole and clung to the roughly woven rope. Bats whizzed by his ears, and musket balls rained down around him. Dodging them as best he could, George flattened himself against the ropes and crawled up until he could see under the railing and onto the deck between the pirates' boots. He searched the pirates' feet until he found Captain Bibble's golden oar. Just barely, he ducked as a bat careened over his head. Its razor-sharp wings snipped off a patch of his hair.

"Captain, I found Oscar!" George screamed.

"I thought I told you to go AWAY!" Captain Bibble bellowed.

"You have bigger problems than worrying about me. Your ship is sinking and your son is in trouble!" George shouted back.

The captain's fearsome face softened a fraction.

"There he is!" George tried to gesture with his chin while still clinging to the rope. The sea was rising inch by inch to cover the rock that Oscar and Ruthie were on. Only a surface the size of a dinner plate was still dry. Terror rose in George's throat. Soon the tide would rise high enough to sweep Oscar and Ruthie away.

But Bibble was too busy fighting off four mechanical bats to leap to his son's rescue. One zoomed straight for the captain's head. He split the bat open with his blade, sending its metal guts spilling out all over the deck.

The pirate captain tossed one of his swords to George, who caught it by the gleaming hilt with one hand. "YOU get my BOY, Lord DEVONSHIRE! And if you don't save him, I'll gut you neck to navel," Bibble finished, slashing the rope George was holding in half with one powerful swing of his blade.

Clinging to the rope for dear life, George felt a mighty tug as the rope was cut loose from the deck. His body sailed through the air and swung from the side of the slanted ship toward the shore...

And landed with a surprisingly soft thud on the beach—right at the edge of a cluster of fighting. When he recovered his breath, George saw that the red-coated men and women had climbed out of the submarines onto the shore. They were locked in combat with pirates who had jumped off the *Kylling* to fight them and their mechanical bats.

The tangled battle was all that separated George from Ruthie and Oscar.

Thinking only of his friends, Lord Devonshire charged into the knot of pirates, fighters, and machines. A bat whizzed over his head, and a roar erupted from his chest as he sliced his sword through the air. The bat's mechanical head fell to the ground, and its twitching body crashed only a few paces away. George raised his arms in triumph and whooped. "I did it! I—"

Something as thick and heavy as a Christmas ham struck him in the back. He stumbled and fell, twisting in midair to see the face of the man who was surely going to kill him.

Silhouetted against the morning sun was a mass of red curls.

The smell of macassar oil filled George's nose.

"Roy." George sneered. "What have you done to my friends?"

Roy sneered back. "Poor widdle coward needs his friends to protect him. OW!"

George struck Roy's knee with the side of his sword. "I. AM. NOT. A. COWARD. ANYMORE!" he cried.

Roy, rubbing his knee, kicked George back down with his other foot. He lifted his heavy brown boot, aiming another kick at George's face. Regrets flashed through George's mind as he steeled himself for death.

He'd been afraid of the world for so long. Now he'd never see any more of it.

He would never go home to No. 8. He'd never see Frobisher again. Or Ada. Or Oscar. Or Ruthie.

He hadn't been able to rescue them.

He hadn't been able to apologize.

This thought was the worst of all. Tears rolled down his cheeks and fell soundlessly into the sand underneath him.

Then a shadow leapt over him, straight into Roy's

chest. Roy staggered back with a frustrated grunt. Able to breathe again, George sat up and saw that the shadow was actually a tiny pirate. This pirate courageously leapt at Roy, and their swords clashed and clanged in a furious tornado of silver. The pirate was far more agile than Roy—but much, much smaller, and quickly losing.

"You're no match for me!" Roy said, narrowly missing the pirate's shoulder with his blade.

"I know I'm not a match. I'm a distraction!" the pirate answered in a high, confident voice.

Roy hardly had time to furrow his forehead in confusion. A lopsided bat came spinning toward him wildly, then struck him in the forehead, knocking him out cold. His body crumpled onto the beach, his face mushed into the sand.

George bolted upright. The pirate plucked the bat off Roy's head and stroked it, congratulating it in a low voice, as if it were a dog that had just performed a miraculous trick. Now that it had stopped whirring through the air, George saw that this mechanical bat was different from the others. Its wings had been elongated and reinforced with twigs. Several spoons were jammed into its middle by their handles, giving it the appearance of a small windmill.

The pirate looked up from the bat and flashed a wide grin. "Hullo, George."

Except, of course, it wasn't a pirate at all.

George's heart almost burst from happiness. "Hello, Miss Byron!"

Chapter Thirty-Five

I'm sorry!" Ada and George said simultaneously, then threw their arms around each other—which, even amid a maelstrom of fighting and clanging swords, seemed like the most important thing in the world.

"I rescued you!" they both cried when they finally let go.

Ada laughed. "That *was* very brave of you, but I don't need rescuing. I need..." She paused, biting her lip as if she were slightly embarrassed.

"A friend," George finished for her. The answer was as simple as a basic arithmetic problem. Panic rose in his chest all over again. "But what about Oscar and Ruthie? Do they need rescuing?"

"I've already rescued them. I instructed Oscar to flag your ship down from that rock, but I lost track of time and didn't factor in the rising tide," Ada said quickly, shaking her head as if ashamed of her mistake. "They're stuck on that rock, and Ruthie's afraid of the bats. She won't come."

"We'll save them, don't worry," he assured her.

"Me, worry? I'm never worried. But we all might need rescuing if we don't get off this island soon." She gripped George's arm, but not in fear—in excitement. "Maybe our attackers aren't the Organization exactly as I imagined, but they're *real*, George, and *very* well equipped. It wasn't all in my head after all! Marvelous, isn't it?"

Even if they were friends again, George didn't have to agree with everything Ada said. He did not think it was marvelous at all.

Together, they ran to the far end of the beach, where Ada had dragged a small dinghy to shore. Clutching her bat-windmill in one hand and George's hand in the other, Ada climbed down into the boat. George followed. In the distance, mechanical bats swooped, but the pirates managed to shoot any that came too close.

"Hurry!" Ada shouted. She fastened her windmill-spoon-bat invention to the back of the dinghy, then flipped a switch in its center. The bat whirred to life again, but this time under the water, propelling their little boat forward—straight for Oscar and his jack-o'-lantern smile.

"George! I'm so glad to see you!" Oscar called when they drew near.

"Oscar! I was wrong about your father. He's here and he's coming for you. You were right about everything. I've been such a crab to you. I'm sorry!" George called back, cramming all his apologies into one breath. When the boat bumped the rock, Oscar and Ruthie hopped aboard, and both wrapped George in a warm embrace. "I'm so sorry for the things I said to you. Please forgive me." He spoke into Ruthie's pleasantly warm fur.

Oscar pulled his face out of George's shoulder. "You can make up for it by finally letting me show you my mineral collection."

"I'd love to," George said through a laugh. "But, Oscar—your father *is* a pirate, just as you said. He got your letters and he's been searching for you all this time. Isn't it amazing?"

Oscar's face broadened into a smile more dazzling than the sun, which had just appeared over the tree line. "I told you! I told you he would find me! Where is he?"

Fizzing with happiness, George unwrapped Ruthie's arms from around his face, turning to point at Captain Bibble's ship. "He's right over—"

His voice caught in his throat. He wasn't pointing to a fearsome pirate ship. He was pointing to a half-sunken carcass of a pirate ship. With their advanced weapons and awful sharpened fins, the mechanical fish had cracked the *Kylling* straight down the middle. A black substance seeped into the water around the ship like spilled yolk, overtaking the blues of the sea in every direction. It must have been the gunpowder and black tar stored belowdecks.

"It'll be all right," Ada said soothingly. Oscar's face looked as broken as the ship's hull. Fear spread through George as quickly as the black substance through the water. Maybe his curse was real and had been biding its time until it could hurt even more people. If he hadn't crashed near the pirates . . .

"George, I can see what you're thinking. It's *not* your fault," Ada pressed.

Ruthie began to whimper, pointing at the ocean below them.

A pod of submarines sat quietly in the water, their sleek dark surfaces glinting menacingly in the sun. From the looks of it, they were the only mechanical fish of the entire fleet that hadn't suffered any damage.

And they had found George and his friends.

One by one, the hatches opened up to reveal red-coated individuals, including Roy, who, George was pleased to see, had a giant reddish-purple bruise where Ada's bat had struck his forehead. In the mechanical pod next to Roy, a very familiar red-haired woman emerged from her hatch.

"*You*," George breathed.

The woman sneered. Her face looked remarkably like Roy's. They must be brother and sister, he thought. A third person stood up in the pod next to her: a tall, thin man whose bald head shone in the sun. They were close enough to hit with a slingshot. Which was saying something, because George couldn't hit his own toe with a slingshot.

As the *Kylling* had been earlier, their little boat was surrounded. The four friends shuffled into a tight huddle, clutching one another's shoulders.

"So you're the Organization." George spat the name like an oath.

"The Organization?" Roy raised his eyebrows, then pointed to his own chest. "You talking about us? We're not called the Organization, you pip-squeak, we're the Society of Nobodies."

"*Enough*, Roy," the bald man snapped. "Next thing, you'll be givin' them our address."

Roy smiled viciously. "Your captain's dead. No one's coming to save ya. Now give us what we want."

George's insides exploded with anger. "The Star of Victory isn't real," he said as vengefully as possible, though he was choking back a sob.

Roy, his sister, and the bald man looked at one another, then all broke into disdainful laughter at once.

"Did you hear that, Rose?" the bald man said. "This child is a nitwit. He thinks this whole mess is about an imaginary jewel. If your brother wasn't such an idiot, we could have had the map days ago, in London." He tapped a cylindrical case tucked under his arm that looked custommade to the exact dimensions of George's map.

"The map?" Ada said. "You want the map?"

But they didn't seem to hear her. Rose glared at the bald man with her hands on her hips. "Roy is not an idiot, Shaw. He had the map in London."

"You all seem like idiots to me," said George. "Why do you want a treasure map that doesn't lead to a treasure?"

Rose and the man called Shaw looked at each other, then burst out laughing again. "The map is worth far more than treasure." Shaw shot a look at Roy, who glared back at him with equal disdain. "If *he* hadn't been so greedy, he would have paid you the money instead of stealing it. Had anyone else located it before Roy did, you would have been relieved of it without a need for international escapades."

Ada's gaze bounced between them as if they were a puzzle she was trying to figure out. "What could you possibly know about the map that we don't know?"

"It holds secrets more incredible than you could imagine," Roy replied. "Secrets that are worth killing for."

The gleam in his eyes made George's heart beat with fear—and rage. If the map held secrets, the 1st Lord of Devonshire had meant for George to protect them.

Ada narrowed her eyes at Roy. "What secrets?"

"Secrets that aren't meant to be told." Roy sneered, but even George could see how he flinched under Ada's steely, appraising eyes.

She laughed. "Never mind. I've no doubt the map holds secrets, but whoever hired you knows you're too foolish to trust with them. So tell me—whom do you work for?"

"Enough!" Shaw barked. "Give us the map."

"The joke's on you," George said triumphantly. "I sold the map."

Rose, Roy, and Shaw stopped grinning at once. "You did *what*?" Shaw said in a dangerous whisper.

Ruthie whimpered, wrapping her long arms around Ada, Oscar, and George to pull them closer. The dark spill from the pirate ship had almost reached their boat, which seemed like an omen of things to come. The smells of coal and sulfur wafted around them.

"I sold it," George replied. "To a man called—" He did not know Il Naso's real name. "Il Naso, an Italian policeman. He boarded a passenger ship bound for Spain yesterday evening."

Rose finally broke the silence. "A passenger ship bound for Spain," she repeated. Her eyes sparkled with glee in a way that made George queasy all over again. "If they don't have the map, we don't need them."

Ruthie whimpered again. George laid his palm on her furry back to calm her.

"Even the girl?" Roy asked. "DJ said—"

Shaw cut him off with a wave of his hand without taking his eyes off Ada, who was glaring at him as if she wanted to bore holes into him. "Never mind about DJ. That girl's the most trouble of all of 'em. Her inventions don't hold a candle to the things we've taken from other geniuses. William Sturgeon didn't make half as much of a fuss when we took his electromagnet, and DJ wanted that ten times as badly."

This insult made George so mad that he forgot his manners entirely. "Ada Byron's inventions can outshine anyone else's. They're the most dazzling, most brilliant!" he shouted at the same time Ada cried, "You *have* been stealing my inventions? How dare you!"

"Shut up!" Shaw snapped. He looked at George, then Ada. "It's been a displeasure doing business with you," he said, saluting in mock respect. Roy and Rose took daggers out of holders on their belts.

George glanced around at his friends. He wanted their faces to be the last thing he saw. But as always, Oscar didn't seem to be paying attention. Instead, his head was bowed over his canvas bag of minerals, his hands rummaging through its contents. Ada also did not seem bothered by the fact that they were inches from having their throats cut. She was gazing fixedly at the black stain that had been leaking from Captain Bibble's ship and now surrounded the mechanical fish. Her hand rested on the dinghy's rudder.

"Ada, Oscar, I'm glad we became friends. It will be an honor to die at your side," George whispered gallantly.

"Shield your face and be ready to jump," she said in a hurried whisper, tucking her face into Ruthie's shoulder.

Clink.

"What are you doing?" Rose snapped. She was crouching next to Roy on the edge of their mechanical fish, both of them readying to leap into the boat with their daggers drawn.

Clink.

Oscar held two stones in his hands just over the surface of the water. They were the same flint stones he'd used to start the bonfire in France.

With a smile, Oscar struck the two stones together again, just above where the black stain met the bluish-green water. George hardly saw the red spark shooting through the air before the ocean exploded into flames.

Chapter Thirty-Six

"Oscar, igniting the fuel with flint stones—that was brilliant!"

The four friends collapsed on the beach, sopping wet after having swum to shore. George's hair was slightly singed and his ears still rang from the explosion, which had given them the chance to escape from Roy, Rose, and Shaw. Behind them, the sea was still alive with flames, but the fire was shrinking rapidly.

"Do you think they're dead?" Oscar asked. George was hardly surprised to hear a note of sorrow in his voice. "Do you think I killed them?"

"No, I don't," Ada replied as she wobbled to her feet in the pebble-filled sand. She offered George and Oscar a hand up. "Their submarine probably shielded them from the worst of it. I have an escape plan, but we need to make it across to the other side of the island. And quickly." She pointed behind them, where the beach gave way to a forest.

"Do you think my father is really..." Oscar trailed off, looking out at the pirate ship, which had sunk almost completely into the sea. A shining object washed in with the tide, skittering like a crab across the sand. It was Bibble's golden captain's hat.

"He's alive, Oscar, I know it," Ada said, steering them away from the sight, toward the thick forest that edged the beach. "Don't give up hope yet. After all, apparently it wasn't farfetched to think I was being hunted by a group of thieving, murderous ruffians. I *am* being hunted by a group of thieving, murderous ruffians who stole my inventions."

She sounded angry, but when George caught her eyes, they were shining with glee. "Ada's right. He crossed oceans looking for you. He probably battled navies and hurricanes and sea monsters along the way. A minor ship-wreck and one measly explosion isn't going to stop him."

Oscar reluctantly turned away from the sinking ship. "He can't find me if I get captured again. Now it's time for escaping," he said, and motioned with a nod of his head for them to start walking. "I'm sorry you lost your map, George."

George frowned, falling into step next to Oscar, behind Ada. "It's all right. We found what we were looking for. Whatever other secrets they think are in the map, I guess I'll never know. It belongs to Il Naso now. The important thing is that we're all safe. I want to keep it that way."

"I knew you would come looking for us," Oscar said.

Red rose in George's cheeks. "Maybe they'll leave us alone now. Frobisher is going to get an earful when I get home," he said. "I forgot to tell you: Frobisher was a *pirate*!"

Oscar stared at him blankly. "You didn't know Frobisher was a pirate?"

"I—*what*? You knew this whole time?" George asked.

"Of course, George. He's the one who taught me the pirate hand signals, remember? I told you, pirates aren't bad people. Do you believe me now?"

George pulled the Star of Victory out of his pocket. Its strange silver rods winked sparkles of light at him. "Neither of you is hiding any other secrets about our priceless treasure?" His voice was slightly bitter, but he breathed a sigh, and the feeling left him.

But Oscar hadn't heard him. He was too busy turning

around in frantic circles. "Oh no!" he said, his voice breathless with fear. "Where's Ruthie? She was right next to me. Ruthie!"

"Don't worry, Oscar. We'll find her." George began to scour the bushes and rocks for any sign of the orangutan. "She's probably just hiding because she doesn't want to be near the fire."

A few steps away, Ada coughed. "No, that's not the reason. Come look," she said, holding her nose.

George and Oscar rushed to the small pine tree at the edge of the forest where Ada was standing. At the base of the tree, they found a large, gloopy brown pile. Above, in the branches, Ruthie hopped up and down proudly, then flung herself down from the branches of the tree into Oscar's arms.

Ada crouched next to the excrement. "Well, you can finally have your pestle back, Oscar. There's no time like the present."

To George's absolute horror, Oscar plunged his hand into the brown gloop, and then they all trotted down to a tide pool so he could wash his long-lost pestle. After a good scrub, he showed off the stone Ruthie had expelled. "My pestle!" he exclaimed.

It was as blue as the sky.

It was as bright as the sun.

It was as radiant as the stars.

It was the Star of Victory.

"H-how? Wh-what?" George stammered.

George took the blue stone from Oscar and held it up to the morning sun. There was no silver, six-pointed star in the stone, but it was a sapphire, just like the Star of Victory his grandfather had always described.

Even Ada's mouth was parted in awe. "Is that...?"

George's lip trembled. Happy tears clung to his eyelashes. "The Star of Victory. I know it. It's real."

Inside the stone, sunbeams turned to moonbeams. There was a frozen world of rippled waves within—indigo swirls and cobalt swells as endless as the deepest sea. The stone wasn't perfect. There was a fractured gash that split it like a canyon. But to George, this blemish made it even more beautiful. It was broken, but it was still exquisite.

"May I?" Ada asked, her voice breathless with wonder. George, beaming now, handed her the stone. She produced a magnifying glass from her pocket to examine the sapphire. "No wonder Ruthie had a stomachache. It's a miracle this didn't perforate her intestines."

"It *is* a miracle," George said softly. Of all the wondrous things he had seen on this journey, this was by far the most incredible. All this time, he had been searching for the Star, never suspecting that it was right beside him in the most unlikely of places.

Next to him, Oscar gasped. He grabbed George's jacket sleeve and tugged hard. "Who's that?" Oscar asked, pointing at a gold flash in the waves.

A lone figure in a golden suit paddled through the clear blue water toward the shore, propelled by the wooden oars that served as his left arm and leg.

"OSCAR!" the captain yelled through choking sobs and huge, gleaming tears. "My BOY."

Oscar splashed into the sea to meet his father, leaving Ruthie behind with George. The captain swept Oscar up into a wet, heartfelt embrace. "I knew you would come back for me," Oscar said, over and over again.

"You've gotten so BIG!" Captain Bibble exclaimed. He hoisted Oscar awkwardly up onto his hip when they were both out of the water. "How did you GROW so quickly?"

"It's been eight years. I couldn't help but grow," Oscar said apologetically.

"EIGHT YEARS!" thundered the captain. "I meant to

317

come back for you later the same DAY. It's all the fault of that blasted devil pirate Jon the Gardener. When he found out I was heading to LONDON, he chased me AROUND and AROUND the Sargasso Sea until my crew and I lost all track of time. He thought I was coming after the DEVONSHIRES, but I was looking for YOU."

"It's all right," Oscar reassured his father. "It's all right." Captain Bibble shook his head so vigorously that water droplets sprayed all over George and Ruthie. He held on to Oscar as if he were afraid to let the boy go.

Eventually, with Oscar riding on Captain Bibble's shoulders, they cut through the forest, following Ada as she led them to one of the Organization's (or rather, the Society of Nobodies') submarines, which, she cheerfully explained, she had tricked them into abandoning before George arrived on the *Kylling*. Oscar happily told his father his life story (which consisted mostly of looking for rocks), and George tallied the revelations of the last day.

It had all seemed so simple at the beginning: follow the treasure map to find the treasure. But at every turn, nothing had been what it seemed. The map was more valuable than the treasure. The treasure wasn't where it was supposed to be. And most perplexing of all, George didn't mind one bit.

Because it was based on Ada's design, she had absolutely no problem piloting the submarine home.

When they were far, far away from Levrnaka, Ada sat down at the steering wheel and took out her magnifying glass to study the new Star of Victory, the cracked sapphire.

George plopped down next to her. Though the miraculous feeling of relief hadn't worn off, dread was pooling in his stomach. He still had debts to pay. Frobisher still needed medicine. George was rich in friends, but was he returning to London only to be thrown right back into the crumbling mansion he'd left? If he wanted to sell the Star, which he didn't, was the chipped, broken stone worth anything?

As if Ada could read his mind, she let out a contented little sigh and put her magnifying glass back in her pocket. "It is not a treasure," she said.

"That doesn't make it any less beautiful and special," George said. "I learned something important today that

I will remember for the rest of my days on this earth. My grandfather chased a dream his entire life, never realizing that the true meaning of life is—"

"I meant this jewel isn't what we think it is," Ada interrupted. "It's something else. Give me the other star, the silver rock, please. I have a theory. There are traces of silver on the edges of the crack in this sapphire."

George handed her the silver Star from his coat. Ada unwrapped the spiky stone, then took one stone in each hand. Squinting as if she were trying to solve a puzzle, she rotated the two stones, then brought them together. When the stones were about two inches apart, the silver Star flew out of Ada's hand, joining the real Star of Victory with a soft *click*, as neatly as a stopper fitting into a bottle.

George stared, openmouthed, at the beautiful sight. The two stones became one: now a silver flower bloomed out of a blue sapphire bulb. Captain Bibble and Oscar looked up from their reunion to gape as well.

"How did you do that, Ada?" Oscar asked.

"Well, I'll be a JELLIED EEL!" Captain Bibble shouted.

"What is it?" George wondered.

"A PAPERWEIGHT!" Captain Bibble said.

Oscar scratched his chin. "A crystal that fell from the moon?" he guessed.

A smile spread over Ada's face. She held up the strange, spiky object, which now fit together so perfectly that it didn't look as though it had ever been two pieces.

"What is it, Ada?" George asked.

"I have absolutely no idea." She met his eyes. "But I'm sure we can figure it out."

"I'm sure we can," George said. He tucked the Star of Victory into his dirty, stained sailing outfit, running his fingers over the stitches fondly. "But . . . can we go home first?"

Oscar and Ruthie wheeled their hands in agreement, as did Bibble, though he looked slightly less enthusiastic about the prospect of land. Finally, a mischievous smile on her face, Ada nodded.

George let out a whoop of glee. At last, they were going home. He couldn't wait to tell Frobisher everything. (Frobisher also had a lot of explaining of his own to do.) It was more important, more urgent than figuring out the mystery behind the Star.

For now.

Chapter Thirty-Seven

In his excitement to see Frobisher, George knocked down the door of his own home. He didn't mean to, of course. It was just that, after only a few days' absence, the mansion was in such an advanced state of disrepair that the slightest pressure sent the door crashing inward. For a terrifying moment, George feared that Frobisher *had* left. Or maybe he'd been standing on the other side of the door, only to be crushed under the weight of it.

But he hadn't.

Except for his usual ailments, Frobisher was just fine. At the sight of his employer, he broke into a sheepish grin. But when George smiled, no hint of anger on his face, Frobisher did not hesitate to beam back.

When he managed to stop smiling, Frobisher wrote a message in George's accounts ledger:

I that you wud nevR RiteRn. The hows and I aR both so cRumblee and old. I that wen yoo saw the woRld, yoo wud fouRget us.

"How could you think I would forget you?" George asked. "No. 8 is my home and you are my—" George wanted to spit out the word *servant*, which once had sprung easily to his tongue. It was the wrong word, and he was no longer afraid of saying the right one. "You are my family."

Under the crumbling roof of No. 8, George reached for Frobisher. They hugged each other as little chunks of white plaster fell from the ceiling and collected in their hair like snow.

When they broke their embrace, Frobisher made a gesture to indicate that the house was falling apart.

George shook the white bits of plaster from his hair, laughing. "I can see that."

Frobisher pointed up at the large cracks running through the ceiling woefully and took up his pencil again.

Haf of the Roof cayvd in aftR a
stoRm. The attic got soked and now
theR aR mushRooms the syz of
Rabits gRowin evRywheRR up theR.

"Mushrooms?" George asked.

"Did you say mushrooms, George?" Ada poked her
head through the wide-open doorway.

He sighed. "Yes, mushrooms."

This news excited Ada significantly. Her eyebrows rose
with interest. "I have a friend in Germany who studies
fungi. He has been asking me to send him some specimens
of native species, but I haven't had the time. I'll clean up the
attic for you and patch the roof if I can have some samples."

"Go right ahead," George said. "I'm glad something
useful can come out of this old place besides slug slime
and squirrel droppings."

"Squirrel droppings are excellent manure," Ada said
over her shoulder as she climbed the stairs. "There is a use
for everything, Lord Devonshire!"

A minute or so later, when he had just finished ques-
tioning Frobisher about a certain pirate named Jon the
Gardener, a loud shriek came from the attic. George

jumped to his feet, but before he could go see what was the matter, Ada ran down from the attic, breathless. She held an enormous white lump of fungus the size and shape of a monstrous, deformed potato.

"You must be the luckiest lord in all of London," she said, never taking her eyes off the misshapen mushroom.

"You must mean the unluckiest," George said, shivering at the sight of the odd thing in Ada's grasp. "Please take that horrid thing away. I can't bear to think of what a ruin my home has become."

"They're everywhere up there. I've never seen anything like it. Your attic is simply stuffed," she said, glowing with excitement.

George groaned. Would there ever be a day when the outside world did not invade his house? No one would rent rooms if they had to cohabitate with fungi. His last hope to make money as a landlord was slipping away. "Maybe No. 8 is beyond repair," he said. "It's probably worth more as firewood than as a residence."

Ada thrust the mushroom under George's nose. "No, no. You have the most amazing house in the entire world. This is no ordinary mushroom. It's the rarest of the rare. It's a miracle. Can't you smell it? It's a *Tuber magnatum*."

Reluctantly, George took a whiff of the whitish lump in Ada's hand. He stuck out his tongue in disgust. "It smells like dirty stockings," he said.

"Everyone smells something different," she said, bringing the mushroom back to her own nose. She inhaled its scent deeply, sighing as if it were a rose. Her eyelids fluttered. "To me it smells like heaven. Like opening the window in my workshop on a warm day. Like a basket filled with freshly baked loaves of bread sprinkled with herbs. Like drinking tea at the mathematics society."

"What is it, in plain English?" George asked after Ada seemed to have recovered her wits.

"A white truffle," Ada said. "This type of truffle usually only grows in the roots of hazelnut trees in a certain part of Italy during the fall. Some varieties of black truffles grow in the beech forests of England, but no one has ever been able to grow them as a crop...until now."

"Of course they haven't," George said peevishly. "Nobody wants to eat ugly potato mushrooms that smell like dirty stockings."

"Oh, but they do," Ada said. "And they'll pay quite a bit to do it."

George's spirits lifted at the mention of money. "How much?"

"I'd say about two hundred pounds," Ada replied.

George's jaw fell open. He whooped, and the noise sent another handful of plaster showering down on his head. "That's marvelous! I don't suppose an attic of truffles is worth as much as a field, but that should keep us going for a little while. Maybe it will even pay to repair the roof so that we'll be free of the fungus for good. You were right, Ada. I am quite lucky, aren't I?"

"No, George. Well, actually, yes," Ada said. "I mean, you are lucky. But you are off in your calculations by quite a bit. Two hundred pounds doesn't even begin to come close."

"Oh." Of course it didn't. Nothing was ever as good as it seemed. "You don't think we can get two hundred pounds for the lot? What about half that?"

"What I'm trying to say is that this truffle is worth two hundred pounds by itself," Ada said, holding up the lumpy mushroom as if it were a precious jewel.

George stared at the truffle in disbelief. "You mean that one truffle is worth more than its weight in gold?"

Ada nodded vigorously.

George continued. "And the attic is full of them?"

"Stuffed full," Ada said.

George's eyes widened. He thought he might fall over. His head began swimming with visions of a ledger book with a positive balance. There were too many zeroes to fit on the credit line. "We're going to be all right, Frobisher! Go find us some cheese to go with our truffles. Actually, I take that back. I'll do it. You stay here, and try not to do any pillaging while I'm gone."

"And eggs," Ada added. "I'd like a hard-boiled egg."

"I'll buy you a dozen laying hens!" George cried.

"Don't get carried away. One egg will be just fine," Ada admonished. "For now."

Epilogue

Thunk. The windowpanes rattled when Ada landed on the roof of No. 8 in her mechanical frog. George no longer jolted out of his chair at the sound the way he used to when Ada had first invented it. In fact, in the month since they had returned home from their adventure, he had almost gotten used to the jumping machine. He had even ridden in it several times, although he preferred to walk when visiting Ada at No. 5.

And Ada had been a constant visitor. The loneliness that had been George's companion was replaced by a house filled with friends, furniture... and fungus. With Ada's help, Frobisher had converted the attic into a truffle nursery in the span of a week. Ada's specially designed retractable glass roof provided the right balance of sun-light and moisture for the truffles to grow to enormous sizes.

The Devonshire truffles, as they were now known, were in high demand all across the globe. Frobisher handled the packing and shipping, while George managed the money. They'd even hired security in the form of Ada's butler, who let no one pass through the doors of No. 8 (which had all been replaced) except for the occasional chimney sweep.

And Ada Byron, who went wherever she wanted, whenever she pleased.

She burst into the room, shouting "George!" instead of "Hello."

The 3rd Lord of Devonshire looked up from his ledger, where he was recording the latest order for five pounds of truffles to the Princess of Portugal, to see that Ada was waving a scrap of yellowing paper in the air.

"I've just gotten a letter from Oscar," she said breath-lessly.

"That's nice," George muttered, his mind fully occu-pied with calculating the exchange rate between pounds and Portuguese escudos. "What did he draw this time? Is it more parrots?"

Ada slammed the ledger shut with a snap. "*Oscar* didn't draw anything. Look." She slid the scrap of paper under George's nose. He gasped. It was a part of his old map. And not any old piece, either. He recognized a sliver of a familiar butterfly wing. It was like seeing an old friend.

"But how did Oscar get it?" He sprang up from his chair. "Did he find Il Naso? Was he discovered by the Society of Nobodies?"

"No, Oscar is safe. Remember when Ruthie bit off a corner of the map when we were in Venice? She must have spit it out and hidden it in her snack bag, because that's where Oscar found it. He thought you'd like to have it."

"I would," George said, cupping the scrap in his hands as if it were a delicate flower (or a very expensive truffle).

"That's not even the best part." Slowly, Ada pulled the Star of Victory out of her pocket and plunked it down on the table in front of George. "With Oscar's help, I've finally figured it out."

"How did you get the Star? I had it locked in the safe."

Ada rolled her eyes. "Never mind that. Did you hear

me, Lord Devonshire? The Star isn't what we thought it was. Not even close."

"You mean it's not a priceless, mystical gemstone?" George asked sarcastically. "I already knew that."

"No, what I mean is it's not a worthless piece of junk after all," Ada said. She picked up the Star and placed it directly on top of the scrap of the map in George's hand, then stepped back and put her hands on her hips expectantly. "See?"

"See what?"

Ada groaned. "The map. Look at the map."

George did as she asked, and—

He clutched the desk to keep from falling over.

The Star had bent the picture underneath like a prism, or a kaleidoscope. Under its spell, the butterfly had disappeared, replaced by an image of something else entirely: a shimmering bluish black angular shape that rose up out of the page, hovering inside the Star in three dimensions.

"What is it?" he breathed. "What does it mean?"

"A hidden picture. I'm not entirely sure of what. But . . . you're curious, aren't you?"

"Well . . ." George wasn't eager to unravel another mystery just yet. Especially if it involved the Society of Nobodies. However . . . "Maybe a little. But only a little."

"Excellent. Because I have a hunch. Relatedly, how do you feel about lost islands, Lord Devonshire?"

"Lost islands?" he squeaked. "Well, I hadn't yet formed an opinion on them."

"Marvelous!" She clapped, then grabbed George's hands and twirled him around the room, dancing in circles until his head spun—not with dizziness, but with the promise of another adventure.

Author's Note

Dear Reader,

I must write you a note of apology. I need to confess that this book contains lies. There are always lies in fiction; most of them are necessary to entertain you.

Some parts of this book are based on real places, real inventions, and real people—therefore, you might be tempted to think that every single detail is correct and historical. Many of them are, but many are not. There is indeed a real place called No. 8 Dorset Square in London, but it was never the residence of any Lords of Devonshire. Charles Darwin was a real person, but he never vacationed in Venice. I can't tell you whether or not a mysterious organization existed in Europe at that time.... I've been sworn to secrecy.

I *can* tell you that Ada Byron was a real person, and the inspiration for this book. She lived from 1815 to 1852 in England. Her father was Lord Byron, the famous poet who is often called the first modern celebrity. He was also called "mad, bad, and dangerous to know." Ada was never allowed to meet her father, who died when she was nine. She struggled with what it meant to be his daughter and inherit his legacy. Her mother was so worried that Ada would inherit her father's worst traits that she insisted Ada study science and logic, rather than poetry.

Here is another truth: when Ada was twelve years old, she dreamed of flying. She attempted to construct wings and talked of building a steam-powered airship and even planned to write a book of "Flyology" that would contain "a list of the advantages resulting from flying and…a complete explanation of the anatomy of a bird."

Ada never followed through on her plans to fly because she became very sick soon after she turned thirteen. Though she was bedridden for years, she relentlessly sought to learn about the world around her. Ada studied many subjects, but mathematics became her passion. When she turned nineteen, she married and became the Countess of Lovelace, and she is best known today by her married name, Ada Lovelace.

Ada thought that her abilities of reason, intuition, and

concentration made her a "discoverer of the hidden realities of nature." In other words, she believed herself to be a scientific genius. She was right. At the age of thirty-six, Ada passed away after many painful bouts of illness. She believed any recognition of her accomplishments would happen long after she died. Again, she was right. Today, Ada Lovelace is recognized as the world's first computer programmer and the first person to foresee that a computer could be so much more than just a calculator.

I'd like to think that Ada would have enjoyed her portrayal in this book. She was very sharp and funny (but rarely humble), just as she is on these pages. As a lonely child, she longed to have friends and adventures in the sky. I hope, then, you'll forgive me for inventing a story for her where she could experience her childhood dreams of "Poetical Science" alongside a little bit of nonsense.

Lastly, Reader, I have one more confession: I hope this book does more than entertain you. I hope it inspires you to be brave in the pursuit of your own accomplishments and adventures. Though it is still far from perfect, the world Out There has infinitely more opportunities than in 1828, when this story takes place. There are new discoveries to be made, friends to be found, and adventures to be had. So the next time you find yourself in a George-ish mood, thinking, *I can't do this—it's impossible*, try thinking like Ada: *Nothing is impossible.*

And now, I leave the last word to the real Ada Byron, aged twelve, who added this postscript in a letter to her mother:

> *P.S. I put as much nonsense as I possibly can in my letter to you because I think it compensates you for the grave dry subjects of your letters, but I suspect the truth is it gives me pleasure to write nonsense.*

Acknowledgments

My sincerest thanks must go first to you, dear Reader, for whom this book was intended. Not many people read this section of the book, so you are certainly special, unique, and very smart. Without you, this book is nothing more than a paperweight.

This book would not exist without the wonderful team at Glasstown Entertainment. They entrusted their precious creation to the hands of an unknown writer plucked from the depths of the slush pile. For giving me the opportunity to tell these characters' story, I do not have adequate words to express my gratitude. Many talented professionals at Glasstown have helped shape this book: Kamilla Benko, who had the first idea for this book's concept; Lexa Hillyer; Lauren Oliver; Emily Berge; Adam Silvera; Diana Sousa; and Stephen Barbara. But my deepest thanks go to Alexa Wejko. She is the genius behind the curtain, and this book is equally hers.

But wait, there is another team to thank! Thank you to Lisa Yoskowitz for giving this book a home at Little, Brown Books for Young Readers. She and Hallie Tibbets have showered it with thoughtful and loving attention, bringing out new depths in the story I didn't know were possible. Thank you to my wonderful marketing team: Emilie Polster, Jennifer McClelland-Smith, Elizabeth Rosenbaum, Valerie Wong, and Victoria Stapleton. A special thanks to my publicist, Katharine McAnarney. Thank you to everyone else at LBYR who has worked on and ever will work on this book: copy editors, editors, compositors, publicists, marketers, and the interns who will one day be running the show. Thank you also to Iacopo Bruno for creating the incredible cover illustration.

Like many people, I have two parents. Unlike many people, I have two parents who are endlessly supportive and always pushed me to be my best. They already know how grateful I am to be their offspring, but I can never say thank you enough. Thank you for everything (especially the help with child care). Thank you, Mom, for being my first reader, my sounding board, and my biggest cheerleader.

Special thanks must also be given to my amazing multilingual friend Claire Smolik, who provided translation assistance and ongoing encouragement. Thank you to the many other friends, family members, teachers, and mentors who have supported me in big ways and small during the writing of this book. You are too numerous to name, but if you bought this book, then rest assured that I'm absolutely talking about you.

If you are curious about Ada (which I hope you are), you should know that her life cannot be contained in a single book of fiction. Many truthful books about her do exist, and they can be found in the nonfiction or biography section of your local library. I would encourage you to read two of them: *Women in Science: 50 Fearless Pioneers Who Changed the World* by Rachel Ignotofsky and, perhaps when you're a little older, *Ada's Algorithm: How Lord Byron's Daughter Ada Lovelace Launched the Digital Age* by James Essinger.

The adventure continues in

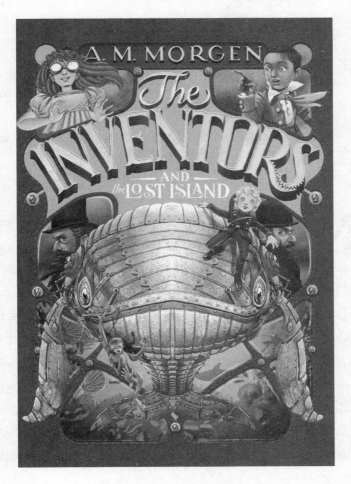

Turn the page for a sneak peek!

Chapter One

Nothing good ever came of a house with no front door. That was what George, the 3rd Lord of Devonshire, was thinking to himself as he strode out the back entrance of his house at No. 8 Dorset Square. All around him, the late-afternoon sun slanted through the trees and made the glass windowpanes of the doorless No. 10 blaze with golden light. His former neighbors, the Mallard sisters, had moved out rather suddenly a week ago, after receiving a generous offer from an unknown buyer. The mansion had been leveled to the ground before the sisters had finished loading their trunks into a moving wagon. Already, the brick walls of a brand-new house had risen in its place.

A brand-new house with absolutely no front door.

George breathed in deeply. The air was crisp and fresh. Graceful starlings flitted through the dimming sky before settling down in the trees for the evening. But No. 10 stuck out like an unsightly blemish in the otherwise perfect neighborhood.

George, who had been the unluckiest boy in all of London, knew that odd things should not be ignored, because they might be dangerous. Even Ada Byron, his genius neighbor and new best friend, had agreed that such a strange house meant trouble, though they had conflicting theories about why.

George was convinced that the owner of No. 10 was a rival truffle farmer who was after him—or, more specifically, after his truffle business. The leaky attic of No. 8 had proven to be the perfect environment for growing the valuable fungi, so it seemed reasonable that the new owners of No. 10 were truffle farmers looking to reproduce the unique environment of George's attic by building a greenhouse and seeding their own operation with George's precious truffles. A greenhouse had no use for a front door.

Ada's theory, however, frightened George more than the thought of truffle thieves. Her theory was that the house's owner belonged to the Society of Nobodies, the criminal organization that had stolen Ada's inventions and chased them across Europe in pursuit of George's treasure map. Ada suspected that No. 10 did have a front door but that it was hidden by complicated mechanisms meant to discourage intruders.

That was why George was setting a trap at his house for the owner of No. 10. Ada was setting her own specially designed trap across the street at her house, No. 5. How else would they know who was right?

Whistling casually, George retrieved a tall ladder from his garden shed and hoisted it onto his shoulder. He held it carefully to avoid the sticky barnacle glue that he'd borrowed from Ada and smeared on the rungs the night before. In plain sight of No. 10, George leaned the ladder against the side wall of his house as if he were going to do some home repairs. To further entice potential truffle thieves, he began chatting loudly to Mrs. Daly, his manservant Frobisher's pet rat who resided in the walls of No. 8, about the incredible truffle crop he was about to harvest. The thieves lying in wait inside No. 10 wouldn't be able to resist climbing the ladder to sneak into his attic now, he thought smugly.

To his shock, Mrs. Daly answered in a muffled voice. "Hmmhoo, Oorge."

George then realized it wasn't the rat's voice he heard. It was Ada's voice, floating through the front door from the speaking tube she had recently installed between their houses. George rushed inside to the trumpet-shaped porcelain mouthpiece sticking out of the wall, next to the front door. "Hello? Ada? Is that you?"

"Are you finished setting your trap?" Ada's voice sounded hollow and tinny.

George grinned. "Yes. Come over and I'll prove you wrong."

"Don't hold your breath. I'm always right," she chirped.

The speaking tube went silent. A shiver raced up George's spine. If Ada was right, a formidable enemy lurked behind the windows of No. 10.

The Society of Nobodies was a gang of vicious thieves Ada had once called the Organization. They had used stolen science to make weapons that could crack a pirate ship in half and machines that could fly through the air or swim underwater. George and Ada, along with their friends Oscar and Ruthie, had barely survived their last encounter with the Society. If the Society was next door, then...well, George couldn't even fathom what it might mean for their safety.

Someone tapped on his shoulder, and he screamed.

"Sorry," said the messenger who'd stepped in through the front door while George's back was turned. "Didn't mean to interrupt your . . . conversation with the wall. I'm here for the—"

"Special delivery for the King?" asked George breezily, as if he hadn't been caught talking into a wall. By now, he knew better than to try to explain Ada's inventions to strangers. They only became more confused. "Yes, I have it right here. One moment."

He darted up to the attic and returned with a smooth, polished wooden box. The engraved words on top, DEVONSHIRE TRUFFLES, seemed to wink in the light of the setting sun. "Please make sure this package arrives at Windsor Castle safely."

"Of course, sir," said the messenger, his eyes bulging—either because he was impressed by the lovely box or because he was trying not to gag from the smell of the truffles inside. To some people, truffles smelled heavenly. To others, they stank. The messenger bowed, then tucked the very fancy box and its very odorous contents into his leather bag.

George ambled to the library to record his latest royal order. He lifted the tip of his quill to record the King's purchase in his accounts ledger—

And was immediately interrupted by a jarring *THUMP* that shook the walls of his house. George's inkpot rattled on the desk. Ada's giant mechanical frog made quite a racket whenever she landed it on his roof. Seconds later, her footsteps rang out on the stairs, followed shortly by the sound of her flutelike voice echoing in the foyer. "George?"

"In the library!" he called out.

Ada appeared in the entryway and paused, smiling. George heard the *clack clack* of several hard-boiled eggs knocking against one another inside the pockets of her yellow dress.

Instead of hello, she said: "Did you get a new clock, Lord Devonshire?"

George frowned. "Not yet. It takes time to refurnish a house."

Ada cupped her hand to her ear. "That is so strange. I could have sworn I heard a clock chiming *wronnnng, wronnnng* as I was coming down the stairs."

"Ha-ha. Very funny. You're the one who's going to be wrong," George said smugly. "I couldn't help but notice, though, that your trap isn't set up yet."

Ada tilted her head to one side, an amused smile lifting

her cheeks. One of her loose curls fell across her face. "My trap's been set for hours."

George scrunched his brow in confusion. He pushed back the curtain to see Ada's house from the window. "I don't see anything unusual except your maid still sitting on the front steps."

Ada laughed. "That's not the maid. That's the trap! Remember the automaton you bought me?"

"Of course! From the Jaquet-Droz workshop in Geneva." George had first seen the organ-playing automaton while they were looking for the Star of Victory in Geneva. She resembled a human woman, but like everything sold in his grandfather's favorite workshop, she was a piece of clockwork made up of gears and mechanisms. With his truffle money, George had bought the machine as a birthday present for Ada. "You named her Hippolyta, or was it Cleopatra?"

"Neither. I named her Hypatia after my favorite mathematician. But I call her Patty now. Don't you recognize her?" she said, nodding out the window.

"That's her!" George squinted in surprise at the figure sitting as motionless as a statue in front of No. 5. Her face was white porcelain and framed with tight blond curls.

George had first noticed the automaton because of her unique pendant in the shape of a butterfly, which looked exactly like a drawing on his grandfather's map. Though he couldn't see it from so far away, he could picture its silver wings. It was another mysterious clue that George would probably never decipher. Had his grandfather copied it on purpose? The 1st Lord of Devonshire loved puzzles.

"She's the most wonderful present I've ever had," Ada gushed. "She's an amazing machine. Her arms are controlled by the gears in her back, so I can program them to perform any sequence of movements. There's no end to what she can do—repairs, navigation, maybe even surgery one day. And she'll be perfect to control my new water cannon."

"She's your trap?" George asked.

Ada raised a gleeful eyebrow. "I made it look as if she had been delivered earlier but no one was home to accept the package. I've rigged her arm to throw a lasso around anyone who walks up the steps toward her."

"That's quite clever. She's excellent bait," George remarked grudgingly. She was the perfect thing to lure the Society. Anyone else walking by wouldn't give Patty a second glance, but the Society of Nobodies loved complicated machines. Turning to Ada, he said, "It's a shame you won't have a chance to see Patty in action, since the owner of No. 10 isn't the Society."

Ada sniffed in disagreement. "I hope you're right. Really, I do. I'd rather it not be the Society after what they put us through in Venice and how ruthless they were about your grandfather's map. But if you were being logical, you'd see that my theory makes more sense. The Society wanted your grandfather's map. They didn't get what they wanted. Therefore—"

"Therefore, they have no reason to come after me anymore," George interjected quickly. "Let's go up to the roof and wait. I made us some sandwiches, and there's a pot of stew on the stove," he added to change the topic to something that didn't make his stomach sour with nerves. The thought of Roy, the redheaded brute from the Society, living next door after trying to kill him was enough to ruin his appetite completely.

While George stoppered his ink bottle and wiped the nib of his feather pen clean, Ada ran her hands along the empty shelves in the library, collecting dust on the edge of her palm. "Are you sure I can't store some of my instruments here? With all the work I'm doing for C.R.U.M.P.E.T.S., my room is full to bursting," she said.

George busily tidied his desk. "This is a library, not a pantry. I have truffles in my attic. I don't want crumpets on my bookshelves. Besides, if we keep any more pastries in the house, Mrs. Daly will invite all her rat friends over for a feast, and Frobisher will insist that we keep them. Oscar may like living in a menagerie, but I don't."

Ada's face fell at the mention of Oscar's name. An undertow of sadness tugged at George's chest, too. He often had to remind himself that his friends Oscar and Ruthie no longer lived a few miles away at the royal menagerie in the Kensington Palace gardens. Once, it had seemed like the journey of a lifetime for George to leave his house and cross the street. But now that Oscar and Ruthie were sailing the seven seas with Oscar's father, Captain Bibble, his friends felt as far from Dorset Square as the stars in the sky.

Ada brushed her brown curls out of her face, discreetly wiping away a tear at the same time. "You and Oscar are always thinking about food. I didn't say crumpets. I said C.R.U.M.P.E.T.S. The Council for Radical Undertakings in Mathematics, Physics, Engineering, Technology, and Science."

"The council for . . . ?" George asked. He knew the next

word wasn't *radishes*, but he couldn't remember what it was. Ada was right. He was always thinking about food.

Ada sighed. "It's a brand-new scientific gathering happening in London. I received an invitation to submit an invention for consideration. If I get accepted, I'll finally be able to prove to my mother that my inventions are worth something. She thinks I'm wasting my time making sloppily built toys instead of devoting my mind to *serious* scientific pursuits."

Ada pulled the invitation from her pocket and put it under George's nose with a flourish. It was printed on creamy white paper and stamped with a gold wax seal in one corner. The date was less than two months away. The location was London. A specific address would be revealed to those who accepted the invitation.

The invitation certainly looked impressive to George, but he wasn't sure Ada's mother would feel the same. Though Ada's inventions were the most wonderful things that George had ever seen, Lady Byron had forbidden Ada to make any more flying machines after her mechanical bird had crashed into the Adriatic Sea. She even insisted that the frog, which had jumped back and forth between No. 5 and No. 8 a million times with no problems, must have a safety harness and an extra braking mechanism. If Ada needed some space away from her mother to build her invention for C.R.U.M.P.E.T.S., then it was George's duty as a friend to help. "Of course there's room for you to store your instruments here," he said, smiling at Ada. "But first, will you join me for dinner?"

In the kitchen, George placed two bowls of truffle stew on a serving tray next to a neatly stacked pile of cucumber sandwiches. Frobisher usually prepared their meals, but the manservant had left for a well-deserved and much-needed vacation at a curative health spa in Vienna. After spending many years at sea as a pirate called Jon the Gardener, Frobisher had developed a terrible case of land sickness when he gave up piracy, and he needed help recovering his land legs. When Frobisher returned from the spa, a brand-new identity would be waiting for him so that his former life as a pirate would be completely erased. All legally arranged by Ada, of course.

They carried their sandwiches and stew up the narrow stairs to the attic, snuffing out all the lights on the way, then climbed out onto the roof to wait for their prey in the shadow of Ada's jumping machine. The contraption vaguely resembled the bottom half of a giant frog or equally large grasshopper, with two long legs that were bent nearly double at the knee joints. Coiled tightly between the legs, the machine's two massive springs were waiting to vault over Dorset Square when they were released, calculated to alight precisely on the matching landing pad on Ada's roof across the street. Though he told himself that the Society had not moved in next door, George threw a tarpaulin over the frog to hide it from view. Just in case.

Darkness fell around them like a blanket. As the stars began to twinkle through the breaks in the clouds gathering overhead, George felt a familiar jumble of excitement and fear prickling in his gut. Something could happen at any moment. Ada adjusted the telescope aimed at her front steps, and George secured the top of his sticky ladder to the gutter, but otherwise it could have been any night spent with a friend. They ate their food and wrapped themselves in quilts to keep warm while they minded their traps like two fishermen waiting for fish to bite.

A few carriages rumbled by, sleepy starlings tittered in the trees, some stray cats yowled in a far-off alley. Soon George's eyelids became heavy. His chin nodded toward his chest. The sound of the wind rustling through the leaves was a beautiful lullaby. With any luck, he'd sleep peacefully all night under the stars and in the morning his ladder would be empty and Patty would be on Ada's front porch, safe and sound.

Suddenly, Ada was shaking his arm. "Wake up! They're here!"

George jolted awake. Ada glared at No. 5, her eyes burning bright as the gas lamps dotting Dorset Square. "It's not a truffle farmer. It's the Society. One of them got Patty's arm. He's heading for No. 10. Hurry."

A shiver of dread shook through George like an earthquake. He looked across Dorset Square. Patty had fallen onto her side. The dark shape of a man raced through the trees away from Ada's trap. But the figure was like something out of a nightmare—he streaked over the grass on thin legs as tall as fenceposts. Patty's disembodied arm dangled behind him like a worm twisting on a fishing line.

In ten long strides, the man crossed Dorset Square and disappeared around the side of No. 10.

"After him!" Ada cried. She was already climbing down from the roof into the attic.

George raced after her, and soon they emerged onto the lawn and skidded to a halt, eyes searching for any sign of the shadowy figure.

"Did you see how tall he was? I didn't calibrate Patty's strength properly to account for someone of that extreme height. Patty's horizontal grip is stronger than her shoulder joint. Her arm sheared off with the rope when the man ran away. He must have gone inside," Ada whispered breathlessly, then vaulted toward No. 10.

George grasped Ada's skirt to pull her back. "Wait— shouldn't we get something to defend ourselves with?"

"There's no time. Our new neighbor is the Society. We can stop them once and for all. Here. Now. Patty's arm is the evidence we need to charge them with trespassing." Ada peeked around the edge of the house. "The coast is clear. I'm going."

She lifted her skirts and raced across the muddy strip of dirt that separated George's house from No. 10. George knew Ada well enough to know that nothing he could say would stop her from charging into danger.

So he took a deep breath and plunged after her.

A. M. MORGEN comes from a long line of engineers and researchers but chose to pursue literature over the laboratory. To her family's surprise, she has managed to make a decent living as an editor with her English degree. In her spare time, A. M. enjoys taking long walks in the forest, trying out new hobbies (then abandoning them), and complaining about her mean cat. Despite what you may think, A. M. is not a morning person.

Come along for even more mysteries and hijinks with

The INVENTORS

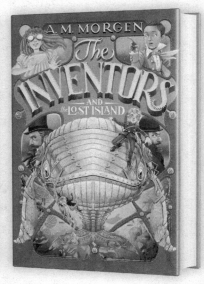

Join Ada and George in this rip-roaring adventure series!